DANCEHALL DAYS

The Life and Times of Ann Brown

Part 1

Sam Young

Sam Young

First published 2024 by Maeday Press

ISBN: 978-1-0686431-0-1

I am grateful to the MS Society UK for permission to use their logo.

Editiorial & typesetting: Averill Buchanan
Cover design: More Visual, Leicester

For my amazing mother, who inspired the story.

For my beautiful, patient wife, Mae, whose diagnosis inspired the choice of charity.

For MS sufferers and their carers everywhere.

All the proceeds from the sale of this novel
are going to MS research.

Thank you to the MS Society UK, which is working hard to find better treatments and, hopefully one day, a cure.

MS Society

Thank you to everyone who buys this book.
I hope you enjoy reading it.

CHAPTER 1

Ann opened the front door of their little two-up, two-down as quietly as she could and tried to sneak up the stairs. Not easy, as there were no treads that didn't creak or squeak.

Ma was in bed in the front room upstairs. 'Is that you, Ann?'

Ann went as low and guttural as she could. 'No, it's Fred.'

'Don't be so cheeky. It's late. Get into bed.'

'Yes, Ma.'

'Church in the morning.'

'Yes, Ma. Goodnight, Ma.'

Ann shared the back room and the only bed with her two older sisters. She undressed in the dark, slipped on her nightie and slid into the sliver of space at the edge. 'Shift over a bit.'

Minimal movement, a half-hearted wriggle and a theatrical, grunting turn created no more room.

Hilda made exaggerated snoring noises and Muriel whispered, 'What time do you call this? We've been asleep for ages and there's church in the morning.'

'Yes, Ma,' said Ann.

'Where did you get to?' Hilda asked.

'I went out to the alley for a fag with Walter.'

'Just a fag?' said Muriel.

'What do you mean?' asked Ann, innocence personified.

'You were dancing with him all night. Did you get a wee kiss?' Muriel persisted.

'That would be telling now, wouldn't it? We had a fag and a chat. Nothing wrong with that.'

'Down a dark alleyway!' Hilda feigned disbelief.

'You've been dancing with him a lot recently. Are you seeing him again?' asked Muriel.

'Maybe.'

'He's very good-looking.' Muriel was fishing hard.

'He's not good-looking. Not film-star good-looking. Not like Gregory Peck,' Ann swooned.

Hilda chipped in, 'He's got a job and all. You could do worse.'

'He drives a bakery van! And he's blond. Film stars aren't blond.'

'You might have to wait a wee while, before you meet a proper film star, much less get married to one. A bird in the hand and all that,' Muriel said.

'We'll see. Sleep. Please. Church in the morning.'

'Yes, Ma,' the sisters said in unison, giggling and wriggling a bit more before drifting off.

* * *

Ann woke with the sun and slipped out of bed without disturbing the others. As she was first up, it was her job to go outside to the tap and fill the kettle.

She put a bob in the meter and the kettle on the gas

burner of the cooker, then she went back outside to the toilet. Being late November, everything was cold, and the seat, like the kettle, would take some time to warm up.

Joe was the youngest of the four siblings. He would be fifteen in a month's time on 27th December. He slept in the back room downstairs. Washing could hardly describe the process he employed over the next few minutes, but he was always ready for breakfast first.

Ma had ironed his shirt on Saturday, but he ate his toast in his pyjamas in case there was an accident with the slab of butter melting on the slice that had just emerged, black, from under the grill. The bread was cut so thick it almost touched the flames. It often went on fire.

Eventually, the girls got themselves cleaned and preened into a state that would allow them to be viewed and admired by the rest of the world.

Ma, as usual, just seemed to be ready. She always wore the same black dress, black hat and black coat. Her Sunday best. They still did the job, she insisted, seeing no reason to spend hard-earned money on 'style'.

The girls wore their Sunday dresses, and Joe had on his best Sunday trousers, which were getting a bit tight.

Coats on, they left the house and turned right. After crossing Abbey Bridge, they turned left up the steep incline of Castle Street, then right onto Church Street, where they passed the chapel. Church Street morphed into James Street, and a couple of minutes later, they arrived at Trinity Presbyterian Church. They were always early and entered the almost empty church by the door at the side of the transept where their pew was.

Everyone always sat in the same place every week. There never seemed to be any strangers who might commit the sin of sitting in the wrong pew. Joe once asked what they would do if they arrived one Sunday and someone was already sitting in their spot. Would they just squeeze in beside them and say nothing? This might depend on the number of interlopers and how intimidating they looked. Or would Ma politely say, 'Excuse me, but you're sitting in our seat', and hope the intruders would meekly apologise and move? This would only move the problem elsewhere, but Joe hadn't quite got to grips with the subtleties of Christianity. In his mind, a problem moved was a problem solved.

Their pew, third from the front, on the right facing the left-hand side of the pulpit, was unoccupied as usual, and the Browns slid in, oldest on the inside. Ma, followed by Muriel, then Hilda, Ann and lastly Joe. Always the same.

Joe's best friend, Harry, and his family came in shortly afterwards. The Johnston family pew was second from the front. His ma went in first, then his younger sister Maureen, his da, then Doreen and finally Harry. Always the same.

Joe thought Doreen was beautiful. He could never tell Harry this of course. One of the highlights of church every week was being able to catch a glimpse of the shape of her bum every time she stood up to sing. And he often wondered, when he saw Harry's da coming into church, what it would be like to have a da. A ma was good, but a da must be great.

There wasn't time to think for too long, as the church filled up quickly. Joe looked up at the hymn board and opened his hymn book. He mouthed the words of the hymns, but Ma and the girls sang their hearts out.

Harry sounded like a drunken donkey gargling glass. He was unaware and didn't care; he sang as if the Lord was profoundly deaf. If this had been school, Joe would have poked Harry in the arse with a ruler, but the potential of eternal damnation made this a non-starter, Besides, he didn't have a ruler.

As always, the sermon seemed to go on forever, but at last Reverend Goodman was saying Joe's favourite words: 'Forever and ever. Amen.'

Outside there was a lot of hello-ing and how are you-ing? Especially if the weather was good and it was comfortable to dawdle. The weather was always discussed. If it was fine, it wouldn't last. If the washing was out, rain was certain. Health issues were another favourite topic. So and so was in bed with her foot or her stomach. There was always an 'it' and there was always a lot of 'it' about.

'These trousers are too tight, Ma,' Joe complained, pulling at his trouser legs as they started to walk home.

'When the arse of them splits, we'll see what we can do,' Ma replied. 'Just don't bend down.'

'Yes, Ma,' Joe said. They smiled at each other, knowing the trousers were done. Ma was saving for a new pair.

They went home the other way, along John Street, past the imposing stone courthouse, down the steep hill of High Street and left into Bridge Street.

Hilda and Muriel always strode together in front, deep in conversation about nothing at all. Ann walked in silence with Ma, their arms linked. Joe dawdled, hopped and skipped along behind.

He stopped just before the corner of Bridge Street to admire a brand-new Austin Princess parked outside the Home and Colonial Store.

'Look at that!'

'Somebody has money,' Ma observed. 'It must be Mr Chestnut's.'

'I want a car like that someday,' declared Joe. He'd never been in a car but he dreamt of it.

'Don't set your sights too high, son, and you won't be disappointed. Get a good job, work hard, save your money and you never know. Remember, a shilling in your pocket is your best friend.' Joe joined in with this last part.

He peered in the front window of the car. Red leather seats. *Fantastic.* He ran his hands over the front wheel arch.

'Don't touch, Joe.' Ma grabbed his arm.

'Yes, Ma. Sorry, Ma.'

Most of the rest of Sunday was spent getting ready for Monday. Shoes polished, shirts and blouses washed, put through the mangle and ironed.

The fire had been set before they left and was lit as soon as they got in. The gas lamps were also lit once daylight faded, which was early now that it was near the end of November.

After dinner, when the work was done and before bed, the chatter subsided and the family settled down to read their books or listen to the wireless. Uncle Louis had given them the radio the week after his brother's – their da's – funeral. Its arrival caused great excitement, as it was the newest, latest thing and must have cost a bomb. Ma reckoned it used a lot of electricity.

The funeral had been on Boxing Day 1937, the day before Joe's sixth birthday. Muriel had turned ten that September. It was a military funeral, but Joe and the girls weren't allowed to go. They had to stay in the house with Ma's friend, Fred. The curtains were kept pulled, as they were in every house on the street. The children could hear the band as it came down Sedan Avenue and stopped outside the house.

Fred always visited on a Sunday evening. He timed his

calls just as the books were about to be put away for the night. He hung his overcoat on the hook on the back of the front door. He never took off his duncher, which looked like it was part of his head. He always brought chocolate – little thin bars of Cadbury's Dairy Milk. It was one of the highlights of the week, especially when they were younger, but still a moment they looked forward to even now.

He asked how they were getting on at work. 'Any boyfriends yet?'

This was met with half-hearted denials and half-truths.

'Muriel is seeing a soldier,' said Hilda.

'I am not. I danced with him once last week. And anyway, you can talk. How many times have you seen that big, long, dozy American?'

'He's not dozy and he's not American. He's Canadian and he's very smart. He works in a secret office doing secret stuff.'

'That's what he tells you.'

Fred turned to Ann. 'What about you?"

'Nobody special. Still trying to find the right dance partner. Most of them are useless.'

'Even Walter?' teased Hilda.

Ann blushed, but in the gloomy light it went unseen. 'He's better than most, I suppose.'

'And he's very handsome,' Muriel added.

'We've had this conversation a million times.' Ann was exasperated. 'He's not handsome. Not like a proper film star, like Gregory Peck … or any of them. He's blond and film stars are not blond!'

'And you, Joe? No girlfriend yet?' Fred shifted his focus.

'He's a bit young for girlfriends,' replied Ma. 'Best if he waits a wee while, at least till he starts work and has a bit of money saved …'

Her children all knew what was coming next, '… for a shilling in your pocket is your best friend.'

'Yes, Ma!' they chorused.

'I know you think it's silly but it's true, and you'll come to realise it someday,' Ma insisted.

'What about the football then, Joe?' asked Fred.

'It's going great. I think I might get a game for the first team this season.'

'Well, if you're good enough, you're old enough. Fifteen next month, eh? Keep at it!'

'It's all right him playing football, but it can't interfere with his schoolwork. He needs to keep his head down till May. Every day counts,' counselled Ma.

Some of the brighter children had the chance to stay on at school for an extra year and Ma had agreed to let Joe do this, for as Mr Lee said, he was very good at maths and should be allowed to learn as much as possible.

Fred had been calling since any of them could remember. When they were small, just before bed, a ritual had developed. Starting with the youngest, they went outside one by one to go to the toilet. Fred accompanied them and stood with his back to the loose rattling wooden door of the privy. He whistled loudly, 'It's six miles from Bangor to Donaghadee.' No one had any idea why he whistled that particular tune. Fred said it was the only one he knew. When they were small and it was stormy, or they were more afraid of the dark than they wanted to admit, this was a great comfort. The ritual ended long ago, but Hilda was still scared of the dark.

The last act of Fred's visits was completed when he pressed a sixpence into each of their hands. It was never long before Bob Campbell's or Miller's shop received it in return for a little bag of treasure, although now, the girls especially had more grown-up demands for the money.

Once in bed, the girls could hear Ma and Fred talking quietly. The radio was on and its muted music was like a lullaby that eased them to sleep as gossip faded into dreams of boys and happy-ever-afters. In his dream world, Joe was playing football for Manchester United, scoring spectacular goals and trying not to look too cocky when the boys whispered in awe as he went past. All the girls wanted to be his girlfriend.

CHAPTER 2

Monday morning was noisy, organised chaos. Hilda let a wee fart to begin the day. The giggling started as Muriel and Ann quickly did the same.

'Open the window,' gasped Muriel. 'We're all going to suffocate!'

Ann opened the window a tiny crack. 'It's freezin',' she said, shivering, and closed it again.

'Must have been the soup,' Hilda remarked as she fell out of bed and began to get ready.

'Lethal lentils,' said Muriel.

'Odious onions,' added Hilda.

'Perfidious peas,' was Ann's contribution.

They had filled their water jugs before bed, so it was teeth cleaned, hair brushed and down for breakfast. The fire hazard remained high from the flickering flames licking the slabs of bread. Sometimes there was jam, but there was always a cup of tea.

Joe's school uniform was a grey jumper over a white shirt that had once been much whiter and his well-worn grey trousers. He wore a pair of black boots, which were replaced every August before the new school year began.

The girls dressed smartly for work. Ma wore a black dress and an apron. None of them could remember her ever wearing anything else on a workday.

Ma worked as a cleaner for three local men. On a Monday she went to Robert Johnston, a solicitor, who lived just beyond the cemetery on the Dublin Road. Jimmy Reed, who lived above his chemist shop on the High Street, was on Wednesdays. Albert Lee lived out near the Manse on the Dublin Road, and Friday was his day. He was headmaster of the Model School.

She had worked for her gentlemen for a long time and was the soul of discretion. As far as Ma was concerned, these people were important and she wasn't. Unlike her, they were educated and rich, but she was reliable, honest and hardworking, and the three small cash payments every week were just enough to keep their heads above water.

That was a lot easier than keeping their house above water at certain times of the year. Large areas of Omagh town flooded almost every autumn, but the aristocracy lived higher up away from the rivers. She never had to clean up after a flood in any of her gentlemen's houses.

Muriel, like her sisters, had left school at fourteen. Her basic qualifications, especially in English, had helped her to get a job in the telephone exchange. Of course, the foot she kicked with had as much to do with it as her qualifications, but the big thing in her favour was her ability to talk.

She knew a little about a lot of things and had an opinion on them all. Gloriously curious, her inquisitiveness could verge on inquisition if the victim was vague or hesitant. Whether any information was true or not mattered little, as it would be twisted and tweaked, embellished and embroidered, before onward transmission.

Working in the telephone exchange with six other like-minded young ladies was as good as it could possibly get. Priceless nuggets of gold travelled incessantly along the wires.

But what happened in the telephone exchange was supposed to stay in the telephone exchange, and while they all tried their best, sometimes the pressure was so great and the nuggets so valuable that they just had to be shared.

These whispered indiscretions always started with a fact like, 'You know, I'm not one to gossip …' or sincere entreaties like, 'Promise you won't tell another soul …' Mostly harmless, never intentionally destructive, gossip was a force of nature as essential as breathing or boy-watching. Every day was an adventure.

At first, Muriel had loved the gossip, but now, after five years in the job, she was good at it, and if the line was engaged, she chatted to the caller with genuine interest.

Every evening there was a debriefing from Hilda and Ann.

'Well, what happened today?' one would ask.

'Anything strange or startling?' asked the other.

Muriel always tried, at least for a while, to be professional. But then she couldn't help herself. 'The craic was ninety as usual. Heather's seeing an American. He's taking her to the pictures this weekend and Wilma is pregnant. Nothing else really,' she replied.

'What does *the craic was ninety* actually mean?' asked Ann.

'No idea,' said Hilda. 'Maybe that's as high as it can go without bursting. I mean the craic is never a hundred, is it?'

'Good point,' said Ann. 'Anyway, what about Mrs Chesney? Did she ring Dr Bowles again?' asked Hilda.

'Perhaps!' Muriel was coy, but the mischief in her eyes gave her away. 'She rings so often now – she might be more than just a patient. But if she is a patient, she must be the sickest person in the world.'

'Maybe the sickest person ever,' said Hilda.

'Maybe, but you'd think the sickest person ever wouldn't be around as long as Mrs Chesney,' Ann noted.

'So she's just the latest sickest person ever.' Hilda started to giggle.

'But she won't be the last!' Ann laughed.

'She did call him today. Can't say more than that,' Muriel blurted out, trying to be serious.

Their imaginations ran wild at the thought of Mrs Chesney having an affair with Dr Bowles. She was definitely not petite, but she had very small feet. She resembled a large wardrobe tottering around on tiny castors. The long loose dresses she wore made it very difficult to determine any shape. The girls felt that it was more likely that Mrs Chesney was simply a middle-aged, bored hypochondriac, but maybe, just maybe, there was something more.

Dr Bowles had been their family doctor for a very long time. Blessed with an effusive, happy personality, he was a pillar of the Omagh aristocracy – a member of the Golf Club, the Rotary Club, the Motor Club and the very exclusive County Club.

There were all sorts of rumours about what went on in the County Club.

One evening Muriel had asked Ma. 'Do you know where Mrs Chesney works?'

'Why do you want to know that?'

'Just wondering. She's always about every time I go up the town, and I was wondering if she actually worked or if she's a lady of leisure?' Muriel knew the latter was unlikely, as Mrs Chesney, like Ma, was a widow with no obvious means of support.

'Maybe Mrs Chesney thinks the same about you. She must see you every time she goes up the town.'

Muriel hadn't considered this.

'She got the cook's job in the County Club a wee while ago,' Ma went on. 'She always buys dear stuff in the butchers. She has to work in the evenings, so she can't often go to things.' Ma gave Muriel one of her probing looks. 'Why the interest?'

'No reason,' Muriel lied.

Hilda and Ann looked up from their books and the three sisters exchanged glances, eyes wide with excitement, wild with speculation. Surely there must be more to Mrs Chesney's phone conversations than discussing meat, menus and malingering illnesses. Planning secret assignations, more like. The flames of the sisters' fiery fiction had been fanned.

CHAPTER 3

Joe had finished his comprehension some time ago and was staring at the clock above Mr Marks's head. Just after five to three. The clock ticked another tock closer to home time but at a rate Joe thought would extend eternity for ever. Time seemed to be suspended. Another loud tick, another hypnotic tock, another, then another. Until the clock was drowned out by the best sound in the world jangling loudly through the Model School.

Joe sat up even straighter, the sun came out, Skid Marks appeared almost human and Doreen looked more beautiful than ever.

'Tidy your desks and leave your jotters on my table on the way out – slowly, for God's sake, or someone will get killed!' shouted Mr Marks as the class exploded in front of him. 'And have a good weekend.'

He looked even happier than the pupils that it was Friday afternoon.

Joe, Harry and a gaggle of other boys raced down Scarffe's Entry to the field at the front of the Academy. A row of cherry trees with large black metal guards around their trunks ran along one side of the enormous grass space that had the prep department at one end and the big school at the other. The trees were perfectly spaced to be goalposts.

The boys usually just played shooting-in. If they had enough people and wanted a proper match, then the goal posts at the other end of the 'pitch' would be two piles of jumpers on the ground.

They took it in turn to be goalie, unless Nigel came. Nigel was huge. Physically and mentally immense. Nobody messed him about. Name-calling was done behind his back. Joe and Harry liked Nigel. He knew everything. Nigel lived above the family clothes shop on the High Street.

When he stood in the goals, Nigel didn't leave much room to score, but he wasn't agile. They had to try and knock the ball in past him off the black metal cages.

Nigel was in goal today. After a few minutes' play, Joe fired a soft shot along the ground straight at him. Nigel couldn't bend down far enough to stop it and the ball went through his legs and trickled over the line.

'GOAL!' roared Joe as he ran around in frantic circles waving his arms above his head.

'You useless big fat fucker,' muttered Harry breathlessly.

Nigel smiled at this far-from-subtle jibe and said nothing. He went to fetch the ball, which took so long that everyone had time to get their breath back. Then he threw it out onto the field as far as he could. Nigel never kicked it because he couldn't.

Minutes later, Harry was closing in on goal. Nigel waited until Harry was just about to tap it past him before he fell forward. Slowly, gracelessly, he wrapped his huge arms round Harry on the way down. Nigel landed heavily on him, smothering him completely.

The air rushed out of Harry's lungs like a blacksmith's bellows. It took Nigel quite a while, with a lot of help, to get vertical again. Harry didn't move, but he was smiling broadly as he lay spreadeagled on the grass.

A universal roar went up. 'PEN-AL-TY!'

However, after a short consultation with the referee – who was always Nigel – they decided the challenge had been fair and Harry deserved to be flattened for being so rude to the referee.

Harry was theatrically outraged and accused Nigel of attempted murder.

'I suppose I better get home then before the cops arrive,' Nigel wheezed. 'I'm fucked anyway.'

'You could hide under the bed,' Joe suggested, laughing.

'The peelers are so thick, it would probably work,' said Nigel. 'They wouldn't notice it was odd that the bed was floating four feet off the ground.'

They all laughed.

'See you tomorrow, big man?' Joe asked.

'Maybe. Though I might have to help out in the shop.' Nigel still had his hands on his knees, sucking in air.

'I hope you do,' Harry said, pretending to sulk.

Nigel smiled at him gently. 'How are you going to make it as a footballer if you can't take a wee knock or two?'

'A wee knock! How could a Nigel knock ever be a *wee* knock? I think my ribs are broken.' Harry rubbed his dirty hands on his clean shirt.

'Are you hurt, right enough?' Nigel was suddenly concerned.

'No. I'm only joking, but next time I *will* tell the cops.'

'If you tell them I tried to kill you, I will have to kill you. And there will be no witnesses.' Nigel looked round questioningly at the rest of the gang; they all shook their heads to confirm their dumb blindness.

'Bugger off,' Harry said, slowly picking himself up. 'See you tomorrow.'

They could hear Nigel wheezing and coughing as he slowly ambled off toward the town.

The rest of the gang slipped away until there was only Joe and Harry left. As the best players, they always stayed late to practise, only stopping when the fading light, the cold and their bellies told them it was time to go home. Their ma's knew where they were and they'd be back in time for tea.

On Saturdays, the plan was to play football all day, unless it was wet, which meant snooker in the YMCA in the morning and the matinee at the flicks in the afternoon. The pair didn't always have the sixpence required, but if they had enough for one ticket, that would do.

One of them would pay to go in, while the other went round the back of the building. The cinema staff must have thought no one could get round the back as it was so narrow. They also had to keep the window open to ventilate the less-than-salubrious facilities. There were always a few willing piddlers to help whoever climbed in through the window.

Nigel always attended the matinees and always had the shilling for the dear seats at the back. He sat in the double lovers' seats, as there was no armrest in the middle and his girth could be comfortably accommodated. Nigel would have loved to sit in the front with Joe and Harry and join in the riotous noise that often engulfed the sound of the film, but he knew it would never happen. He was too fat to fit in the cheap seats. Besides, no projectiles could hit his head if he sat at the back.

Like Joe and Harry, Nigel loved all kinds of films, but especially war movies and westerns – tales of goodies and baddies, cowboys and Indians, right and wrong, except he often wanted the Indians to win.

Initially, Joe and Harry thought Nigel was just being Nigel when he argued that the Indians got a bad deal. *Fort Apache* changed everything. Suddenly they could see that every story had at least two sides, with the truth sandwiched somewhere in the middle. Sometimes it oozed out and became visible. Often it remained hidden between the thick slices of prejudice and hatred. They agreed that it was easier on the brain when it was a simple 'black hat/white hat' story where the baddie was bad, and the goodie was either a saint or misunderstood and struggling with inner demons.

They reviewed every movie. On the way out, Joe and Harry would sit in the big seat next to Nigel and ask, 'Well, what did you think of that?'

Nigel always picked holes. 'John Wayne's six-gun had about a hundred bullets in it,' he'd observe. 'And yer man was a particularly stupid baddie. Why are they always so thick? You would make a brilliant baddie, Harry!'

'Fuck off! I'd be the fastest gun ever seen. Faster than Wyatt Earp.'

'Nobody's faster than Wyatt Earp,' remarked Joe. 'Get a grip.'

'He's right,' said Nigel. 'Harry the Half-wit, the slowest gun in the west.'

Joyce, the usherette who was also the ice-cream lady during the interval, would always come past and ask them to leave as she had to get the place cleaned. It always looked as if a sweet shop had exploded with the remnants and wrappers of love hearts, Parma violets, and penny chews, along with half-eaten gobstoppers and sherbet dab dust under every seat and strewn in every corner.

'Did you both have tickets today?' she asked with a smile.

'Must have,' said Joe. They all knew this meant no.

Last to leave, as usual, they made their way down the street to the imaginatively named Cake Shop for a snowball. Joe and Harry only went if they had enough money for at least one that they could share. The snowballs were enormous, so one was often enough, especially if they'd had sixpence-worth of sweets.

Nigel always went, but often he was on his own.

CHAPTER 4

Ann had left school in May 1944, a month after her fourteenth birthday. She started work straight away and was now sixteen. Though she was bright and picked things up quickly and intuitively, continuing her education was never discussed. It was just accepted that education meant spending money they didn't have and starting work meant earning the money they needed. Her life path was to get a job and a husband, in that order, then have children.

Ma's views on marriage were: fall in love with someone with plenty of money, and if that wasn't possible, marry someone with plenty of money. At least you would be miserable in comfort. Ann intended to follow her dream and marry a film star – the who, how, and when were mere details.

Her husband would be dark and handsome like Gregory Peck. He would be a great dancer. Together they would be like Fred and Ginger.

Her first job at Black's Solicitors was as a junior clerk. She didn't know what this meant, even though she'd had an interview, but she thought she'd be good at clerking, whatever it was. She was excited at the thought of being paid. Imagine having money of your own!

After putting some of her wages into the tin for the household, she would be able to buy make-up, stockings and perfume, and go to the flicks whenever she wanted without having to ask Ma for sixpence. Her dreams for the future were limitless.

In her new adult world, she learned quickly about office life and human nature. Her initiative and intelligence led to rapid progress. Ann took on all the tasks that didn't seem to belong to anyone else or that the senior clerks considered beneath them.

She got faster and faster at shorthand and typing. Now she was Mr Black's go-to person if he wanted work done quickly and accurately. Ann was eager, efficient, faultless and blissfully unaware that these stellar qualities might cause upset among the more established employees.

At first, Ann listened a lot and only spoke when necessary. As time passed, she became more confident. Now she loved her job.

Ann had first encountered Walter at Black's on a wet Wednesday, seven months earlier. It was April, just after her birthday. He was a few weeks into his new job as a trainee van driver for the Model Bakery. He had been driving the bread van up Market Street and tried to turn left into Scarffe's Entry. This was a very narrow lane and he turned too sharply. Walter thought the van wasn't going to fit and panicked. Crashing the gears, he reversed out, straight into a coal lorry that had turned in behind him. With a sickening crunch, the back corner of his van hit the front corner of the lorry. Walter jumped out. The bread man doing the training jumped out. The coalman jumped out and a crowd gathered round.

The coalman said it was Walter's fault and the breadman said it wasn't. Everybody was talking at once when a policeman appeared. He tried to take notes but couldn't keep up. Walter and the breadman eventually made their statements and returned to the bakery. Walter was advised to speak to his employer's solicitor to get advice on who should pay for the brake light on the van and the headlight on the lorry. He was sent to Torney's garage to see about getting both fixed. After many sharp intakes of breath, the mechanics reckoned it wouldn't be cheap. It wasn't just the glass that needed to be replaced; the bulbs were broken as well *and* there were dents.

Walter also had to visit the police station to make, complete and sign his statement. The police said they couldn't be certain as to who was at fault until all the facts were known, and they wouldn't know all the facts until all nine and a half witnesses had been interviewed.

The half witness was Mrs Chesney, who'd heard the crash and hurried up Market Street from Willy Coate's shop as quickly as her wee castor feet would carry her. Even though she hadn't actually seen anything, she insisted on her right to make a statement. After all, she was at the scene *almost* immediately afterwards, before the dust had settled.

In her opinion, it was 'obvious that the coal man was too close to the bread man because he probably drove into Scarffe's Entry every day and thought it was easy. But if it was your first time, you might be inclined, quite rightly, to be a little more cautious, as it is a very narrow entry. The young boy driving the bread van had every right to go as slow as he thought necessary to navigate the tight space safely. If he thought he couldn't make it the first time, then he should have been allowed to reverse out and try again.'

Of the other witnesses, two old ladies had nearly fainted with shock and another needed a stiff sherry in Bogan's to recover. Another couple escaped death by inches, inches that got shorter with each telling. However, all agreed with Mrs Chesney that the coalman should have been more patient and alert. Thus, the police concluded that the accident might … possibly … be the coalman's fault. But Walter should speak to a solicitor 'to get a proper legal opinion'.

And so Walter had walked into the office of Black's. Ann smiled and asked how she could help.

After he explained his problem, Ann asked if he didn't mind waiting as Mr Black was with another client but shouldn't be too long, and would he like a cup of tea.

Walter had said that that would be very nice and asked if there would be biscuits.

'Milk and sugar?'

'Lovely,' confirmed Walter. 'Not too much milk, and two sugars.'

Ann brought him a cup of tea. 'No biscuits, I'm afraid,' she said. 'Mrs Black usually makes shortbread at the weekends, but it's always gone by Wednesday.'

'Not to worry.' Walter grinned. 'Maybe I could buy you a bun in the Cake Shop someday,' and his grin widened.

Before she knew what she was saying, she'd said, 'That would be lovely.'

Mr Black emerged and said goodbye to his client.

'Mr Green to see you, Mr Black.'

CHAPTER 5

The quietest of the three girls, Hilda had turned eighteen a few months earlier on the fourth of July. She didn't have Ann's striking looks or Muriel's lively imagination, but she had a strong intelligence and knew her own mind.

She worked in the Reform Stores and so was able to provide welcome additions to the normal rations. Rationing wasn't as severe or as rigidly applied in Omagh as it was in Belfast. The rural setting meant there was a steady supply of fresh seasonal fruit and vegetables. But it was the little luxuries, like the odd wee tin of fish or spam which found their way to Sedan Avenue, that produced welcome smiles.

Ma asked the same question every time Hilda brought something home. 'Are you sure Mr Porter knows you took these? We don't want the police knocking at the door.'

'Yes, Ma. They would spoil if they stayed in the shop much longer.' Hilda didn't know if this was true or not, but it salved Ma's fear of being accused of unlawful activity, or worse, embarrassing social exposure. 'Mr Porter makes sure we all get something now and again.' This bit was true.

Like her sisters, Hilda went regularly to the dances in the Starr Ballroom across the street from their house. She didn't go as often as Ann, who would be out every night if there were enough dances to go to. Instead, Hilda was trying to save some of her meagre wages. She was planning to escape and that required money. She dreamt of working in a posh shop in Belfast and staying in a nice dry house that didn't flood, a house with an inside toilet.

Hilda had met Dan, a tall, lanky Canadian, earlier in the year. He was based at Knock-na-Moe Castle with the US Army 8th Infantry. This meant he was important. Only officers stayed in Knock-na-Moe. The ordinary soldiers stayed in St Lucia Barracks.

Dan had an angular face dominated by a large pointy nose. 'He's no picture,' as Ann would say, but he wasn't bad-looking.

He had asked Hilda to dance and he was proficient. Maybe not good enough for Ann, but adequate.

She loved his exotic foreign accent and that he was from somewhere so far away it was almost mythical. Dan came from a place called Winnipeg. The very name sounded foreign. He explained it was an Indian word meaning Muddy Waters, and that the Indians roamed all over North America long before there was America or Canada.

Between sets, Dan described his home. 'It gets so cold there in the winter that the rivers freeze solid enough to drive trucks over them. Our rivers are ten times the size of the Strule. Further up north, polar bears wander the streets looking for food, which includes people.'

Hilda had seen a picture of a polar bear in an encyclopaedia. She thought they were beautiful and dreamt she might see one for real someday.

Dan said, 'They are very dangerous, especially when they're hungry, which is nearly all the time. They can eat a grown man in five minutes!'

'Seriously?' Her eyes grew enormous.

'Coat, hat, shoes everything! And they always start at the head.' He knew he was scaring her, so he smiled and said, 'Only joking. They hardly ever kill people unless the people are stupid enough to get too close.'

Dan asked her for another dance and wondered if she went to the Starr every Saturday night.

'Not every week. I'm trying to save up to move to Belfast and get a proper job. Then I want to save really hard so I can go and see the world.'

'Maybe see a polar bear?'

'Wouldn't that be something!' Her eyes shone. 'That really would be something.'

Every time she went to the Starr after that, Dan was there. He asked her when she would be coming again, and he stopped going in between times. Hilda knew this because Ann went every week and confirmed that Dan wasn't there when Hilda wasn't there.

'What do you think that means?' Hilda asked in bed one night.

'It means he likes you,' said Muriel.

'It means he likes you a lot,' said Ann.

Hilda's thoughts were crashing all over the place.

'Has he tried to get fresh in any way?' asked Muriel.

'No, absolutely not. He's a gentleman.'

'That's a bit disappointing,' said Ann and they laughed. 'He seems to be a good sort. You should try and hold on to him as long as you can.'

'What about a sense of humour?' asked Muriel.

'He's funny when he's telling me about Canada and polar bears and stories about the army. Although sometimes I wonder if he's in the navy. It's hard to tell what's true and what he's making up.'

'He's obviously trying to impress you,' Ann observed.

'He is quite impressive,' said Hilda, 'especially his nose.' They giggled again.

'You know what a big nose means?'

'Don't be so cheeky.' Hilda turned around to face the wall.

'Work in the morning!' Ma shouted through the thin walls.

'Yes, Ma!' they all chorused.

After Christmas, Dan started appearing in the Reform Stores now and again. Never in uniform, always in a smart suit. 'Just passing,' he would say.

Like all soldiers, he seemed to have plenty of money. Nothing much to spend it on, thought Hilda. No food to buy, no rent to pay, no coins needed for the meter and a free uniform to wear at work.

Dan didn't need to buy groceries, so there was no good reason for him to call into the Reform Stores. The pair chatted about the weather and the number of cars on the streets nowadays. The other girls' ears were out on stalks listening for anything juicy as they distractedly served their customers. Eventually, Mr Porter would come out from the back of the shop and Hilda would have to resume work. Dan always bought her a bar of chocolate to share with the others at home.

Other little gifts started appearing. A scarf from the Arcade Store. A little brooch from Love's.

Wednesday was half-day closing, and if Dan was free and the weather half decent – a rare combination of events in the winter – they started going for strolls. The Lovers Retreat, just outside town, was one of their favourite places. This was a local beauty spot with a small waterfall on the Camowen River. As they walked along arm in arm, often in silence, they watched the herons and kingfishers.

Without thinking about it, they grew closer. Dance partners became friends, and then one Saturday night in the middle of February, just after the last waltz, Dan dropped a thunderbolt.

'The Americans are leaving soon' – he held both her hands in his giant paws – 'and unfortunately, that means I have to go too.'

Hilda had not allowed herself to contemplate what she had known would be inevitable.

'Can you not stay and do whatever it is you do with the next regiment?' she asked, her eyes pleading.

'I train people about radios and communications and stuff, so I have to go where they tell me. I can't really say much more, I'm afraid.'

Beyond saying he was in the Canadian navy, all Dan revealed about his job was that it was very boring but sort of secret.

Hilda realised he was very young to have such an important job. Dan was ambitious and loved what he did. But he also loved Hilda more than he could say, or so he said. But orders were orders and there was no question of him staying.

Hilda went back to his quarters in Knock-na-Moe Castle that night, and friends became lovers. Nothing seemed more natural or beautiful.

She slipped into her house in the early hours of Sunday morning. Even Ma wasn't awake. The living room was still warm from the fire that glowed in the grate. Rather than disturb anyone, she slept fitfully on the small settee for a couple of hours.

The day passed busily with no time for questions. But her sisters could tell Hilda wasn't her usual happy self. So that night in bed, Ann started the interrogation.

'Well? Tell us. What happened?'

'He's leaving,' Hilda sniffled. 'End of March. He invited me back to Knock-na-Moe after the dance, and ... well, he says he loves me. One thing led to another, but he can't stay. He has to go back to Canada.' She dried a tear with her hanky.

Ann gasped. 'You mean you two actually ... did it?'

'Work in the morning girls!' Ma shouted from the front room.

'Yes, Ma,' they said altogether, laughing now.

'So that's it then? Even after ... ? You'll miss him,' whispered Muriel. 'I was sure he was the one for you, but he's a soldier I suppose.'

'I thought so too. Crazy as I am about him, they all leave at some stage. It was stupid to think it might be different with Dan.'

'If he really loves you like he says, then maybe he could transfer to another regiment or something and stay. Train other dopey soldiers in whatever it is he trains them in. He's so smart he could be a general in the Inniskillins in no time,' Ann suggested.

'I don't think it works like that,' said Hilda. 'If only it did. Anyway, as Ma says, work in the morning.'

'Yes, Ma,' Ann and Muriel said together.

Hilda was sniffing and sobbing, attempting to be quiet, as they tried to get to sleep. She struggled to fight the sad darkness with memories of the joy she and Dan had shared. She was madly in love with the big eejit, but Winnipeg seemed as far away as the moon. Other soldiers had come and gone. Most of them were idiots with two left feet, one big ego, and no manners. Only recently, Ann had met a brilliant dancer – an English guy, a corporal with the Green Howards called Chester Burnett. He was actually able to teach her a few things and she had been looking forward to dancing with him regularly, but he left a few weeks later. Those encounters were exotic and transient; sunny days, with good stories and free stockings. Then it rained again.

Hilda decided she had to be pragmatic. She and Dan would make the most of the next few weeks. That's all they could do. Lots of walks and tea in the Cake Shop. Maybe more magical nights in Knock-na-Moe.

Dan was very subdued. Preparing to leave seemed to be taking up much of his time. This, and the poor weather, meant they never went back to the Lovers Retreat. Or Knock-na-Moe. He explained that it was now impossible to bring civilians into their barracks. But they did meet for tea and buns in the Cake Shop a few more times.

One Wednesday afternoon a few weeks before he was due to leave, Dan said, 'Today is the last time we'll be able to do this, Hilda.' He put his big hands on top of hers on the small table.

She was determined not to cry, especially in front of everyone in the shop. Ma would be affronted by the speculation and gossip and the 'I-don't-mean-to-pry-but' questions.

'It had to happen sometime,' Hilda said. 'We've had a lovely time. Well, I have anyway. I've loved every minute since I met you in the Starr that night.'

'Me too.' He lowered his voice. 'I've never met anyone quite like you. So easy to talk to. So easy to …' and he looked down at their entwined fingers.

'Are you all right?' Could he be trying not to cry, just like her? Hilda wondered.

'Come with me, Hilda.' He looked up into her eyes.

Confused, she replied, 'Where to? It's bucketing outside.'

'Come with me,' Dan repeated, 'to Canada.'

'What!'

'Marry me and come with me.' He let out a long breath and his shoulders lifted.

'How can I do that?' Hilda's brain turned to mush. 'I've got work and …'

'And what? Please, come and live with me in Canada.'

'Have you been drinking?'

'No,' he said with a smile. 'I love you. I didn't plan this. It just came out, there now. But the more I think about it, the more right it seems.'

'You haven't thought about this? It just came out? Are you serious?' Hilda's mind was exploding in all directions, like fireworks at Halloween.

'Absolutely, and if you really, really love me, you'll say *yes* and come with me. Because if you don't, I'll be the saddest man who ever lived. I'll end up wandering alone in the frozen wastes and will probably get eaten by a polar bear.'

'So I can only go with you if I really, really love you?'

'Yes, it might even need three reallys, just to be really sure.'

'And I'll save your life? I'll save you from getting eaten by a polar bear?'

'Yes, absolutely.'

'Well, I don't want to get arrested for murder. Ma would never get over the shame, and I really, really, really love you, Dan Page, so I suppose I will have to say yes.'

'Jeeze. Fuck. Sorry. What do we do now?' Dan brushed his hands over his short hair and smiled so much his face almost split in two.

Hilda had never heard Dan swear before, but it sounded good. It sounded right. The moment was that important, so significant that proper words were useless.

'Fucked if I know,' she replied, and they giggled like naughty children who had just said a bad word for the first time.

CHAPTER 6

Ma looked shocked and delighted, all wrapped up with her natural caution and normally justified cynicism. Hilda knew what she was thinking – that dreams don't come true, and poor people had to work for everything and still got nothing.

'Page?' she asked the morning after Dan's proposal. 'Is he one of *them*?' They knew this had to be asked!

'I've never asked him, but he knows I'm a Prod and we'll be getting married in Trinity, so I doubt it.'

'And he's an officer?'

'Yes. A commander in the Canadian navy, which is very high up for a young man like him. He's not an ordinary soldier or sailor or whatever. He does secret stuff.'

'What age is he?'

'Twenty-four.'

'Five years older than you. Are you pregnant?' Ma was always blunt.

'Of course not!' Hilda was horrified that her mother should ask.

'Where will you be living?' Ann started her inquisition. 'Does he have a house? What do his ma and da do? Where do they live? Are they rich?'

'Hold on a minute!' Hilda protested. 'Dan wants to come round and meet everyone, especially you, Ma. I told him it would have to be a Saturday as we all work and Joe has school.'

'You're going to bring him here? This Saturday? We've no proper cups. Will he want sandwiches or spuds or something? What will we give him?' Ma was going into inferiority complex overdrive.

'It'll be fine,' reassured Hilda. 'He's walked me home often enough. He knows where we are. He won't want anything. He just wants to say hello and ask your permission to marry me. Then you can fire off all your questions. He'd like to do it properly. If you're happy, then he'll be happy and I'll be happy and we'll all be happy.'

'And we'll all live happily ever after,' said Ann. 'Like in a fairy tale.'

'Exactly. Like in a fairy tale.'

There was hardly a wink of sleep that night. Plans were made, unmade, then remade and dreams were dreamed.

Two days later, Dan came to visit. The family had spent the morning cleaning the front room as best they could. Before he went off to play football, Joe was sent out to sweep the yard, clean the toilet with bleach and put a proper toilet roll on the wire hook behind the door. No cut-up squares of newspaper; not today. Ma raided the tin and sent Muriel over to the Model Bakery to buy a small fruitcake. They had two good cups with pictures of horses on them. Ma and Dan would get these. Everyone else would drink from the stained, chipped everyday mugs.

Ma wore her Sunday best and the girls their best work dresses. Joe had to settle for his school trousers and nearly-white shirt.

Dan arrived at exactly two o'clock as arranged. He was wearing a blue suit with a very white shirt, a navy tie and brown brogues.

The meeting was a great success, mainly due to Hilda's detailed briefing and Dan's ability to take instructions. Hilda had provided hints on how to respond to the most subtle movements of her head, hands or eyes.

Ma seemed impressed with his manner and his manners. He called her 'Ma'am'. He was obviously educated but not patronising. There was no way of knowing whether he or his family had money. He told them his father had been in the army and was a brigadier when he retired. His folks had moved back to Winnipeg and now ran a small shop, or 'store' as he called it, selling, among other things, jumpers and other woolly items that his mother knitted. She had always knitted copiously as she followed her husband round Canada before the war and while she was on her own during large parts of it.

Hilda had never knitted much, but she was good at embroidery. Could you sell embroidery? she wondered. Imagine having your own shop or store and selling things for money! Dreams blossomed in her head, but she had to concentrate as Ma had moved on to the tricky topic of asking Dan if his parents went to church.

'Yes, Ma'am. They go more regularly now Pop has retired and you'll be glad to hear that they're proper God-fearing Presbyterians.'

Glory be to the Lord, thought Hilda, and she wondered if this was true or had Dan just known the best answer. It didn't matter; Ma was now a convert to Danism. Ma announced she would be proud to welcome him into the Brown family. It was obvious that he loved Hilda and would look after her, even though they would be on the other side of the world.

Joe was mesmerised by the big foreign soldier, and his mouth dropped open when Hilda asked Dan to describe polar bears and how they prowled the streets of settlements above the Arctic Circle looking for anything they could eat, including humans!

'Does everyone have to stay indoors all winter since it's freezing and there's man-eating bears everywhere?' Joe was wide-eyed.

Dan tried to put their minds at ease. 'People are used to the bears and know how to treat them with respect. They chase them away by making lots of noise or firing shots over their heads.'

Joe gawped. 'Does everyone have to have a gun to scare the bears?'

'Most grown-ups have guns. We do a lot of hunting in the forest – mostly rabbits and deer. There are grizzly bears as well, and we have to scare those off too. Sometimes you have to shoot grizzlies if they get too close.'

Joe was in heaven.

Dan went on. 'Hunters skin whatever they kill, butcher the carcass and store the meat to eat in the winter. It's so cold the meat keeps fresh for a long time. We also do a lot of fishing in the rivers and lakes, mostly for trout and salmon.'

This was mind-boggling for Joe. Salmon came in tins.

'Would you eat a bear if you had to shoot it?' asked Joe.

'Good question. I've never tried it myself. Mostly they're left for the scavengers. People sell the skin and fur, or keep the heads as trophies.'

'If I go to Canada,' Joe went on, 'can I get a gun and go hunting and shoot a bear?'

'Sure, but it's a long way to Winnipeg,' said Dan. 'Hilda and I will have to sail across the Atlantic Ocean, travel right across Canada on a train, and then get a bus to the fort where we will be living.'

Joe was fit to burst. Ships, trains, buses, fishing, hunting with real guns *and* living in a fort! Wait till Harry and Nigel heard about this!

Ma changed the subject and asked about Dan's work. He explained that he was a specialist in radios and communications. He ran training programmes and shared his expertise with other forces, which was why he was in Omagh with the American army.

Joe asked if he had a gun here in Omagh. Dan told him all soldiers were issued guns, but he only used his on the practice range. Joe thought it was very disappointing that Dan hadn't killed any Germans. He, Harry and Nigel had seen every war film ever shown in the County Cinema and now he'd met a real live soldier in his own house. He could make a great story out of this. Better than one about a Canadian who never fired a gun and who trained people how to use radios, that's for sure.

'I appreciate you must be worried about Hilda going off halfway around the world with a stranger, a foreigner,' Dan admitted. 'And sad to say goodbye to her.'

Ma considered for a few moments before she replied. 'Of course I'm worried, and sad too. She's young, a dreamer. Dreaming is a great thing, but dreams don't always come true. When that happens, the dreamer can stop dreaming and might never dream again. If dreams get shattered, life can be very hard and desolate, but it doesn't stop. You still have to go to work to buy food and pay the bills.'

It was clear to all the children that Ma was talking from

personal experience. Her eyes took on a certain look for a split second and then it was gone.

Noticing her children watching her closely, Ma continued on a cheerier, more familiar note. 'These ones will tell you what I always say, "A shilling in your pocket is your best friend and will never let you down".' She paused. 'So go and live your dreams. I'm sure you'll have a long and happy life together.'

'Thank you, Mrs Brown. Your blessing means everything.'

Ma started twiddling her hanky in her hands, wrapping it tightly round her fingers. 'I know I'll never be able to go to Canada, but maybe you'll come back someday to visit or work or even to live. I don't want to sound maudlin or anything, but it would be nice to think I will see you again before, you know, the good Lord calls me home.' At this, she looked heavenward.

Ma had rarely said so much in one go before. Listening to her, the Brown siblings realised for the first time that their mother had once been like them, with dreams of her own. And it was she who had actually had those dreams shattered, yet had carried on day after day after day. It struck them, too, that they might never see Hilda again. Sniffles broke out.

'I know what you mean, Mrs Brown.' Dan knelt in front of Ma and clasped her hands in his.

'I promise to look after Hilda and do whatever it takes to make her dreams – our dreams – come true. I'll even try to take her to see a polar bear. From a safe distance, of course. I love her more than I can say. I *will* look after her. And I know she'll take good care of me too. Rest assured I'll never let her down.'

Ma noticed a tiny bald patch on the top of his head.

'Hilda only ever wanted to go to Belfast and get a job in a fancy shop and now look at her. Traipsing off halfway around the world,' said Joe.

'Shush, Joe, you're just jealous, that's all,' Ann replied as she blew her nose.

'I believe you, Dan,' Ma said. 'I think you two are made for each other.'

'Thank you again. You don't know how much this means to me. To both of us.' He stood up and took another piece of cake.

'Thanks very much for the tea, and I must congratulate you on the cake. It's delicious.'

They all looked at each other, but nobody said anything, not even Ma. Her eyes looked moist.

The silence stretched a bit until Dan broke it. 'So then, if it's okay with everyone, I'm going up to the church tomorrow to meet Reverend Goodman and get things moving about the wedding. We don't have long to get everything sorted before I … we … have to go.'

'Just have to keep 'er lit,' Hilda said and seeing the confused looks, went on, 'Don't worry he knows what it means.'

'I'm a fluent Norn Iron speaker now, Mrs Brown, and I'll keep 'er lit till it's done.'

'I don't doubt it for a second,' Ma said, smiling at him.

Hilda walked him to the front door and pulled it closed behind them. 'That was nice, what you said about the … cake … and everything.'

She had told him there would be a cake because it was a special occasion, and they would have to dip into 'the tin' to buy it.

'I meant everything I said. Your mom has had a tough time bringing you all up on her own, and now you're leaving for the far side of the world with a complete stranger. That's hard for any mother, but I hope I've eased her worries, at least a bit.'

'I think you did. Ma's not easily impressed by anyone, especially not soldiers. I think she's sad but happy, if you know what I mean. And she'll have a few less spuds to peel or clothes to wash!'

'That's a terrible thing to say, Hilda Brown.' He was smiling.

They shared a kiss before he strode off up the street.

CHAPTER 7

The family met Dan outside the church and introduced him to Reverend Goodman who was delighted to meet him and marry the couple, once it became clear that Dan wasn't 'one of them' and that Hilda wasn't pregnant. The wedding would be in two weeks.

With the date set, planning began in earnest. It was to be a small affair due to lack of time and money. Muriel and Ann would be the bridesmaids, Joe the usher and Fred would give Hilda away. Dan's best man was an army colleague. Because Dan was attached to the US Army, his best man was not someone he knew well but a guy he worked with. They would likely never see each other again.

Joe borrowed Harry's bike and cycled out to the Tyrone and Fermanagh Hospital at the edge of town to deliver handwritten invitations to Uncle Louis, Auntie Brenda and cousin Jim who was sixteen.

Joe didn't like going out to the T&F, as it was known. It was a hospital for the bewildered and the mad, surrounded by high black stone walls. Nobody really knew what went on inside there. Uncle Louis never spoke about what he did, so rumour was the only source of information. Joe had heard tell of people being murdered walking past the walls at night. Screams and ghostly moans could be heard coming from inside. Joe had never been near it at night. Even on a sunny day, it was scary going inside the grounds, through the huge metal gates, past the gatehouse and up the long gravel drive to the big house where Uncle Louis lived.

Louis seemed to be the boss of the hospital, but he wasn't a doctor. He had meetings all the time and sometimes went to Belfast. He had a car, a black Wolsey 10, but Joe had never been in it. His uncle didn't drive it much around Omagh, but Jim said he went to the Golf Club in it. Sometimes he forgot that he had taken the car and had to walk all the way back the next day to get it.

Ann and Muriel called at all the neighbours' houses to tell them the good news and explain the wedding had to be soon because Dan had to leave shortly. And no, Hilda was not pregnant. Sedan Avenue only had six houses on one side, with the Model School, the bakery and the Starr on the other. Some housed Prods and some, 'them uns', but they were all good neighbours and everyone was invited.

The girls took pains to ease the guests' fears by explaining that as Hilda would be going away soon, there was no need to buy presents. The newlyweds wouldn't be able to take much with them. The relief on some faces was less well hidden than on others.

Ma said there was no time to send invitations to the Browns who lived out at Beragh. She had no time for her late husband's family. Joe and the girls didn't know why. She never talked about them and they lived far enough away that she never bumped into them. She assumed they came in to the market on Saturdays, like most farmers, doing whatever farmers did. Ma never went, but Joe and Harry often strolled round it to see the hustle and bustle, the animals and to absorb the farmy smells. They always tried hard not to get shit on their boots, but it wasn't easy.

Before they knew it, the wedding day arrived. Uncle Louis left Brenda and Jim at the church, then drove down to collect Hilda and Ma. Ma was wearing her Sunday outfit, and Hilda looked a picture in her gown. It was Ma's old wedding dress, an off-white colour and very old-fashioned. Hilda loved it.

'Can we go up the town rather than Castle Street, Uncle Louis? More people will see us.'

'No problem at all,' he replied.

And so they turned right, out of Sedan Avenue and up Bridge Street. Then turned right again up High Street and veered left past the courthouse, over to Trinity Church.

Hilda beamed. 'I feel like a princess, Ma.'

Ma smiled and squeezed her daughter's hand.

Muriel and Ann wore summer dresses, as it wasn't Sunday and it was a wedding. Joe was made to wear his school trousers again and his nearly-white shirt, having nothing else decent. He was forced to wear a grey tie with blue dots that had belonged to Da.

Dan and his best man, Doug from Arizona, wore smart blue suits with brown brogues.

Weddings didn't go unnoticed in Omagh and the whole town knew about it. Everyone who knew anyone even remotely connected to the family – and a lot who didn't – turned up to pack the church. Some of the girls from the Reform Stores were there; it was a Saturday so the shop had to be open. Mr Porter could not attend, but he sent a card with a big white fiver in it.

The ceremony was beautifully simple. Muriel read Psalm 67, the Song of Songs. Reverend Goodman read from Romans Chapter 12, and the two hymns were 'Love Divine', and 'All Things Bright and Beautiful'. Nigel and Harry had squeezed in at the back of the church. Joe could hear Harry 'singing'.

Hilda and Dan exchanged rings. Dan had bought them in Paddy Bogue's and Hilda's eyes filled up when she saw her gold band.

'Where did you get this?' she whispered.

'Out of an apple tart from the Cake Shop,' Dan whispered back and even Reverend Goodman smiled. 'It makes up a wee bit for the lack of an engagement ring.'

He sounds nearly like a local, she thought.

Having exchanged traditional vows, the register was signed and they were married!

Outside Hilda threw her bouquet of red roses over her shoulder. Muriel caught it, and Uncle Louis took photographs on the church steps.

* * *

In the church hall, the Women's Institute laid on a spread of tea and meticulously prepared sandwiches and traybakes. The feast was supposed to be just for the wedding party, but Harry and Nigel were doing their best to make sure nothing was wasted.

'Will you miss your big sister?' Harry asked Joe between bites of cake.

'Like a boil on the bum. She farts like Tommy Smedley's motorbike, but she did bring nice things home from the shop now and again. I'll miss those.'

'You could get her job in the shop when you leave school,'

Nigel said helpfully, 'and then you could bring us nice things now and again. You'd look lovely in that wee uniform, as long as the pinafore was long enough to hide your knees.' He feigned lifting a skirt up to his waist.

'Bugger off.' Joe tried to push Nigel. It was like pushing an oak tree. 'I'm going to be like Dan and join the army and do clever secret things that nobody knows about and travel all over the world. I'm even going to go and see a polar bear and shoot a moose and eat it. Da was in the army, so it can't be that hard to get in.'

'Are you saying your da was thick?' Nigel's eyebrows went up.

'Dunno. Don't really remember him, but I suppose he must have been all right if Ma married him. Ma wouldn't have married a dope.'

'No, your ma's not stupid,' agreed Harry. 'So your da must have been smart, 'cause your Ma married him, which means you have to be smart to get into the army, which means you have no chance.'

The logic was too good to argue with, so they grabbed another clatter of sandwiches and queen cakes and went outside.

* * *

There was no time for a honeymoon. Hilda moved into Dan's quarters in Knock-na-Moe and they left for Canada a week later.

There were tears aplenty at the station as the enormity of it all sank in and the Browns realised this really was goodbye.

Ann hugged Hilda. 'There'll be more room in the bed now, and we'll not have to open the window so often.'

Hilda tried to smile.

Muriel asked Hilda to write as soon as she could and tell them all about everything.

Ma quietly slipped a fiver into Hilda's handbag. It was all she had.

'Good luck, love. Be careful. Look after Dan. I'll miss you.' She blew hard into her twisted hanky.

'Don't cry, Ma. You'll set me off.' Their hug was intense.

Ma wagged her finger at Dan. 'You look after her and bring her back before I'm too old to know.'

'I will, Mrs Brown, and you never know what might happen in the future. I'm very fond of Omagh.'

'I'll write as soon as I get there,' Hilda promised, wiping her nose. And as Ma dabbed at her eyes, she slipped the fiver back to Ann.

Joe didn't know what to say. He couldn't think of anything funny. He just stood with his hands in his pockets and tried not to cry.

Yet more hugs and kisses, which made Joe increasingly uncomfortable. Then the whistle blew and Hilda and Dan boarded the train that would take them to Belfast on the first part of their epic journey. The big engine puffed to life, the whistle blew again and the train moved off, wrapped in a cloud of steam.

Hilda had only ever been on a train on Sunday school excursions to Portrush. But now they had their own compartment and they sat opposite each other, with Dan facing backwards.

'People say it's better facing the way you're going,' he remarked. After the train got going properly, he asked, 'How are you, love? So much has happened so fast. It's been a blur.'

Hilda didn't reply for a while.

Dan looked at her.

'I'm trying to find the right words.' After a moment she went on. 'This is the start of the biggest adventure ever. More than I could have imagined. I just wanted to live in the city, work in a shop that sells lovely things and live in a nice house. Now I'm going so far away, I can't even begin to imagine it. To say I'm excited isn't enough. And to say I'm scared isn't enough. But I'm with you and that's all I need. You know where we're going and what to do. To say I'm happy is not enough either. It's hard to take it all in. Do you know what I mean?'

'I certainly do. And I feel exactly the same – excited, happy, scared – but mostly happy. I'll miss the snowballs in the Cake Shop, that's for sure.'

'There'll be real snowballs where we're going,' Hilda said.

Dan came and sat beside her and Hilda snuggled her head onto his broad shoulder.

CHAPTER 8

'It's very quiet,' Ann whispered as they woke on the first morning after Hilda left. It felt like the first day after a funeral when everyone has departed and the reality, finality and enormity of what has happened sinks in.

'I hope she'll be okay,' said Muriel.

'Of course, she will. Dan will look after her. I hope I find someone as steady as him,' said Ann.

'You have Walter.'

'Walter's all right, but I doubt he's going to take me away to see polar bears. He'll be happy to stay in Omagh and drive his wee van around. Anyway, you'll have to get yourself a man soon. You're not getting any younger!'

'True. Nearly twenty and no man. Sad, but it's good fun looking.'

'He's out there somewhere, Mu.'

'I hope so. I don't want to end up like Gladys in our place.'

'She must have been quite pretty when she was younger. Maybe she didn't want a man,' Ann speculated.

'Or like Mrs Chesney, chasing married men at her age.'

'Allegedly. Was she ever young do you think?'

'Allegedly! You sound like someone who works in a solicitor's office. She must have been young once, or she's a bigger medical marvel than we thought.'

'Seven o'clock, ladies. The kettle's on,' Ma shouted outside their bedroom door.

'Yes, Ma.'

They went to church and life went on.

* * *

Five weeks later, a letter arrived. Letters caused great excitement in the Brown household. Like rare jewels, they dropped through the letterbox only once in a blue moon. They were exotic, alien things, and this one wasn't even in a normal envelope. It was lightweight and light blue. Battered and creased like it had come a long way.

The postman handed it to Ma as she was out washing the front step. It was the middle of May, the front door was open and dust dots danced in the sunlight, which lit up the threadbare carpet on the bottom two steps of the stairs. She carried the letter in like it was made of glass and would shatter if dropped. It was passed around all four of them and Joe read the address aloud:

'Mrs K Brown and family, 12 Sedan Avenue, Omagh, County Tyrone, Northern Ireland, United Kingdom.'

The few letters they got were simply addressed to Mrs Brown, Sedan Avenue, Omagh, so this extended effort was of great interest.

'Taking no chances with the address anyway,' Joe noted.

'I suppose not everyone in the world knows that we live in No. 12 and that Omagh is in Tyrone, which is in Northern Ireland, which is in the United Kingdom, even though it's in

Ireland. Easy for it to get lost if it's coming from somewhere far away,' said Ann.

Even the assortment of stamps was odd. All said *Canada* and displayed images of the King in his uniform.

'Open it, Ma. I'm going to wet myself!' Ann was fidgeting with the treasure in her hands.

'Get me my glasses then.'

Ann reached the glasses case down from the mantelpiece. Ma opened it, lifted out the glasses and slowly wiped each lens with her apron. She took a deep breath and unfolded the letter. Then she began reading silently, muttering the words to herself.

'Come on, Ma, read it out loud,' implored Muriel.

'It's from Hilda,' Ma announced.

'Seriously?' Ann grinned. 'Are you sure it's not from Fred to say he can't come round this weekend because he's getting married?'

'Don't be so cheeky!' Ma snapped. 'Fred wouldn't waste the money on paper and stamps. He'd just come round. And there's more chance of me finding an extra fiver in the tin than there is of Fred getting married.'

This was Ma's first mention of the fiver. The girls now knew she'd twigged what had happened.

'It's just a wee joke,' Ann said. 'Who would marry Fred, for goodness sake?'

Ma looked over her glasses at Ann, who noticed a fleeting, questioning sadness.

Ann changed the mood. 'What does she say?'

Ma began to read.

Dear Ma, Muriel, Ann and Joe,

We arrived in Canada around 4 weeks ago, but it will probably be 5 weeks or more by the time you get this. It was a very long journey, and we were very tired when we finally got here.

To start with, we had to go across on the boat from Larne to Stranraer, then all the way down through England to the port of Southampton on the south coast. We had to wait in the barracks there for 3 days before we got a troop carrier ship that took us all the way across the Atlantic Ocean to Canada. We were at sea for more than a week! The cabin was very small and the crossing was mostly fine, but sometimes the sea was very rough, and everyone, even Dan, was seasick. This was a horrible feeling and you thought it was never going to end, but it did, and we finally arrived in a place called Quebec.

'I hope she didn't fart in that wee cabin,' said Ann.
'Ann,' scolded Ma., 'there's no need for that.'
But it broke the tension a bit and they all laughed.
'Go on Ma,' said Muriel.
Ma began again.

We had to stay in Quebec for a few days in the Army camp. Dan called it a 'ship' even though it's on dry land. It's called Her Majesty's Canadian Ship Saint-Hyacinthe to be precise.

Everyone had funny accents like Dan's, and a lot of people spoke French as well as English. Sometimes they would start speaking French, but when they realised, I didn't understand a word they were saying, they quickly changed to English. I would love to learn to speak French. Imagine speaking two different languages.

'What are Frenchies doing in Canada speaking foreign to our Hilda,' Joe asked.

'That doesn't matter right now,' said Ma. 'We'll find out later. Ask Mr Marks on Monday.'

'Nigel will know, but if he doesn't, I'll ask Groucho.'

'I hope you don't call him that in school.'

'Ma, go on,' urged Ann.

Ma continued:

> *When we left Quebec, we got on a train which took us all the way across Canada to a city called Vancouver. The train journey took eight days. It had a lovely dining room with nice food and our own sleeping compartment! It stopped at least once a day to get supplies, so we were able to get off for a wee while and stretch our legs.*

'A train with a dining room. How posh is that?'

'Shut up, Joe,' Ann said sharply. 'Go on, Ma.'

> *For most of the way, the scenery was very boring, just miles and miles of flat grass. Dan called this the prairies and said that it went on for thousands of miles in every direction. As far as your eyes can see and even farther. This is where the Indians used to live and hunt buffalo, but there's no buffalo now.*
>
> *Once we got near the end of the journey, the scenery became far more exciting and we went up through the Rocky Mountains. The mountains were bigger than huge and there was snow on top of most of them. There was lakes everywhere and it was just so beautiful to look at that the days passed very fast. The lakes were as blue as your sparkly brooch, Ma.*

We even saw a big brown bear on the side of one of the mountains. Dan said it was a grizzly. It was very far away but it still looked very big. Dan said polar bears were bigger.

'There *were* lakes everywhere,' Muriel corrected. 'Very bad grammar. Anyway, carry on, Ma. What a journey, eh?'

Dan couldn't take his eyes off the scenery, even though he had made this journey before. He says that every time you do it, it's different, and it's different at different times of the year. He said it's really beyond description in the fall, which is what the Canadians call autumn. The leaves all fall in the fall!

'How big is Canada?' asked Joe. 'We have a globe at school and Canada looks very big and very pink.'

'Shush, Joe,' said Ma. 'We've a lot to get through.' She rustled the flimsy paper pages. 'We'll be here all day reading it if we don't get on. Where was I?'

'Leaves,' Joe said impatiently.

'Oh aye.' Ma stabbed a finger at the letter. She pushed her glasses up on her nose and proceeded.

We have settled into our quarters in Vancouver now and Dan is back at work. He seems to be very important and a lot of people call him Sir. I still don't know exactly what he does, but I know he can speak French, and I heard him speaking what sounded like complete gobbledygook to another officer the other day. When I asked him what language it was, he said Russian! That's four languages he can speak, if you count Northern Irish! So, he's got a big brain to go with the nose.

'Russian?' exclaimed Ann. 'Where do you learn that?'

'More to the point, why do you learn that?' said Muriel.

'Quiet, quiet,' Ma shushed them testily. 'There's still the washing to get out.'

> *I spend my time keeping our little house clean. It's even smaller than our house at home, but the toilet is inside and there is a bath inside as well, and you get hot water out of the taps. There is a rubber hose thingy that you put on the tap, and it has a sprayer on the end of it like you would get on a watering can. You use this to wash your hair in the bath! It's magic. I sometimes just lie in the bath for ages.*
>
> *We have one bedroom, a small sitting room and an even smaller scullery with a gas cooker.*
>
> *Canadians burn logs all the time. No coal. And they've never heard of coke or damping down the fire. I told them that we do this to make the fire last longer in the winter and they just laughed at me.*

'Somebody needs to go and get some coke,' Ma said, looking up. 'Good job Hilda mentioned it.'

'It's Hilda's turn,' smirked Joe and they all glared at him. 'Only joking. I'll go as soon as we finish the letter.'

'The Gasworks will be shut by then, if we don't get a shift on,' Ann said.

It took Ma a minute to find where she had left off.

'They burn logs instead of coal,' Muriel prompted.

> *It's very warm at the minute, but Dan says it will get very, very cold in the winter and there will be lots of snow covering the mountains, and even down low where we are. He's talking about going up into*

the mountains in the winter and doing a sport called skiing.

Ma pronounced it 'sking' and nobody corrected her.

> Sking *is where you strap two planks of wood to your feet and slide, standing up, down the mountain on the snow. It sounds like great craic, but you would need to be well wrapped up, with at least a couple of ganzies on, a good coat, a scarf and a warm hat to keep from freezing. I hope we can make a snowman as well. It doesn't sound like there will be any shortage of the stuff.*

'They could probably build the biggest snowman ever,' sighed Joe. 'Bigger than Dan.'

'They'll need a really big carrot for his nose.' Ann quipped and the siblings chuckled.

Ma didn't seem to notice. 'Shuush. I'm concentrating.'

> *There is no rationing here and Canadians eat lots of meat. Huge big steaks like you would never see in Kenwell's. They eat chips, but they call them 'French fries'. They aren't as nice as yours, Ma. Too skinny. For breakfast, they have pancakes with maple syrup poured over. There's lots of maple trees here and the syrup comes out of the trunks. It's very sweet. It's beyond lovely. You would all love it too.*
>
> *They have porridge as well, but they call it oatmeal. Canadians have different words for lots of things, and it takes a bit of getting used to, but everyone on the base is very nice, and they seem to love the way I talk. They're always asking me to slow down so they can understand me better.*

'Good luck to them trying to understand Hilda,' said Ann.

They love my accent and the words I use for things. Imagine, they've never heard of a sheugh. They just say ditch, but I suppose I'm the stranger here, just like Dan was in Omagh. Dan is keeping well and is very busy, but he wants to go to Winnipeg this summer to see his ma and da, or his Maw and Paw, as he calls them. It will be great to meet them. I hope they like me.

I've got lots of new clothes. In a few months, I will have to get some really warm things, but for now it's skirts and summer dresses. Dan says that we will have to go to fancy dos and get all dressed up, so I will need a fancy dress for that. Imagine dancing in a proper ball gown! Are you still dancing as much as ever, Ann?

I've met a few of the other wives and they are all lovely, in a Canadian sort of way. There is one lady who is the double of Mrs Chesney. She is married to a General or an Admiral or something.

I'm going to try and get a job soon. Dan's pay is very good, but the days can be very long with Dan away working so much and I'm used to working. I'm also going to join some of the ladies' clubs and societies to get to know some of them better and try and make real friends.

Dan and I are very happy and in good health, as I hope you are as well. I hope you are keeping out of trouble, Joe! And that there won't be any floods this year. It never floods here, apparently. Can you imagine!

I miss you all very much. Give my love to everyone, and tell the girls in the shop that I was asking after them.

Yours sincerely,

Love Hilda (Page) XXXOOO

'Well, that's some letter,' concluded Muriel. 'What do you think, Ma?'

'She sounds a bit lonely, but happy. Dan's a good man, but she has no friends yet. I must go to the library and look at the atlas to see where Vancouver is.'

'It sounds like she went so far round the world one way, that it's probably closer returning the other way,' Ann said. 'I hope she likes the food. It sounds very different from soup and champ.'

'Hilda won't be long making friends. She was only in the Reform Stores a day when she was best friends with Sadie and Maud,' assured Muriel.

'Ah, but they're Omagh girls and were just like Hilda. It's different when they don't understand what you're saying and you don't understand them. They speak English, I suppose, but you'd never have thought it could be so different, with different words for things. It must be very hard for her,' said Ma, wiping a bit of dust from her eyes.

'She'll get fat eating all those chips. Especially if there's no dance hall to go to. What do they call them?' Ann asked.

'Dance halls,' said Joe.

'No, you bloody eejit – chips.'

'French fries. There's a lot of Frenchie stuff out there.'

'She didn't say much about Dan either. A Canadian navy officer in Omagh training American soldiers how to work radios always seemed odd,' said Ann.

'He must be very smart, so he must, that's all I can say,' said Ma.

'He speaks Russian and French and he lives in a fort,' Joe enthused. 'How brilliant is that? Nigel will know what he does.'

'Remember, walls have ears, Joe,' Ma warned him. 'Loose lips sink ships.'

Joe puckered up, 'How can lips—? Oh never mind!' and even Ma laughed. 'Seriously, do you think there might be spies in Omagh?'

'Them uns supported the Germans, remember. So just be careful, is all I'm saying.'

'I'll tell the lads out in the middle of the Academy field and make them swear not to tell anyone else on pain of death,' Joe said. 'That should be safe enough.'

Ma glared at him.

'When can we write back?' asked Ann.

'In a day or two, after I've read it a few more times. I hope she's happy. She sounds happy.'

Ann and Muriel exchanged looks. Ma didn't seem totally convinced.

CHAPTER 9

Joe left school for the very last time on the last Friday in May. The next afternoon he made his debut for the YMCA team. It was an important match in the first round of the Omagh and District Cup.

He rose early, excited and nervous, but mostly excited.

'Can I have eggs for breakfast, Ma? Billy says I need to build my strength up.'

'You can have one egg. We're not made of money.'

'Fried on toast? I'll do it myself.'

'I'll go over to the fire station and warn them,' said Ann.

'Very funny. I think I can do an egg on a bit of toast.'

'Just be careful with the hot fat, son. It can spark out at you.'

'Yes, Ma.'

Ann and Muriel peered at him as Joe sliced off a doorstep of bread, struck a Bo Peep and lit the grill. He put the bread under the flames and placed the battered, blackened pan on the hob after lighting the gas ring. A little nob of Cookeen soon melted and he tapped the egg on the side of the pan to crack it. Then he prised it open and poured the egg into the hot fat. He sighed with relief when the yolk didn't break. The egg sizzled and started to go white. He flicked fat over the top of it with the ancient fish slice, until the yolk looked pale and cooked. He turned the toast, and in a few seconds, it was nearly black on the other side as well.

The carbonised toast went onto his favourite enamel tin plate, like the ones cowboys used, and he smeared it liberally with butter. Then he deftly lifted the egg from the pan and set it on top.

'Masterpiece,' said Joe.

'Not bad for an eejit,' Ann conceded, 'When did you learn to do that?'

'I watched Ma. It's easy.'

'It must be if you can do it.'

'Pass the salt.' Joe looked very smug.

He knew he was getting a game for the YMCA earlier than he could have expected, given his age, but the war had taken its toll on the pool of players to choose from. Besides, Billy said he was good for his age – as good as he'd seen; he just 'needed to build himself up a bit.'

Harry was on the bench. Joe hoped he would get on. He was as good as Joe, maybe even a shade quicker, but Joe had the knack of finding the right pass to the right player at the right time, and he had an eye for goal.

Harry knocked the door.

'You're early. Could you not sleep? I've been up polishing my boots since seven and had fried egg on toast, so I'm rarin' to go.'

'Me too! I hope I get on and get a chance to show Billy what I can do.'

'You will. Big Jack is like a donkey. He'll be knackered in no time, and then you'll get on and we'll take them apart.' Joe's face was shining with glee.

'Are Clanabogan any good?'

'Dunno, but they can't be as good or as fit as us. I bet you they don't play every day. We should just go on round. We can have a kickabout till the others turn up.'

'It's great not having to put our kit on in the house. Proper changing rooms, eh? Big time, Joe, big time.' Harry put his arm round his mate, buzzing with excitement.

It was just after half eight when they got to the Showgrounds. Somehow Billy had managed to get this game played at the Omagh version of Wembley, with actual changing rooms and a nearly flat pitch. Although its current condition was more brown mud than green sward, at least the mud had been rolled, which made the newly-painted lines shine very white. This was where the people of Tyrone held agricultural shows and horsey-type events – show jumping and gymkhanas and such – the place where all the posh people mingled and walked through the expensive horse shit in fancy green wellies.

Kick-off was at eleven, but it wasn't long before Billy arrived with a big bag of kit and a few footballs.

'All right, lads? Nice and early. Excited?'

'Rarin' to go, Billy,' said Joe. 'Are Clanabogan any good? What tactics are we going to use?'

'Tactics? Our master plan, as always, is to score more goals than them. Then there's a fair chance we'll win. But take nothing for granted. Skinny cubs like you will need to be careful you don't get maimed. Clanabogan play rough. Tackles will come from all angles, and where the ball is won't matter. You'll need eyes in the back of your head and be ready to jump if you want to avoid a broken leg, which wouldn't be good. Too much paperwork.'

'When will Harry get to show his blistering pace down the wing?'

'When most of them are fucked. Clanabogan will be big and strong. Farmers mostly, but they won't be fit. Not used to running, unless after sheep.'

'Just like most of our team then.' Harry smiled.

'Very funny. Can't all be as fit as you whippets. We've only two fat farmers, Big Jack and Finbarr, and then we have you two. If you can stay in one piece.'

'Is there a proper referee?' asked Harry, suddenly worried about his well-being.

'Fonsie Gallagher, with his two cubs running the lines.'

'Jesus. Linesmen as well. Big time, Joe, big time.'

'It might be stretching it a bit to call them linesmen' – Billy grinned – 'or Fonsie a referee, but they're better than nothing. If there's a bust-up over a penalty, I doubt we'd win a fight with these bastards, so any sort of referee is better than none. Anyway, give me a hand to set the kits out, and let's hope all our boys turn up.'

The changing rooms were under the sole stand, which was at the Sedan Avenue end of the ground. They were basic, very basic. But Harry and Joe thought they were at Old Trafford. Awestruck, they stared at the wooden benches, pegs and flooring. They inhaled the smells of old wood, liniment, sweat, farts, socks and BO. Very grown up. Very manly.

Their sense of wonder mushroomed when they found the showers. Four along a wall that had once been white, but now green garlands of slime dripped down below each shower head. The floor was bare concrete, a yellowy-green colour. It smelled of mould and piss.

'I've never had a shower,' whispered Joe in reverential tones.

'Nor me. Everyone'll be able to see your willie. It might be embarrassing.'

'Aye, for them, when they see the size of my massive toot.'

Harry laughed. 'I'll look forward to seeing this impressive appendage.'

'Prepare to be amazed, Harry boy.'

The team arrived in dribs and drabs and stood around smoking and chatting, eager to give their opponents the once-over.

Eventually, Clanabogan arrived, crammed into two well-used boggin', old, dented Land Rovers. The players spilled out the back like giant bags of spuds – not all of them landing on their feet. They were big. Some looked fairly young and big; the rest were just big.

'Right lads,' Billy called out. 'Let's get kitted up. It's half ten.'

Shorts and shirts were provided by the YMCA, but players had to wear their own socks and boots. Harry stripped down to his pants and pulled his shorts on.

'These are fuckin' massive. Billy, I must have the wrong ones. I could wrap these round me about four times.'

'They're all the same size,' said Billy. 'Costs less. I told you, you need to eat more spuds, build yourself up.'

'Nigel would fit into these. I could use them as sheets.' Harry was trying to pull his shorts up above his calves by turning the waistband over and over.

'Stop gurning and get a move on.'

Joe pulled the waistband of his shorts out about a foot and a half from his belly. 'It'll take a lot of spuds!'

'A few pints of stout and you'll soon fill out,' Jack said.

'Looks like that does the trick,' returned Harry, scanning his teammates, who laughed at his cheek.

Billy's pre-match pep talk was always the same. 'Run or walk as fast as you can. Pass the ball to one of your *own* team as often as possible. Don't let any of the other side get past you, especially if they have the ball. Keep your eyes and ears open for potential broken legs or other serious physical damage at all times. You may not necessarily see your attacker – sorry, tackler. And if we score more than them, we will probably win. But the referee is such an arsehole that it can't be guaranteed.'

Joe and Harry already knew most of their teammates, and there were perfunctory introductions and confirmations of positions and roles.

'Frank will take all the free kicks in their half and all the corners. Big Dunc will take the frees in our half. He'll hoof it up into their box, after which it could go anywhere. Good luck lads! Remember, if in doubt, kick the shit out of them.'

They ran out onto the pitch and were greeted by an actual cheering crowd – at least fifteen people leaning against the railings that surrounded the field.

The match kicked off at five past eleven. Fonsie Gallagher was wearing a proper referee's kit. He looked like a giant black snooker ball, his head a bright red balloon perched on top. He looked like he could burst at any moment. Joe thought he might find it difficult to keep up with play, but he soon realised Fonsie's plan: stand long enough in one place and the game would occasionally come to him. Joe hoped his eyesight was good, but of course Fonsie had his two sons, Pat and Paddy, to help. The pair looked exactly like their da, except the red balloons sported more hair. They didn't seem too bothered about the colour clash between their florid faces and their bright ginger hair.

Three minutes in and Joe knew this game was quite a step up. A wee bit faster and a huge bit more brutal. He was playing inside right and got his first pass after a couple of minutes. Joe had his back to the goal just outside their penalty area. He trapped the ball and was about to pass it to Big Jack when he got flattened by a train. If Nigel could go at a hundred miles an hour, that's what it felt like. He ended up face down on the ground, sprawled out like a starfish. He'd never seen a starfish but he was seeing stars.

The whistle didn't go. He hauled himself up, gasping for breath. A toothless mountain was smiling at him.

'Are you okay, son? Need to be quicker next time,' and the behemoth moved off like an avalanche back into position.

Soon Omagh were attacking again. Joe feinted to run past the Mountain to his right. As the ball came to him, he darted the other way, but the Mountain stuck out a huge leg. It connected with Joe's skinny leg and he cartwheeled up in the air and landed face down in the mud again.

'*Ref-er-fuckin-ree*!' shouted Big Jack. 'Yer man's goin' to kill the cub!'

Fonsie blew his whistle. 'No need for the language, son. Free kick to Omagh.'

Frank planted the ball on a tee of mud, and when every player, bar Omagh's goalkeeper, was crowded into the Clanabogan box, he lofted the ball towards the penalty spot and their centre forward, Geoffrey. Joe and Harry called him Giraffrey, which they thought was very clever because he was a couple of years older than them and at least a yard taller. Ma saw him in the street once and reckoned he would never be out of work as there was always a need for clothesline poles.

The ball drifted into the grey sky towards Giraffrey, and he leapt up amidst the throng of bodies. It was like a set of Uillean pipes and bagpipes had been thrown into the air at the same time. Arms and legs – and he seemed to have three or four of each – went in all directions. At least six people got clattered as he soared like a burst bag of sticks. At the apex of his graceless leap, the ball hit Giraffrey on the back of his head and arced away from the goal, directly towards a waiting Joe.

He had avoided joining the dangerous-looking scrum in the box. Time slowed … the ball slowed as Joe shifted off his right foot onto his left. The ball was inches off the ground when he hit it as hard as he could. It screamed towards the goal, rising as it went and crashed into the crossbar. A waterfall of raindrops cascaded from the shaking wooden bar. Giraffrey was just getting up; still on his hands and knees, he stretched out his neck like a heron on a riverbank. The ball struck the front of his head and trickled over the line.

Fonsie blew his whistle and the crowd went wild. Joe revelled in his volley that was as sweet a strike as you could wish for. Though the goal was credited to the giraffe, everyone knew the part Joe had played in it and the obvious touch of class.

Until half-time, the score was stuck at one–nil. Then it started to rain again, turning the wet mud into mud soup. Harry and the other three subs could only huddle in their coats and pace up and down the touchline. 'On the bench' was just a technical term. Billy's half-time talk, being much the same as his pre-match talk only shorter, was missed by half the team who were either off for a wee or a smoke. In it, Billy took full credit for the tactical masterclass that led to them being one up.

The sodden leather ball became even heavier as the match continued with mistakes of all magnitudes – terrifying tackles, acrobatic escapes and the occasional pass that went where it was intended. The Mountain continued to try and cripple Joe and anyone else he could get close to, but he was running out of steam and Joe was skipping away from him more and more often. As they predicted, Big Jack was breathless after fifteen minutes and had to stop for a fag. He rubbed the front of his thigh, reckoning his hamstring had seized up. Billy shook his head, feigned sympathy and brought Harry on.

Initially, Harry got kicked all over the place like Joe, but the instinct for self-preservation meant he quickly found out how to avoid the worst of the lumbering, bone-crunching assaults. Before long, he and Joe were weaving beautiful patterns down the right-hand side of the pitch. The giraffe became a hard-to-miss target and went on to score a hat trick. The second and third goals were proper headers that actually went where he meant them to go.

'How long to go, ref?' Billy roared from the touchline.

If he'd actually been moving, Fonsie would have stopped to look at his watch. Instead, he just looked at his watch. 'Ten minutes.'

He was still checking his watch when Joe got hacked down again on the edge of the penalty area and went sprawling full length in the quagmire.

'PEN-AL-TY!' roared the whole Omagh team and the crowd in unison.

'It was outside the box, ref,' wheezed a knackered giant.

'I'll have to consult my linesmen,' said Fonsie, who was still in the centre circle, as he had been for the entire match. 'My view was obscured.'

How useful this consultation would be was dubious, as Pat was in the other half of the pitch and Paddy was chatting to someone on the sideline.

'Definitely a penalty, Da,' Pat reported. 'They've been kicking the shite out of that wee lad all day and he's been running rings round them. He deserves a penalty.'

'Didn't see it, Da,' chimed in Paddy, 'but it looked like a penalty to me.'

Fonsie knew the rules didn't facilitate issuing a penalty just because someone deserved it, but it sounded like it could have been a penalty and that was good enough to warrant the drama of giving one.

He blew his whistle so hard the pea shot out. 'Penalty!' he roared and was immediately surrounded by tons of sweaty flesh.

'You didn't even see it, you useless fat bastard.'

'Are you blind as well as stupid?'

'Can you not see without your stick?'

'Shut up the lot of youse, or I'll send you all off for abusing the ref. I'll not change my mind, so give my head peace.'

Frank would take the penalty. It was suggested that maybe Joe should take it, but he was still getting to his feet in the ooze that threatened to suck him in completely.

The Clanabogan goalkeeper stood like a massive monolith in the middle of the goals, with only a sliver of daylight down each side of him. But Frank was one of their best players.

Fonsie had had to move from the centre of the pitch. He ceremoniously placed the ball on the penalty spot, once it had been identified. Frank stood over the ball. He stared at their keeper. Without a functioning whistle, Fonsie stuck two fingers in his mouth and blew loudly. Frank stepped back five steps, strode forward slowly and deliberately, and walloped the leaden ball into the bottom left-hand corner of the net.

The Omagh players whooped and rushed over to clap Frank on the back. Frank made a point of shaking Joe's hand.

The rain became a torrent and Fonsie blew the whistle five minutes early. Billy, the only other person with a watch, said nothing.

The home team trudged off the pitch, very happy, very dirty and very heavy with mud.

'Glad we don't have to wash our own kit,' Joe said, smiling at Harry.

'I've bruises everywhere,' Harry complained, panting. 'How did they manage to kick me on my shoulder?'

'At least you haven't got stud marks in your bum.'

'We're lucky to be alive. But we won, that's all that matters.'

Billy's post-match team talk was short and sweet and to the point: 'Well done lads. Good result. No serious injuries. Get showered and I'll see you in McAleer's for a pint.'

The smell in the changing room was incredible. Joe and Harry were amazed at the sight of the naked bodies. The boys were very conscious of their smooth boyish skinniness as large hairy arses, wobbly torsos and legs with bulging calves walked round them. The heads at the top of these shapeless bodies were all shouting and laughing at once as they bellowed to be heard above their own din.

'It's like the market, but with different animals,' Harry whispered.

'Same smells.'

The boys waited until the mass of flesh in the showers thinned out. The hot water was all used up, but they were happy to be in a shower, even if it was only a cold trickle, and to have free soap. They used the cracked bar of Sunlight to wash their hair too. It made it squeak in their fingers.

They got dressed in the now-empty changing room.

'Did you see the size of Giraffrey's willie? A real giraffe would be proud of that thing,' said Joe.

'I'm disappointed that yours isn't nearly as prodigious as I was led to believe.'

'Were you looking at my willie?'

'Only because you said it was huge. I wanted to be impressed and I'm sorry to say the whole experience was extremely underwhelming.'

'Are you a fruit, Harry? Fruits look at other men's willies all the time.'

'You're a very attractive man, Joe Brown, but I prefer your sister.'

'Which one?'

'Ann.'

'You fancy Ann?'

'I'm just saying she's very pretty, but maybe a bit old. She must be nearly eighteen.'

'You really believe she's better looking than me?'

'Sadly, yes. She has bigger tits for a start.'

Joe patted his flat, almost concave chest. 'She's only seventeen, I think, but still far too old for you. She'd kill you. Time for snooker?'

'Let's go.'

They talked about the match all afternoon to anyone who would listen. The truth got stretched to breaking point.

Joe could smell the liver and onions as he turned into Sedan Avenue. His favourite! He was a grown-up. No more school. Man of the match. What a day!

CHAPTER 10

Joe found a job right away. It was in the tax office because he was good at sums. Harry started work as an apprentice mechanic in Torney's garage, partly because he was good with his hands, but mainly because his da was the senior man in the place.

The informal football gang had largely broken up, but Joe and Harry began training on their own in the long summer evenings, as well as going to team training every Tuesday and Thursday. At first, they just had a kickabout, but soon, without any real plan, they started running. They were naturally lean and fit and quickly found they could run for miles.

'Like two bloody greyhounds, Kathleen,' Joe overheard Fred saying to Ma one evening. 'You could make a fortune with those two down at the track.'

'At least it keeps them out of mischief.'

'Too tired for mischief, I imagine, the amount of running they do.'

One Wednesday afternoon, when his family's shop was closed, Nigel wandered over to watch and have a chat. He was wheezing.

Harry said to him, 'You should have a go at running Nigel. Get a wee bit fitter.'

Nigel shrugged his enormous shoulders in a that's-not-bloody-likely sort of way and looked down at his feet, which he knew were there somewhere.

Joe immediately knew where Harry was going with this. Harry was worried for their friend. Only sixteen, Nigel couldn't walk very far, or very quickly. He always seemed to be short of breath. Maybe if they could get him to run, even a little, it might help.

'Just try it. A short jog, then stop. Then do another wee bit. You'll find that all the wee bits gradually join up.'

'Joe's right,' said Harry. 'Only do it when it's just us. At least to start with. No one will see you. It will make you feel great.'

Nigel looked like he might want to do something but was too embarrassed and didn't know how or where to start. He slowly nodded his huge head as if to say, *I know what you're trying to do here and I love you for it.*

The following week, he began running. On the first day, he shuffled less than a hundred yards before he was punctured. His face looked like a busted turnip.

Harry and Joe ran laps of the Academy field. Nigel waited for them to come round. Then he would shuffle along with them as far as he could before stopping and waiting for them to come round again. The first time he completed one of these intermittent laps, Harry and Joe had circled the field ten times.

Over the following days and weeks, after work and after Harry's and Joe's match on a Saturday, they ran. The number of times Nigel got lapped before he got all the way round decreased. He was stopping less and less, but still hadn't gone all the way round without pausing for breath.

It was hard work, but Nigel was determined and convinced he was beginning to feel better. He had to make a new hole in his belt. Only an inch from the last one, but it was in, not out.

Then one Monday evening, Nigel declared he couldn't do any more running. Just like that. He was done.

'Why not?' asked Joe. 'We thought you loved it. And you're making headway. We can see it.'

'My ma says I'm overdoing it and I need to be careful of my heart. She's frightened I'll have a heart attack like Da had.'

'Your da's still alive, isn't he? Still working. Still fleecing people in the shop. He might never have had a heart attack if he'd done more running when he was younger. That's the whole point,' insisted Harry.

'Is there anything wrong with your heart?' asked Joe.

'Dunno. Don't think so.'

'If your heart is in proportion to your body, then yours is big enough to drive the Belfast train. Imagine, if your heart stays gigantical, but your body gets smaller. You'd be able to run to Belfast and back. No need for the train,' said Harry.

'You should keep going and only stop if you want to stop,' added Joe.

'I don't want to lie to Mum. She'll find out. I'm always panting and knackered when I get home.'

'It's not like real lying. It's like telling her you only had one snowball after the flicks when you really had two, or not telling her at all that we were caught in Jimmy's orchard. What she doesn't know and all that,' said Harry.

'I dunno.'

'Wait before going home. Get your breath back. Tell her you're going for a walk with your friends instead,' Harry suggested.

'What you do isn't that different from walking anyway,' Joe quipped as he moved out of striking distance.

'Cheeky bastard,' Nigel said with a grin.

'Cheeky maybe, but I know who my da was. He was a soldier.'

'So your Ma says,' Nigel shot back.

'And there was lots of soldiers,' said Harry.

'Were. Were lots of soldiers, you thicko, and Ma was only married to one of them.'

'Sorry, Mr Marks,' Harry whined like an obsequious schoolboy. 'Me don't do grammar too good.'

They laughed and Joe said, 'Tomorrow if it's dry? Tell your ma you're playing snooker after work.'

'She'll think I'm bonkers.'

'Wise woman, your ma,' Harry smiled.

'She knows I don't know one end of a snooker bat from the other.'

They all laughed.

'Tomorrow?' Joe persisted.

'We'll see.'

In his own quiet teenage rebellion, Nigel kept running and one day, without saying a word, he got right round. No stops. The boys only lapped him three times. He still wasn't properly running, but he was jubilant. All three were doubled over with their hands on their knees, gasping for air, sweating and flushed with effort and pride.

'An extra scoop is called for,' proclaimed Joe.

'And extra sprinkles,' Harry chimed in.

'And chocolate,' finished Nigel. 'My treat.'

They went to the Cake Shop and Nigel bought them all a big whippy ice cream with sprinkles and a bar of Dairy Milk.

Nigel said, 'I don't even feel stiff.'

‘The girls don’t like it if you’re not stiff,’ said Harry.

‘Like you would know,’ Joe answered.

‘I know more than you think I know.’

‘I think you think you know more than you think you know.’

‘That doesn’t make sense.’ Harry scratched his head like Stan Laurel.

‘There’s lots of things that don’t make sense.’

‘Where you’re concerned anyway.’

‘Now, now, children,’ Nigel cut in. ‘Let’s not fight.’

‘Seriously, Nigel, you’re getting on great.’ Joe tried to put his arm round Nigel’s shoulders and got about halfway.

‘No stopping me now. Next stop the Olympics,’ he said and a big grin split his big face.

CHAPTER 11

As summer drifted into autumn, the rain began. Everyone expected flooding almost every autumn. It was a real cause for celebration if the cold set in and the rivers stayed where they belonged, but it rained heavily throughout September and Omagh's rivers burst their banks in early October.

Joe was at the gasworks in Spillars Place getting coke for the fire when word reached him. When it flooded in Omagh, word spread as quickly as the water.

He raced home pushing the old pram full of coke, lumps scattering the streets as he ran. He could already see brown water at the edge of the bus station.

He banged open the front door, gasping, 'Flood!'

'Shit,' said Ann, who was sitting in the living room fixing the hem of a skirt.

Ma stopped peeling the spuds. 'Ann! What sort of language is that.'

'Sorry, Ma, but I was supposed to be meeting Walter tonight at the Starr.'

'The dancing can wait. Everything upstairs. Quickly!'

This was a familiar routine, and they started grabbing everything they could. Joe's mattress, sheets, pillows, blankets and clothes were bundled up and deposited in Ma's room where he would sleep on the floor. Downstairs, his flimsy wardrobe was put on top of the bed frame. The two old armchairs in the living room were piled onto the settee and it was hoisted up off the floor using ropes strung over two hooks in the ceiling. The curtains were gathered up and tucked into the rails holding them up.

The mat in front of the fire was lifted along with the coal bucket. Joe filled another rusty bucket with coal and lugged it up too. Ann helped him carry the pram full of coke up the stairs and put it in her room at the back.

They only had one toilet roll, but Muriel grabbed last week's *Conn*, the local newspaper.

'Don't forget your po,' Ma shouted from halfway up the stairs, carrying the bread bin and a load of spuds.

'Already done!' called Joe. 'I'll get the wee stove.'

'And a couple of pots, Joe.'

'Yes, Ma.'

'And the radio.'

'Yes, Ma.'

'And the matches. Don't forget the matches.'

'Yes, Ma. I mean no, Ma.'

Joe rolled the raggedy stair carpet up five steps.

Finally, they laid a couple of the mouldy sandbags that were out in the yard across the bottom of the front door. The sandbags were completely useless, but it was all they had. It was part of the routine. Once the sandbags were put in place, the family trudged upstairs.

They made space amidst the clutter as best they could, then went into Ma's room to watch the advance of the water.

'There it is now,' said Joe, pointing to the corner of the Model School wall. Slowly at first, but increasingly quickly, the water turned into Omagh's fourth river. It was eerily quiet as the deluge flowed down the street; chocolate brown and randomly swirling into little whirlpools that appeared, spiralled and disappeared chaotically. Twigs and larger branches raced past and became entangled to form small rafts at the lampposts.

'Looks like it might get quite high this time,' Muriel said, glancing at her mother questioningly.

'Hard to tell, but it's rising fast. Two days is my guess.'

'Why does it always happen at the weekend?' moaned Ann. 'We won't even get a day off.'

'No work, no pay,' said Ma, 'and you know what I always say.'

'*A shilling in your pocket is your best friend*,' they chanted together.

'Exactly.' She smiled. 'Get the wee stove lit, Muriel, and let's have a cup of tea.'

The smell of paraffin filled the small room as the kettle slowly came to the boil.

They lit fires in both bedrooms; the buckets of coal and coke were laid out on the floor on pages of an old *Conn*. Ma thought there should be enough for a three-dayer. The gas rarely went off. They had candles, but it was hard to read without the gas lamps.

The dirty brown river turned into a lake and rose as high as the downstairs windowsills. It rarely got any higher; a line around the walls downstairs testified to this. They had long given up trying to wash this line away. It was a constant reminder of why the house always smelled of damp and mildew, with earthy undertones of mud and more than a hint of sewage.

They made do with a loaf and a pot of homemade jam for lunch. The bread would be mouldy by morning in the stuffy heat, and the milk would be off as well. The lump of cheese would last longer; they could always cut the blue bits off the outside. Ann reckoned these blue bits added flavour, but Ma said they'd make her sick. Having anticipated the flood, Ma had hard-boiled ten eggs.

There was no feeling of anger about the floods; they just happened. They were as much a part of the annual cycle of life as the first frost or snowdrop.

All the lower areas of Omagh flooded. Harry lived in Campsie at the eastern end of the town. There, the houses were built on a narrow, crooked finger of land, with the Drumragh river on one side and the Camowen on the other. Their confluence at Campsie Bridge formed the Strule River, which flowed along the south of the bus station, under Bell's Bridge at the end of Bridge Street, before curving round to flow north under Abbey Bridge at the end of Sedan Avenue. Then on around the Showgrounds before veering off to the north-west.

The ground rose quickly away from the rivers, so the main shopping areas of Market Street and High Street, the churches and the chapel and the more affluent houses on the Dublin Road and Derry Road never flooded.

But because Harry's family lived in a two-up, two-down like the Browns, they also got flooded and they dealt with it the same way. There was a stoic acceptance that this was the way things were and there was nothing that could be done about it.

In Sedan Avenue, the Browns boiled spuds and ate them out of the pot, along with the eggs. They couldn't waste water washing plates. Then they settled down for the evening.

'Can we listen to the wireless for a wee while, Ma?' asked Ann 'There might be a dance band on.'

'The 'lectric might run out soon. I put a couple of shillings in this morning, but we need to be careful.' She said this even though there was nothing upstairs or downstairs that used electricity other than the radio. The sockets downstairs were set high on the walls, safe from the water.

Ann tuned the radio to the BBC Light Programme and they listened to Benny Goodman, Lily Ann Carol and Martha Tilton for an hour.

'I like Lily Ann Carol's singing,' Ann said. 'I wish I could sing like that.'

'I wish you could sing, full stop,' said Joe.

'Don't be so bloody cheeky. Even Harry sounds better than you!'

'Ann! Your language is getting worser and worser,' chided Muriel.

'It's the way our clients talk. In any case, "worser and worser" isn't very good English either.'

'I don't bloody care.'

Even Ma was laughing. 'Girls, girls, now don't be so common.'

'But we are common,' protested Ann.

'A bit more decorum, please.'

'What's decorum?' asked Joe, anticipating the answer.

'It's the middle of the de-apple-um,' Ann responded quickly and everyone groaned.

Muriel was reading *Great Expectations.* Ma was darning a pair of Joe's socks. He was trying to study. It was basic tax stuff, and while he liked the maths, he got bored quickly. He put his jotter down.

'Homework done?' asked Ma.

Joe shook his head, exasperated at Ma thinking he still did homework 'Naw, I'll finish it tomorrow. It's pretty easy. I'd actually like to try harder stuff.'

'Smart alec,' teased Ann.

'Alec is as thick as you are,' said Joe. 'He's digging sheughs for the Council. Smart Joe, you mean.'

'Smart—' *Arse* was about to slip out but Ma intervened with a sharp scowl.

Later, Joe suggested a game of whist. 'We can all play, now there's only four of us.'

'Poor wee Hilda,' said Ma. 'I hope she's okay.'

'Do you think they play whist in Canada?' Joe wondered. 'Cowboys only play poker, but maybe that's just America.'

'Can't imagine John Wayne sitting round the campfire playing whist after a hard day shooting train robbers,' said Muriel.

Ann opened the much-used deck of cards. 'I'm sure we'll win as usual, Muriel.'

Joe put on his most superior voice. 'I think you'll find that Ma and me always win because it's a known fact that I'm the smartest. And I'll huff for a week if I lose.'

The cards were dealt out. The gaslights were lit, the music turned down, and they were snug together in the flood.

After a while, Joe said, 'It's not the same without Hilda, is it?'

'She's living her dream,' answered Ann. 'And I will too. I'm going to marry a film star and dance in the flicks like Ginger Rodgers.'

'Dream on,' said Joe. 'It's your go.'

Joe and Ma won with hands to spare. He seemed to have an almost photographic memory of the cards.

They went to bed to the sound of the now-muted rumbling

of the water outside. As the water levels peaked and the flow slowed, the smell got worse.

* * *

'You can come in now love,' said Ma, and Joe crept into her bedroom. He kept his clothes on as he curled up on his mattress under a pile of blankets. Ma was lying facing the wall and wouldn't have watched him getting undressed, but for him the very idea of undressing in front of Ma was unthinkable.

He turned to face the window and remembered how it wasn't that long ago he used to sleep in Ma's bed when the floods came. And not just during the floods. A wee crack of thunder was enough of an excuse.

That was when it hit him that his mother must be very lonely. When everyone was worried about the floods and the mess they left, Ma always appeared completely calm and in control of everything. She must be very tired too, he thought. She never stopped doing stuff. Maybe she'd sleep better if there was someone there to give her a big hug.

'Night, Ma.'

'Goodnight, son. Sleep tight.'

He heard her making gentle, elegant, moaning sounds as she slept.

He had to have a pee during the night. He knelt down close to the po to be as quiet as possible and not wake her, but her steady breathing stopped for a minute. He knew she had stirred.

They rose with the light. The day was brighter and the rain had eased off to a downpour. The water in the jugs and washbasins would have to do them until after the flood, so washing was quick and basic. That suited Joe, who noticed no difference from his normal routine, but the girls were delighted not to be going to church so no one could see them.

Once the girls were up, Joe went into their room to give Ma privacy as she dressed. Within minutes all was normal again, and the pos were emptied out the window at the back into the fetid lake. The contents added little to the filth levels of the water. The smell was getting worse by the minute. It would be really potent once the sun came out, but that wouldn't happen today.

They had tea with slightly stale bread and jam for breakfast. Then Ma leaned out of her bedroom window and called, 'Jean! Jean! Are youse all all right?'

The sash window next door was pushed open and Mrs McGartland roared back, 'We're grand, Kathleen. And you?'

It was odd to hear anyone calling Ma 'Kathleen'. She was Ma or Mrs Brown. Kathleen made her seem more fragile; like an ordinary somebody, with brothers or sisters or friends.

'Yes, all safe. Has Charlie gone across yet? The milk's nearly off.'

Charlie Hunter lived two doors down and worked in the Model Bakery. In the floods, he would wade across to the bakery, which was set back from the street, and, whether by accident or design, never flooded. A few other hardy souls would make it into work and get the ovens going.

Charlie would then slosh across to each house in turn. They would each lower a basket and pull up a fresh loaf and milk, which the bakery always kept in their big fridges. Ma couldn't imagine having a fridge.

'He went over a wee while ago,' Jean shouted, 'so he shouldn't be long. I wonder how long this one will last?' She looked down at the swirling water.

'I'm guessing tomorrow afternoon at the earliest,' said Ma.

'Aye, sounds about right. Pat says it might be Tuesday, but what does he know?'

'You and I both know that what Pat knows isn't worth knowing and what he thinks he knows is worth even less.' Ma knew Pat could hear this exchange and he and Jean would be having a wee laugh.

Half an hour later they watched Charlie leave the bakery down the ramp at the side where the vans went in and out. He was wearing full-length green fishing waders and the water quickly reached his waist. He held his basket above his head and slowly traversed the stinking water. Joe lowered their basket and Charlie shouted up, 'Your usual, Joe? Bread, milk and five snowballs?'

'Four.'

'Sorry, I forgot there's only four of youse now. I've five here, but call it four.'

Joe pulled the basket up and the heavenly smell of fresh bread wafted in the window, wiping away for a moment the stench of the turgid lake hiding the street below.

'Thanks, Charlie!' shouted Ma, as Charlie waded next door.

'No problem, Kathleen!'

Joe pulled a chunk off the loaf before it was even in the window.

'Joe!' Ma scolded and slapped his hand. 'Have some manners.'

'Can I not have the heel now?'

'You'll just have to wait like everybody else.'

'There's four sides,' argued Joe.

'If we all have a heel, then all we'll be left with is the soft middle bit which will go off in no time,' explained Ann as if talking to a toddler.

Ma put a cloth over the loaf. 'We'll have bread and cheese at twelve, and don't let me catch any of you picking at it in the meantime.' She glared at Joe.

'No, Ma,' said Joe.

'Have you no homework to do?'

'I left school at the end of May, Ma.'

Ann and Muriel giggled behind their hands.

'I mean aren't you doing an exam soon? Have you no homework you could be doing for that?'

'It's called studying, and anyway, it looks easy. Just lots of adding up.'

'Fine. Just make sure you do the work. There'd be no need for experts if it was easy.'

'Yes, Ma. I mean no, Ma. I mean you're right, Ma.'

The extra snowball was quickly divided up and devoured. It was still warm, and they all closed their eyes and made *umming* noises of heavenly satisfaction.

The morning drifted by until the mantel clock downstairs chimed twelve.

'You forgot the clock, Joe.' Ma smiled.

'Me? Everyone forgot the clock!'

'You're right, son!' Ma gave him a squeeze.

The cloth was lifted off the loaf and they discovered that all four of the soft corners had been eaten. All hell broke loose. Ann and Muriel were outrageously outraged. They glared and pointed at Joe, who was the picture of innocence. He put his hands together in front of his face like a choir boy and said he wouldn't be that stupid after Ma's warning. Then they caught Ma with the slightest hint of a smile and the mock tension vanished.

'Couldn't resist it. You can have the crusty bits now.'

'If there's any left.' Joe was bereft at Ma's duplicity.

The rest of the day dragged on as Ma continued to work at repairing various items of clothing, while the girls read their books and Joe devoured *The Hotspur*.

They had tea at three and shared two snowballs.

For dinner, there was champ made with boiled spuds and fresh milk, and scallions from their garden. All agreed it was tasty, but needed butter, which they didn't have, and Joe was blamed for not bringing up the salt.

Music came on the radio, the fires were lit, and later – after the last of the bread and cheese – the cards came out. Joe and Ma won again, much to the girls' chagrin. It was very close this time, with only one point in it after nine hands. They couldn't accuse Ma of cheating, but Joe! The sisters knew, or thought they knew, he was cheating, but if he did cheat, he was very good at it.

Monday morning dawned brighter and occasional vaguely sunny shafts shone through the cracked dark sky.

Breakfast was the last two snowballs.

As the floodwaters began to recede, the stench intensified. By the afternoon, the water was low enough to allow them to venture downstairs and begin the clean-up operation. They had to run the outside tap for ages before anything like clean water began to flow. Then it was boiled and the floors and walls scrubbed with diluted Jeyes Fluid. The clean antiseptic smell battled to replace the smell of muddy sewage. After several flushes, the toilet became useable again and a debate over who would go first ensued. Ann suggested alphabetical order. Muriel turned to get Ma's opinion, but she was already gone.

As the light faded, they lowered the settee back down and lit the fire with the remains of the dry coal from upstairs to try and dry the place out. The curtains were let down and pulled across and life returned to normal.

Soon the rain would start again and it would clean the garden.

As the Browns ate boiled potatoes with salt for dinner, they realised they'd all lost a day's pay.

CHAPTER 12

The next day, the flood was briefly discussed – dismissed by those affected and ignored by those who weren't. Nobody died, not even a dog or a cat, although Joe did find a dead rat in the coal shed. But the hidden damage lingered. Conditions got even worse in houses already riddled with damp and mould.

The man called to clean and empty the gas meter. He asked for a bucket of water to rinse the pennies. He wiped the inside of the meter with a dirty rag, closed it up and left twelve pennies piled up on top.

Back at work, Muriel took a call from an Englishman who sounded very posh. He was in the Royal Arms Hotel in Omagh and wanted to be put through to Mr Louis McKeown at the Tyrone and Fermanagh Hospital.

'I'll try him for you now, sir,' she answered in her best voice. While they waited for the call to be picked up, she said to the posh Englishman. 'Mr McKeown's my uncle, so he is.'

'Is he now?' Muriel could hear him smiling. 'Is he a good uncle?'

'Oh, aye. He's very kind and very smart.'

'I haven't had the privilege of speaking to him yet, but he must be very smart if he's in charge of the Tyrone and Fermanagh Hospital.'

'We call it the T&F. It's shorter.'

'Shorter indeed.'

The call was picked up and Muriel said, 'I have a call for Mr McKeown, from … who shall I say is on the line?'

'Dr Algernon Tolleshunt-Darcy.'

* * *

'You'll never guess who telephoned Uncle Louis today,' she said that evening at home.

Ma looked up over her specs. She was putting new elastic in a pair of Joe's underpants.

Ann turned down the corner of the page of her book to mark her place. She knew old Bertha, the librarian, hated people doing this. While Ann understood that books should be respected and others would be reading them after her, this sounded like important gossip and her bookmark was on the mantelpiece, three feet away.

'Was it loony Larry from Limavady,' asked Joe, 'or bewildered Bernie from Belfast?'

'No.' Muriel laughed. 'It was a very posh gentleman from England called Dr Algernon Tolleshunt-Darcy. Calling from the Royal Arms.'

'About what?' asked Ann. 'I'm sure you earwigged!'

'God, no! Uncle Louis would go mad if he found out.'

They all smiled at the unintentional pun.

'He might take the radio back,' said Joe.

'I'd have to kill him,' Ann said.

'We could get Dr Tolleshunt-Darcy to poison him,' proposed Joe.

'He's probably not a doctor doctor,' Muriel observed. 'I think he's a mental doctor.'

'I hope Uncle Louis knows he's mental.'

'You know that's not what I meant.'

'You mean he's a patient?' Joe asked.

'Don't be daft. He speaks just like what's his name in that film we saw the other week.'

'David Niven?' suggested Ann.

'That's him. Like David Niven, but with extra plums.'

* * *

Dr Tolleshunt-Darcy rang the T&F again the following afternoon. Seeing the call was coming from the Royal Arms, Muriel nearly broke Esther's arm to get it.

'Hello again,' he said in his lovely plummy voice. 'Are you the only person who works in the telephone exchange?'

'No, there's heaps of us here, so there is. Just coincidence, I suppose.'

'A happy coincidence, I'll warrant. I've met your Uncle Louis – Mr McKeown – and he is all you said he was and more. Very kind, and generous with his time and expertise. Not to mention clever. Can you please put me through to him again?'

'Of course. Please hold for a moment.'

'Thank you.' As the doctor waited, he began to whistle.

'I know that tune! What's it called? It's on the tip of my tongue.'

'I believe it's the "Missouri Waltz" by Glenn Miller.'

'It's a lovely tune to dance to,' Muriel said. 'Such a pity what happened to Glenn Miller. Just disappearing like that.'

'Most unfortunate.'

'That's you connected now, Dr Tolleshunt-Darcy.'

'Most kind of you, and please, call me Al.'

'Al.' Muriel sighed, loving the sound of it, and he was gone.

* * *

At teatime, Muriel announced, 'He phoned again today.'

'Who?' asked Ann, exasperated by the vagueness.

'Dr Tolleshunt-Darcy.'

'He's nearly as bad as Mrs Chesney.'

Joe asked, 'Do you think he's getting treatment over the phone for being mental?'

'Don't be so thick. Anyway, Uncle Louis isn't a whatdoyecallit?"

'Psychiatrist,' said Ma, without looking up from sewing a button onto Joe's shirt.

'That's it. He just runs the place.'

'So why is Dr Whatshisname over here?' asked Ann.

Muriel shrugged. 'He's had a meeting with Uncle Louis.'

'How do you know that?'

'Al told me.'

'Who's Al?' Ann was now confused.

'Dr Tolleshunt-Darcy. He told me I could call him Al.'

'Very familiar,' said Ma without looking up. Her tone suggested caution.

'He must be mental if he's chatting you up on the phone,' Joe said. Muriel clipped him round the ear. 'Hey, Ma! Did you see that? She punched me on the head!'

'No, son. I didn't see it. Don't hit your brother, Muriel.'

'Yes, Ma. Anyway, he wasn't chatting me up. He was just being friendly. I could listen to his voice all day.'

'Maybe he does lectures. You could pretend to be clever and go along, just to hear his lovely accent.' As Joe continued to wind her up, he got a clip on the other ear.

'I'm away!' he said. 'Reading about tax is better than listening to you cooing over Dr Al, who isn't even a real doctor.'

* * *

Al was back on the line on Friday morning and the other girls knew better than to pick it up.

'Well! It's you again!'

'Good morning, Dr Tolleshunt-Darcy.'

'Al, please and you haven't told me your name yet.'

'It's Muriel. But we're not supposed to tell people our names.'

'Mu-ri-el.' He rolled all three syllables around like he was tasting a glass of vintage port. 'What a lovely name. Greek, I think. I hope you won't be in trouble for divulging it.'

'It's fine. Do you want me to connect you to Mr McKeown again?'

'Not today. We're having lunch. I met him yesterday, and in the course of our discussions, I told him how helpful his niece has been. He said he always admired your discretion.'

Muriel had to put her hand over her mouth to stop herself from laughing out loud. Nobody had never called her discreet before.

'He said you were the best niece he'd ever had and easily the most beautiful.'

'I'm sure he never said any such thing.'

'Not in so many words, I grant you. The point is, I am leaving tomorrow morning and was wondering if you would like to join me for a drink this evening at the hotel?'

Muriel was never lost for words, but this was close, very close. It took her nearly a full second to recover her breath and her poise.

'That would be lovely. What time?'

'Eight. I could meet you in reception?'

'Good. Excellent. Yes, lovely. That will be lovely. Good. Excellent. Yes, good!'

'Right-o. I'll see you at eight.' And he was gone.

Muriel never moved as fast as she did after work that day. She ran all the way home and burst into the house, face flushed red and gasping for breath.

'He's asked me out for a drink!'

'Who?' asked Ann, as she stirred the Irish stew.

'Al! Dr Al. Posh Al. English Al. Al who sounds like David Niven with an extra plum.'

'Tonight?'

'Yes, at eight!' Panic was setting in.

'What about Derek?' Ann lifted the pot off the hob.

'Damn – sorry, Ma – Yes, Derek!' Muriel had completely forgotten her arrangement to meet him that night at the town hall. 'Can you go and tell him I'm sick or something? Will my hair be dry in time if I wash it now?'

'Quickly, then,' said Ma. 'Build up the fire, Joe.'

Ann helped Muriel with her hair. She wolfed a bowl of stew into her, then dried her hair at the blaze Joe had created with a couple of dry blocks. She put on her best Friday-night dress and a quick dab of make-up and she was ready.

'I can't go yet. I can't be early. Ingrid Bergman would never be early.'

Ma said calmly, 'Take a breath. You'll be fine. You look beautiful.'

'What's the story with this eejit anyway?' asked Joe.

'Other than that he's a psychiatrist, I can't tell you anything more. You know what happens at work is confidential.'

Joe and Ann burst out laughing.

'Maybe he wants to practise his *psychiatricality* on you. If he's a beginner, like. He might need nutters to practise on.' Joe covered his ears, just in case.

'You're just jealous. Where's your girlfriend then?' taunted Ann.

'She's a secret.'

'Keep her that way. I wouldn't want to see any girl that would go out with you,' said Muriel.

Joe was still thinking up a witty reply when Muriel said, 'Got to go' and donned her coat.

'Be careful,' Ma counselled. 'He might sound posh, but you don't know him from Adam. He could be married. Or divorced. He could even be one of them uns. You never know.'

'Yes, Ma.' English taigs don't count, do they, Muriel thought.

Al was waiting in the small reception area, next to the door to the bar. He stood out like a film star surrounded by extras. He was tall, handsome and looked in his late twenties.

Muriel spotted him before he spotted her. She steeled herself to walk straight up to him, something not normally done by young ladies. To her great relief, his face registered surprised pleasure.

'Muriel! Good evening. I must say, your face matches your beautiful voice. Your uncle painted a glowing picture of you, but I'm afraid, he didn't do you justice. Shall we find a table?'

Muriel followed him through the crowd, nodding and mouthing silent hellos to the people she recognised, and parking any information gleaned for future use. She was sure they were doing likewise, wondering what a girl like her was doing with an obvious gentleman.

Then he actually took her hand – or more like he took the tips of her fingers with the tips of his – and guided her in as she sat down. She hoped her hair had survived the walk up the town.

He took her coat and hung it on a peg on the wall beside their table.

'Can I get you a drink?'

Muriel thought he sounded nervous, which surprised her. She was as jumpy as a cat in a kennel. She looked around nervously to see what the few other women were drinking.

'What are you having, Dr—'

'Al.'

He raised a finger to summon the waiter. 'Your uncle has been extolling the virtues of Bushmills whiskey. Black Bush to be precise.'

'I've never had a Black Bush. I'll have one of those, if that's all right.'

The drinks arrived and he raised his for inspection, swirling the golden liquid slowly around the small glass. He held it up to his nose and took a long deep sniff. Then he sipped it and looked like he was in heaven. 'It's as smooth as …' He pondered for a moment. 'It's as smooth as the smoothest thing you can think of.'

'That's very smooth,' agreed Muriel. 'Difficult to think of anything smoother than that.' And they both smiled as their nerves settled. *You're the smoothest thing I can think of right now*, Muriel thought.

Muriel took a sip and couldn't stop herself grimacing.

Al laughed in a rumbling sort of way. 'Well?'

'It's very strong,' she paused. 'And smooth. Very smooth.' She coughed a little before taking another tiny sip.

'Apparently a small, or should I say *wee* drop of water will loosen it up a bit. The barman told me it helps to release the taste and the aroma better.'

Al went up to the bar and got a small jug of water with 'Jameson's Irish Whiskey' on it. Muriel thought he looked very smart – tailored tweed suit, shiny black brogues, both probably handmade, and a pricey-looking shirt with cufflinks. He seemed to glow through the haze of cigarette and pipe smoke.

He poured the tiniest amount of water into each glass, drank and sighed with approval.

Muriel was dubious that a *wee* drop of water could make any difference but it did and after another sip, she began to enjoy it.

'Now. Tell me about your work. It must be fascinating working in the telephone exchange,' Al said.

Muriel didn't think he was being sarcastic and patronising; he sounded genuinely interested.

'I love the little intrigues.' she began. 'I like to chat to the callers if I can, even if it's only for a few seconds. I try and guess why they're phoning, what they say to each other and all that.'

'Like little mysteries.'

'Sort of. I imagine the story behind the call, even if there isn't one. You must think I'm terribly nosy.'

'Imaginative, curious and caring, I would say. I'm sure you hope each conversation creates a little joy in the lives of the participants. Even if it's only for a brief moment.' Al sipped his drink contentedly.

'I never thought of it like that. I just want to know what's going on, and if I don't know, I make it up.'

'So, you *are* nosy then.'

They laughed together.

'Imaginative, curious and caring is what I would say.'

'Touché.' Al raised his glass in a toast.

'What?'

'Another?' He signalled to the waiter.

'I don't think I should be drinking whiskey. It's not very ladylike.'

'The ladies in London do it all the time.'

'They must be very drunk.'

Al smiled. 'Do you like it?'

Muriel realised she had finished her drink. 'Yes. It's very sort of warm and glowy.'

'Glowy? That's a good word.'

'It's a local expression. Well, it is now 'cause I've just made it up.'

'I like it.'

'Well, doctor – sorry, Al – you know what I do, but what do you do?' she asked when the waiter returned with their drinks. 'I know it's something to do with mental patients, 'cause that's what the T&F does.'

'You *are* nosy.'

'Interested and caring.'

'Indeed.' He explained his work in the psychiatric unit at Guy's Hospital in London. 'Many of my patients are soldiers, or ex-soldiers. They may look as though they survived the war physically intact. But what they saw and heard has damaged their minds. A broken brain is much trickier to fix than a broken leg. Often the men struggle to explain what they're going through. They feel it shows weakness to admit they've been affected by the war like this. Especially when so many of their brothers-in-arms didn't come back at all or are living with terrible injuries. But the men I treat are probably hurting just as much. Hiding it from themselves and everyone else and trying to carry on as normal only makes it worse. The trauma eats them away from inside.'

Muriel was gripped. 'I never heard it explained like that before. Everybody just thinks the T&F is full of loonies that have to be kept locked up. Nobody thinks of it as an illness that can actually be fixed. What can you do for them?'

'That's partly why I've been here to see your uncle. The T&F has a small farm on the grounds and the patients get involved in growing vegetables and looking after the chickens and pigs. I'm interested in doing something similar in London. Space might be an issue, but a farm or allotment would be of great benefit.'

'Aye, so they have something to do. They're outdoors enjoying a bit of company, getting exercise, instead of sitting in bed all day. That has to be good for your brain.'

'That's the idea. Having a purpose and learning new skills helps promote feelings of self-worth. And it's important that the patients work with others. I've seen the benefits here, so I'm sure we can do a lot more along the same lines. It's a very exciting area and I'm keen to develop it as far as I can.'

They chatted on, easy in each other's company. Another drink and Muriel looked at the clock above the bar and suddenly realised it was eleven o'clock.

'Where did the time go? I'd better get home.'

Al glanced at his expensive-looking watch. 'My train leaves at seven in the morning, so I suppose it would be sensible to call it a night, although I'd much rather stay here and learn more about you.'

Emboldened by the whiskey Muriel said. 'That's a very romantic notion.'

'That's me! Mr Romantic. Nothing better than a good romantic film, I say.'

'What's your favourite then?'

'You're very nosy, Miss Brown.'

'Seriously. Your favourite film of all time.'

'*Casablanca*. Great story, great acting. I fancy myself as Humphrey Bogart. On second thought, I'm probably too good-looking to be Humphrey Bogart. I like *Brief Encounter* too.'

'Ingrid Bergman is beautiful.'

'Just like yourself.'

Muriel blushed at the compliment. Even in the smoky gloom, it didn't go unnoticed.

'Perhaps we could go to the cinema the next time I'm over.'

Next time! More than a brief encounter! Muriel's heart leapt.

He stood and held out his hand. 'May I escort you home, Mademoiselle?'

Muriel panicked. How could she possibly show this posh London doctor with cufflinks the tiny terraced house where she lived?

'That would be very gallant of you, doctor. It's Friday night and there's always a few hallions about.'

If he was put off by her home, then too bad, but her instinct was that he wouldn't care.

They left the Royal Arms and crossed the street. On Bridge Street, Muriel pointed out Kenwell's butcher's shop and explained that Oliver Kenwell was the OK in the OK Showband who played in the Starr all the time.

'You like dancing?'

'Love it. We all do. Well, Hilda did, but she's away in Canada now. She married a spy! Ann goes all the time. She wants to be a dancer when she grows up – well, she is nearly grown up – but you know what I mean. I go as often as I can.'

'Maybe we could go dancing the next time I'm over.'

'The pictures *and* dancing?'

'Not both at the same time.'

'You will be back then?'

'I hope so.'

They crossed Bell's Bridge and turned left into Sedan Avenue.

'Is that your school?' he asked as they passed the Model School.

'Yes. That's where *my* brain got damaged.' They had reached the end of the short terrace. 'This is it,' Muriel said. 'That's the Starr Ballroom over there, and that's the Model Bakery. Best snowballs in the world.'

'Snowballs?'

'Big round buns covered in coconut flakes with raspberry jam in the middle.'

'Another local delight I'll have to try the next time I'm over.'

'You're going to be busy.'

'Busy hands make light work … or something.'

'You and Ma would get on well. She loves all those old sayings.'

'Maybe I could meet her the next time I'm over'; 'Maybe you could meet her the next time you're over,' they said simultaneously and laughed.

He took her hand and kissed it gently. 'Goodnight, Muriel.'

'Goodnight, doctor … sorry … goodnight, Al.'

He turned and walked back up Sedan Avenue. As he disappeared into the night, she could hear him whistling the 'Missouri Waltz'.

* * *

Ann wasn't even feigning sleep. She heard the creak of the first step on the stairs, followed by the squeak of the second one.

'Is that you Muriel?' Ma called out.

'Yes, Ma.'

'It's very late.'

'Sorry, we got chatting and lost track of time.'

'You can tell me all about it in the morning.'

'Yes, Ma. Good night Ma!'

Everything was as it should be. Everything was normal. Except it wasn't.

Ann turned to face Muriel. 'You look like you're about to burst. So, come on, tell me all about him. What's he like? Young, old, married, plump, short, tall? Is he really posh? What did you talk about?'

In the gloom, Muriel changed into her nightie without saying a word.

'Come on, Mu. Put me out of my misery here! What happened?'

'I don't think there's words enough to describe tonight, so there's not.'

'I hope you mean in a good way. You sound like you've been hypnotised. Tell me something, anything. Does he have all his own hair and teeth?'

Muriel did a fair impression of the Mona Lisa, smiling like she had just seen God.

'He looks a bit like Gary Grant, only better. Fair hair. Not as blond as Walter.'

'Nobody's that blond.'

'And he has deep blue eyes. He wears expensive clothes. Oh, and he has cufflinks!

'Oooh, very posh.'

'Shiny black shoes. And he's tall, slim, not skinny, with a voice that you could listen to forever. You could fall asleep to his voice, except he's so interesting. We had three drinks. Whiskey! Can you believe it? Ann, he's gorgeous! He sounds like the King and he's a gentleman. He walked me home. And did I tell you he's a doctor who looks after soldiers whose brains are broken?'

As she went into detail, rabbiting on about unseen war damage and mental conditions, Ann cut her off.

'Stop! This bloke sounds almost too good to be true.'

'And he's coming back soon,' Muriel said dreamily.

'Can we mention any of this to Uncle Louis?'

'It was Uncle Louis who suggested he ask me out. Apparently, he said nice things about me.'

'He must be going mad. Is insanity infectious? Anyway, work in the morning, so stop grinning like a Cheshire cat. Some of us need our beauty sleep!'

'Yes, Ma.'

'Sweet dreams,' Ann whispered and kissed her sister lightly on the forehead before rolling over to face the wall. Muriel had forgotten to ask her about Derek, she noted.

CHAPTER 13

Winter began cold, dark and wet. No clothes could be dried outside, so the old wooden clothes horse was smothered, dripping, every day. The house smelled of damp washing and mould, mixed with smoke and soot from the fire, which took ages to heat the little sitting room. But its heat never reached any other room in the house, so the small fires upstairs had to be lit too.

Ann got a modest pay increase at Black's. No longer officially junior, she would have a little extra for the tin and herself. She couldn't go dancing more than she already did, but she wanted to start entering competitions with Walter. For that she would need new dresses, dancing shoes and make-up.

She had grown very fond of Walter and he could dance. He often gave her little pecks on the cheek at the end of a dance, but they had never gone further than that. Sometimes she thought Walter might be a bit odd, but then she caught herself on. Just because he could dance and was good-looking didn't mean anything.

Muriel was going out with Derek. She told Ann that she liked him. He was 'nice'. Quiet and gentle, but he'd never bought her three drinks in the Royal Arms. He liked a pint of Smithwicks in Bogan's on a Saturday afternoon. She had never seen him drunk, and he was always on time and clean. He was a so-so dancer, but happy enough to sit out dances, or not go at all. He still liked cowboy films with lots of shooting. Sometimes Muriel had to go to the flicks with Ann and Walter to see something more challenging, like *Laura* or *Gentleman's Agreement*.

Fred regularly called to sit and chat with Ma and listen to the radio. He liked to talk football with Joe. He was a Blackpool fan, but Joe didn't mind. Fred and Ma often had a wee drink. He smoked a pipe stuffed with Sweet Afton, which was pleasant compared to the normal smells in the house. Ma rarely smoked, except at Christmas, mainly because she couldn't bring herself to waste money on cigarettes.

Joe and Harry had become valuable members of the YMCA team. Joe was scoring goals and getting mentioned in the *Conn* now and again. He started cutting out the reports and was saving to buy a scrapbook and glue. However, saving seemed such an alien concept. Hilda had always been able to salt some cash away, but Joe couldn't get the hang of it at all. There were always more entertaining alternatives.

'Maybe Santa will bring me a scrapbook,' he said on the evening of the day his name appeared in big letters on the back of the newspaper.

JOE BROWN HITS HAT TRICK FOR YMCA

'If he comes this year,' Ma said without looking up from her knitting. 'You might be too big for Santa.'

Joe looked outraged and spluttered, 'Too big for Santa? When did that happen? How big is too big?'

'Stand up,' Ann said.

Joe stood.

'That big,' Muriel said, extending her arm so it was level with Joe's head.

'Your head's a marley! What use is Christmas without Santa?'

'It's supposed to be a celebration of the birth of Jesus, not Santa. I'm not sure Santa was – *is* – even a Christian.'

'You mean he might be a taig?'

'Catholics are Christians, you ignoramus.'

'What?' Joe exclaimed, looking comically stunned.

'Enough nonsense,' interrupted Ma. 'Money is scarce, is all I'm saying, but you should make a list like always, just in case.'

'Yes, Ma,' chorused all three together.

December marked the start of Christmas and all the wish lists and to-do lists that came with it. Ann and Muriel had long ago moved from toys to make-up and magazines. Joe was obsessed with footballs, boots and books, and now a scrapbook and glue.

It seemed real when the wireless began playing carols, and even Joe was happy to go to the carol service at the church.

They all went down to Anderson's, Ma included, to see the window display and the impressive toy train that circled the huge seasonal toy department. The train set was built every year by Gareth Moore, who was also so good at being Santa that all the children thought he was the real thing. Somehow, when they were younger, Ma made sure each had the sixpence required to go up and tell him they had been good all year and what was on their list. They came home with a small paper bag containing a balloon, sweets, crayons or short colouring pencils and a wee colouring-in book. When they were small, this kept them quiet all day, but they all knew they were getting too old when the colours stayed inside the outlines and the balloons didn't get blown up straight away.

Fred brought a little tree from Scarffe's, and the same few ancient baubles were hung on it. They had no lights.

Socks were pinned to the mantelpiece on Christmas Eve and a small glass of milk and a gnarly old carrot was left on the hearth.

Fred also brought chocolate ornaments to hang on the tree on Christmas Eve. There was always a clamour to pick one and hang it up, and always a 'can we have one now?'

'No, they're for tomorrow,' Ma always said, pretending not to notice as Fred slipped each of them a spare one.

Fred's generosity stretched even further. Every year, Ma was given a bottle of Harvey's Bristol Cream, which never lasted very long.

Fred liked a wee Bushmills himself. On Christmas Eve, when the children were small, the two old friends would have a drink and listen to Christmas music on the wireless after the weans had gone to bed, early and over-excited.

'Santa won't come if you don't go to sleep.'

'Yes, Ma.'

Starting in January, Ma saved a few shillings when she could in Anderson's Christmas Club so that Santa could bring them simple treasures like dolls, or a tin train, or a cowboy outfit, or a teddy bear. There were always new handmade socks in the stockings, along with an apple, an orange and a few sweets, usually a little bag of brandy balls or clove rock.

Christmas morning began very early when they were wee; Ma said it sounded like there were fourteen weans in the house, not four. It was the only day that she could get a cup of tea and a biscuit in bed. The children would bring her a box of Milk Tray chocolates, and she'd always feign surprise and tell them there was no need for them to get her anything, that they should save their money because *a shilling in their pocket was their best friend*. But they all knew this was nonsense. It was just Ma being Ma. It didn't really matter what they got her, but it couldn't be nothing.

The spuds were peeled. The sprouts and carrots were trimmed and prepared, and the fire was set before they went off to church. Even Joe sang the familiar carols. The church had a huge tree festooned with decorations and the flower arrangement was a big spray of holly and mistletoe. Candles flickered everywhere. It was a wonderland, and their small world was filled with optimism that God would make the world a better place, where good people did good things. Next year would be better.

Back home, after church, the small turkey that Jimmy Reed gave Ma every year was filled with a basic stuffing made from breadcrumbs, onion, parsley and an egg.

The bird always arrived in its entirety and Ma and Fred decapitated it, plucked it and cleaned out its guts in the yard on Christmas Eve. The giblets and neck were used to make soup, and the last sharp bits of the feathers were burned off by holding the turkey over a metal plate of burning methylated spirits. This was one of the more pungent, unpleasant, unforgettable smells of Christmas, soon replaced by the aroma of soup bubbling away in the largest pot and the bird roasting. Ma and the girls always made plum pudding in the autumn and it would be steaming in their second biggest pot.

Dinner was ready when it was ready, but it was always after they had gathered around the radio to listen to the King's speech.

A pile of gorgeously crispy roast potatoes, a few sprouts, which they all loved – except Hilda – carrots, and Bisto gravy poured all over completed the feast.

They had no fancy special occasion plates or serving dishes, and the size of the meal meant that nearly every piece of delph in the house was pressed into use. Bowls had to be washed after the soup, so they could be used again for the plum pudding, which was always served with custard.

A small table with fold-under wings, which served as a sideboard the rest of the year, was unfolded and a linen tablecloth made by Ma's ma was smoothed over the top. Only four could sit round the table, so Joe ate his dinner off a tray on his lap, constantly running in and out of the kitchen to get another spud or to pull another piece off the turkey. This year, though, he finally had a seat at the table.

Christmas dinner was always long, chaotic, noisy and hilarious. Joe was always the first to succumb to the effects of the sprouts, to everyone's indignant protests, but soon they all joined in and their sides were sore with laughing.

Neighbours called in. Fred returned and received a box of five little cigars from the family. Harry and a few of the girls' friends dropped in to see what everyone had got. Uncle Louis, Brenda and Jim called in for a drink, a mince pie and a chat. Louis was keen to hear how Muriel had got on with Al.

For all the jollity, Christmas that year was not the same without Hilda. They joked about her being the odd one out for hating sprouts, but they missed her sorely and realised the holidays of their childhood were over.

The dead days between Christmas and New Year were for reminiscing about the year past. Ma always insisted the coming year would be even better. It would be the best yet, because they were a year older and a year wiser. And a year had passed without another war. So they closed in around each other and looked forward, dreaming about what 1948 would bring.

CHAPTER 14

Walter's da, Mr Green, worked at the train station. He was a porter, and Walter had loved being in and around the massive trains when he was younger – the noise, the smells and the grown-up language.

The main duties of a porter were to look after all the various needs of the passengers – everything from helping with luggage to getting taxis. But other duties included having to walk along the tracks to light the oil lamps at the signal posts.

In the evenings, Walter would often walk with his da to these signal posts as the light faded. He stood at the bottom of the ladder while his da ascended to light the lamps. As they walked back, these lights became a ghostly glow in the gloom, their flames flickering in the mantels.

The last time they made this walk together was on 2nd February 1945. It was Walter's fifteenth birthday. It had started to snow just as the last low light of the day turned the sky orange in the west. Father and son always did the Londonderry line first, as that train was due an hour before the final train of the day from Belfast. By the time they had gone fifty feet, they couldn't see a yard in front of them. The wind picked up strength and the snow became a blizzard. Walter's da had a Tilley lamp that he used both as a light and a flame to ignite the taper used for the signal lamps. It shone a dim pale yellow at the end of his arm. Walter clung to his other arm so he didn't get separated and lost.

'You okay, son?'

'I can't see. The snow's burning my eyes.'

'And I need wipers on these bloody glasses,' chuckled his da. 'Haven't seen snow like this for ages. Not far now.'

His da had walked this section of track so many times that he probably could have done it blindfolded, but this was different. They had wrapped up pretty well, but the wind still went through them.

He never wore gloves. 'Too footery getting the mantel off and lighting the taper,' he said, as the lamp almost slipped from his frozen hand. 'Can you take the lamp for a minute son, so I can try and warm my hands up? I don't want to drop the bloody thing.'

Walter was wearing gloves, so he let go of his da's arm and took the lamp in his right hand. Now he could just make out his da's big black shape and smell his oily, tarry, coat. He stumbled along, getting increasingly nervous. What if they got lost and buried in the snow, and nobody found them for days?

They swapped the lamp from one to the other until his da reckoned they must be at the signal point. His da felt for the tracks with his foot, then nearly bumped into the pole. He put his hands on the ladder.

'Are you going to climb up in this?' Walter asked, fear creeping into his voice.

'Have to. No choice. They need to see the signals.'

'Will the train even be able to get here in this?'

'Maybe not, but we have to assume it will.'

His da stepped up one rung. Then another. Soon he was just a dark shape above Walter, clinging on with both arms as he reached the signal lamp.

'This will be good fun!' he shouted above the howling storm. His da hunched over the Tilley lamp, but had to let go of the ladder to get the taper out of his pocket.

Walter saw the shape lurch to the left, then steady. Somehow, his da got the signal lamp open and lifted the mantel off. Using his body and his coat to protect the frail flame, he got the lamp lit. He slipped the mantel back on and closed the lamp. The flame flared, then steadied to its normal dull yellow.

His da slowly crept down the ladder and they embraced with relief.

'I'm not sure if a driver could see that in time, but I suppose he'll be creeping along. Let's get back before we freeze to death. I'm not sure if we'll have to do the Belfast line, but best to find out first.'

'I was certain you were going to fall.'

'That doesn't bear thinking about, son! Let's get a hot cuppa into us.'

The wind was behind them on the slippery trudge back to the station. They could only see its welcoming lights once they were within a few yards. The windows shone orange from the fires inside the waiting room and office.

Station Master Bob Carson, a lifelong friend, was waiting for them, puffing on his pipe. 'Do you want the good news or the bad news,' he said.

'You decide,' his da said to Walter.

'Good news,' Walter replied.

'The good news is you don't have to do the Belfast line,' Bob Carson said.

'And the bad news?'

'You didn't have to do the Derry line either. All trains have been cancelled. The snow is up to their oxters at Strabane.'

'Bloody hell!' his da blustered. 'All that for nothing.' He sipped the tea his friend had brought them.

Later, his da said to Walter, 'You did well out there, son. That was as bad as I've ever seen, but we done it. I know you're foundered with the cold, but don't keep your boots too close to the fire. They'll dry out all hard.'

Walter moved his feet back a few inches. 'I'm not sure I want to do that again,' he confessed, shivering and cupping the warm teacup in both hands. 'My feet are like blocks of ice. Everything's soaked.'

The snow lasted for a week. Spring came and Walter never went along the line with his da again.

When he left school at fourteen, he started doing odd jobs around the station – running errands and making tea. He'd always wanted to become a porter like his da, but changed his mind after this episode. Walter had no idea what to do with his life until a year later when he saw an advert in the paper. The Model Bakery was looking for delivery men. Cars and vans had replaced horse-drawn carts, and drivers were in demand. Driving sounded exciting, modern, warm, and dry. He decided to apply and learn to drive.

As a trainee, Walter was required to pass the driving test before he could go out on his own. He quickly realised he was a natural, enjoying the banter with his customers, adults who weren't teachers, preachers or parents.

He hadn't been working long when he met Ann in Black's.

Their Cake Shop date was a big success. They had loads in common. Yet Ann was so bright and confident. She seemed so professional and grown up that by the time he got home, Walter was convinced she was out of his league. Thus, he didn't have the courage to ask her again.

Still … he knew Ann went to the Starr Ballroom every Saturday night, so he made sure he was there as often as possible. He had seen her there before, but he was always with his mates who weren't much into dancing. They took to the floor sparingly, drank less sparingly and hoped to get lucky without trying too hard. Most of their time was spent making comments about the women and which ones they wouldn't say no to, though their language was less polite. And they'd boast about conquests that had only ever happened in their imaginations.

He was heartened, if surprised, to discover that Ann didn't seem to be dating anyone. The first time he finally summoned up the courage to ask her for a dance, he had watched her on the floor with Sammy Hopkins. He was a soldier and a footballer, but not just any old footballer. Sammy was a professional who played on the wing for Tottenham Hotspur no less. His nickname was 'Lightnin' because he was so quick. He was big and gangly, with a horsey but not unattractive face.

Ann caught Walter's eye, smiled at him and a firework went off in his head. At the end of the set, Walter took a deep breath and went over to where Ann and Sammy were standing. 'Sorry to intrude,' he said politely, 'but may I have the pleasure of the next dance?'

Ann looked at Sammy 'Do you mind?'

'Not at all. I need to get my breath back and I could murder a pint.'

The next dance was a set of waltzes. As Walter put his arm around her waist, he could smell her perfume.

'You took your time,' she said.

'Whaddaya mean?'

'I've seen you looking at me all night.'

'So you must have been looking at me.'

'Hard to miss you with that white hair. Has anyone ever told you that you glow in the dark?'

'It's not white, it's blond.'

It took a little while for them to get started because Ann had to explain a couple of the steps. But Walter, for all his inexperience, was very light on his feet and a quick learner. They were a good match.

They danced together for the rest of the night. Ann caught Sammy's eye at one stage and mouthed 'sorry' to him. He smiled and mouthed back, 'It's grand.'

Soon Ann and Walter were regular dance partners. She teased him about his missteps. Walter took it as a compliment that she liked to take the piss out of him. He didn't mind, because he fancied her like mad and it meant she liked him. Didn't it? And it was worth it to be with the best-looking, best dancer in the place. He knew people must be wondering what she was doing with the likes of him. Surely she could have any bloke she wanted.

He just liked being close to her, letting her teach him how to dance properly. After a few weeks, he escorted her home from the Starr, even if it was only across the street.

Ann was beautiful. She looked like a film star. She smoked, she drank, she swore, she was confident, she was funny, she was perfect. She talked about films, music, dancing and books. He had to start reading so he could have a sensible conversation with her. He liked Charles Dickens, especially the scary characters, like Magwitch and Fagin. At home, he surprised his family by asking if he could listen to the radio when the dance bands were on. He liked whatever Ann liked.

His ma reckoned he was either in love or had gone soft in the head; there wasn't much difference between the two. 'No money in books, son, better out working like your da.' When his da wasn't working, he was in McAleer's or asleep.

Ann had opened Walter's eyes to a new world where even people like them could dream, laugh and have fun for no good reason at all.

Now, eighteen months on, it was New Year's Eve, the night of the Gala Ball in the courthouse, and he was going with Ann. It was snowing as he left his home on the Hospital Road. Walter walked up Campsie, over the bridge, up Market Street, then right into Bridge Street. The buses were lined up in regular rows to his right as he turned left into Sedan Avenue. It was a good half-hour walk, but he slipped along in the deepening snow. He'd borrowed his da's galoshes, but the bottoms of his best black trousers still got soaked. Heavy flurries swirled around him. He didn't care. He pulled the collar of his heavy tweed coat up around his neck. He was foundered with the cold, but the happiest man in the world as he knocked on the door of No. 12.

Just as he thought things couldn't get any better, they did. Ann opened the door.

'Crikey!' he gasped as he stepped backwards off the icy step, nearly slipping.

'What's wrong?' she asked.

'You look … the dress … you … it … I … it's the most beautiful thing I've ever seen.'

She twirled round in the doorway. The gown was a fiery, satiny red flame that took Walter's breath away. It accentuated her shape, showed off her bare shoulders and swept down to her ankles. He'd never seen anything like it. It was like something from a movie.

Ann swished the skirt. 'Iris made it for me. I bought the material in Anderson's. It's just like a dress I saw in *Claudine*, one of the posh magazines Black's has in their waiting room. Iris is brilliant. And Muriel did my hair. Isn't it the best thing ever?'

'I … it's … I … you look like a film star. Like Hedy Lamar. How are we going to get you up to the courthouse without it getting wrecked?'

'Come in out of the cold!' Ma called from her chair.

'Hello, Mrs Brown. Happy New Year.'

'Happy New Year to you too, Walter. You're looking very dapper.'

Walter blushed at the unexpected compliment.

Ann went out to the scullery and came back with a pair of black wellies and a length of binder twine.

'Tie the dress up with this.' She handed the rough hairy string to Walter. 'At the back. Careful. Keep the folds as neat as you can. Good. Now help me into these.'

Walter knelt and Ann put her hands on his shoulders as she wriggled her stockinged feet into heavy socks and then the wellies. Her long winter coat hid everything except the wellies.

'Me next, Walter,' said Muriel, who had the same plan. She was meeting Derek at the courthouse.

On any other night, Muriel would have looked stunning in her dark blue gown, but compared to Ann, she was, well, sort of okay.

'He only lives round the corner from the courthouse in James Street, so I told him you'd escort us both,' she explained when Walter asked why he wasn't calling for her.

'Be careful and don't be too late home,' Ma said without getting up from her seat by the fire.

'Yes, Ma. See you next year.'

Walter was in the middle with a beautiful woman on each arm as the storm worsened and they slipped and slithered their way up the hill to the courthouse. The girls never stopped jabbering, both at the same time. Walter didn't care.

Their faces were red from the cold and the sting of the snow.

'It's hard to tell where you end, and the dress starts,' Walter said with a shiver.

'I'm not red, I'm glowing,' Ann corrected him.

Derek was waiting just inside the big double doors.

Ann's shiny red shoes were in her coat pockets. Walter undid the knot in the string and in slow motion the wondrous dress cascaded and flowed down to its full shimmering crimson glory. Then they deposited the coats and wellies in the cloakroom.

'What are you having?' Walter asked.

'What are you having?' Ann replied.

'I fancy a pint of Guinness.'

'I'll have one of those as well,' Ann said.

'A pint? Are you sure?' Muriel looked at her.

'Only joking. I'll have a Martini, if that's okay.'

'Muriel?' Derek was grinning at them.

'I'll have a Martini as well, thanks.'

'So, a Guinness, a Smithwick's and two Martinis.'

Derek went up to the bar with Walter to help with the drinks.

'I hate asking, but can we split this?' asked Walter. 'I'll probably only have one 'cause Ann won't miss a dance. But apart from that, I'm not sure I have enough for four drinks. They're probably dear in a fancy place like this.'

'Put your money away, Walter. I'll get these. You can get me again sometime.'

'Cheers, Derek.' Walter saw the price list behind the bar. 'Bloody hell. I owe you one, or three.' Walter was embarrassed that he couldn't afford to buy a round. He hoped Derek wouldn't say anything in front of Ann.

As Walter returned with the drinks, he noticed all eyes were on Ann. She was the star of the show and it hadn't even started yet.

The dance itself was a glorious, glamourous, glittering affair. The Swing Earls Orchestra were in fantastic form and Ann and Walter jived until their feet were sore.

'I must be getting better. I don't think I've stood on your feet once,' he panted at one stage.

'Don't be getting carried away, Blondie, but I must admit, you *are* getting better.'

'Better than Sammy Hopkins?'

'Better than Sammy Hopkins.'

Walter's chest puffed out.

'Who's all pleased with himself?'

'I think you've just paid me a compliment, but I'm not sure.'

'It's a good job, then, that you use your feet for dancing and not your head.'

At midnight, a piper warmed up to play 'Auld Lang Syne'. Walter got brave and slipped his arm around Ann's waist as the crowd stood and counted down the last minute of 1947. He squeezed her gently. Ann looked at him with a smile that said, 'I like that.' He felt a gentle stirring in his loins.

'It's 1948!' was what she said out loud and she gave him a peck on the cheek.

He was going to ask if he could kiss her, but he didn't have to. The peck became a proper kiss, her gorgeous glossy lips on his pale pink ones. His loins stirred again, a bit less gently this time, as the piper played and everyone sang along.

'Happy New Year, Ann Brown.'

'Happy New Year, Walter Green.'

After the last waltz, the four retrieved their socks, wellies, string and coats and slipped and slid back down the hill. There was plenty of giggling and endless chatter about the band and the style. Did you see what so and so was wearing? Was that one really with him? Who was drunkest … best dancer … worst dressed? And was that the fastest Lindy Hop they'd ever seen?

Derek held onto Muriel and Walter held onto Ann. The snow stopped as they reached the corner of Bridge Street. The world was silent and white.

'You could get lost in this, Walter.' Ann ruffled his hair.

'It's blond, not white.'

'Ooooh, touchy. Just don't get a white coat, that's all I'm saying. We'll never find you.'

They walked arm in arm. Omagh was beautiful. Ann was beautiful. The Christmas tree twinkling in the window of Mill's shop was beautiful. Life was beautiful. Walter thought things couldn't get any more beautiful, but they did when he received another kiss on the doorstep of No. 12.

He didn't leave any footprints in the snow as he floated home.

CHAPTER 15

Dr Al returned in the middle of March. Muriel met him for drinks and he walked her home again.

'He's got a new job,' she told Ann later. 'He's going to be one of the top dogs in the psychiatric department at the Maudsley Hospital. It's in London somewhere, so that means he may not be over again. He's learned all he needs to know about gardening and chickens from Uncle Louis and the docs in the T&F.'

'It was good while it lasted, I suppose. You got a few drinks. Learned about brains. Not the kind of person you meet every day in Omagh. You won't forget him in a hurry. Does Derek ever buy you Black Bush?'

'He's the nicest person I've ever met. Smart, considerate, funny.'

'Derek?'

Muriel just looked at her.

'You forgot rich,' Ann added. 'He might still ring you now and again for a chin wag. After all, it was your chat that attracted him to you in the first place.'

'Do you think he was attracted to me? Or was it just my accent and the conversation? Maybe he was just looking for company?'

'I don't really know him, Mu. But you obviously like him, and from what you've said, he wouldn't mess you about and let you think he fancied you if he didn't.'

'He's never even tried to kiss me.'

'That's definitely rare behaviour in these parts.'

'Work tomorrow, girls,' Ma reminded them through the thin wall. 'Get to sleep.'

'Yes, Ma.'

Muriel liked Derek a lot. He was kind, thoughtful and generous. He had a good job in the bank and reckoned he could be a manager in a few years. He often bought her beautiful gifts and somehow always seemed to choose the right thing. He wasn't hard to look at either. Tall, dark-haired and classically handsome.

'He looks more like a proper film star than wee white Walter ever will,' Muriel would tease Ann.

The only problem with Derek was that he was a bit dull. In fact, he was too serious all the time. Yet he was a good swimmer and a proper paid-up member of the Lough Muck Swimming and Lifesaving Club. Last summer, he had taught them all to swim.

Joe had looked impressed when Derek told him earlier that spring that he was saving up to buy a car and would own one before long.

'Don't dump Derek like you dump every other boyfriend,' Joe warned Muriel. 'He'll have a car soon. Imagine, a proper car. We could go anywhere.'

'Derek and I could go anywhere, you mean. Why would we take you?'

''Cause we're friends now, Derek and me, and I'm your brother and you love me,' Joe said. 'Anyway, he has to take me or I'll tell him what you're really like and that would ruin your love life.'

'Go and boil your head. You know nothing about my love life.'

'That's 'cause there's nothing to know.'

'Is your girlfriend still secret? You seem to spend a lot of time with Harry these days.'

'Don't be horrible. We're training for the team.'

'I'm winding you up. I'm sure you'll get a spin in his car, just as soon as he gets it.'

'I hope it's something decent and not a wee fart of a thing.'

Muriel knew Ma liked Derek. Her eyes misted in ecstasy at the thought of having a bank manager for a son-in-law. That would be the best thing that could ever happen … to Ma.

'Job for life in the bank, and you know what I always say about a shilling in your pocket,' Ma would say every time Derek's name was mentioned.

'He says he might have to move away if he gets promoted,' Muriel said.

'Are you sure? Soldiers move away, bank managers stay forever. At least until they die or go to the T&F. Look at Dan. He's a good man, but a soldier. Granted, not an ordinary soldier, but even he has to move about. But a bank manager? There isn't a better job in the world, even if he has to move.'

'Would he have to move even if he's married?' Joe asked.

'I think the bank would expect his wife to go with him. I'd have to leave my job, and I like my job.'

'You like the gossip.' Joe pulled his head back, but no blow came.

'Exactly.'

'And the calls from Dr Al,' said Ann.

'And the calls from Dr Al,' said Muriel, and her gaze drifted off into a different place at the thought of Dr Algernon Tolleshunt-Darcy.

'Has he rung recently?' asked Ann, knowing he hadn't because Muriel recounted every word as soon as she got home.

'Not since he was over a few weeks ago.' Muriel shrugged.

'Derek's a good man,' counselled Ma, 'and more importantly, he's here, and even more importantly, he has a good job. A job for life. People like us can only dream of what life is like for folk like Al. You need to know your station and not dream about the impossible. Ann has the right idea. People will always need bread, and if you can drive a bread van, you can drive anything. A good, honest, proper, secure job without any need for high falutin' fancy nonsense.'

Muriel and Ann exchanged exasperated glances.

A few weeks later, early on a Saturday morning in April, Derek parked his new car outside the house and tooted the horn.

Joe nearly flattened Muriel into the wall as he rushed out to see it. It was an Austin Princess! The very motor that was always parked outside the Home and Colonial.

'You bought Mr Chestnut's car? It's beautiful!'

By this time Muriel and Ann had made it safely to the front door to admire the shiny machine.

'Yeah, I had to borrow a wee bit to make up the money,' Derek said, getting out, 'but I'll pay that back in no time. He was going to sell it to someone else, so I had to act quickly. It's not new, but it's as good as. He was very careful with it. Never raced or rallied her.'

Muriel knew Ma's ears would have pricked up at the word 'borrow'. Muriel also knew that this would be a big blot on Derek's copybook. Borrowing, along with gambling and drinking to excess, was a sin that would lead to damnation and financial ruin in Ma's mind. Muriel could hear her already: 'Pride comes before a fall. You mark my words.'

Joe was inside the car, sitting behind the wheel, smoothing his hand across the red leather of the passenger seat. The interior smelled of leather and polish, the best aromas ever. The steering wheel was covered in dark brown leather that matched the wooden trim on the dashboard and the insides of the doors.

'It still smells new. The clock says she's only done fifteen hundred miles. It's not even run in properly.' Joe was awestruck.

'It was much cheaper than a brand-new model and there's not a scratch on it,' said Derek, proud of his new status symbol. Nobody else he knew had a car yet, much less an Austin Princess.

'Can we go for a spin?'

'Muriel?' asked Derek. 'And you too, Ann.'

'Try and stop me. I hope all the neighbours are watching,' beamed Ann, who knew all the neighbours were watching.

'Pride comes before a fall. You mark my words,' Ma intoned as she stood in the open doorway.

Muriel and Ann looked at each other, smiling.

'It's only a bit of fun. Don't tell me you don't want Mrs McGartland and the rest of them to see us all getting into this and driving off?'

'Well, I hope they don't think we've come into money.'

'Unlikely, Ma. They would've known before you if we'd come into money.' Ann ran her finger along the bonnet.

'Probably,' Ma said with a little laugh that turned into a cough.

'Are you okay?' asked Muriel.

'Yes, yes, don't fuss.' She cleared her throat. 'Away and enjoy yourselves.' Another cough, racking this time. Ma was bent over with the effort.

'You go ahead,' Ann said to Muriel and Joe. 'I'll stay with Ma.'

Derek ejected a reluctant Joe from the driver's seat, then Joe and Muriel piled into the car and Derek drove them up, down and around the town so as many people as possible could gawp at them.

Ann helped Ma into her chair. 'Have a wee rest, Ma. I'll get on with things.'

She filled the kettle and, when the water was boiling, poured it into the tin bath and added a little Persil. On the box it said there was enough for fifty washes, but they made it extend to a hundred and fifty. Then came the hard slog – scrubbing the clothes on the washboard until her hands went red. The mangle was outside in the yard and everything was squeezed through this antique machine. Its rollers were nearly worn away, but while they still resembled rollers, the mangle would not be replaced.

'Have you seen the price of a new mangle in Crawford and Wilson's?' Ma would say. 'Twice the price they were twenty years ago! Daylight robbery.'

It looked like it might be a dry day and there was a good breeze, so Ann went out the back and hung the washing on the line that ran the length of the gravel path in the middle of the narrow garden. On either side were vegetable beds. Once the washing was pegged out, she raised the line in the middle with a wooden pole.

'Cup of tea, Ma?'

'That would be lovely. Have we any milk?'

'A wee drop and it smells okay.'

Ann often took her tea black if there wasn't enough.

'There's one digestive. Do you want it?' asked Ann.

'I'll have it if you don't want it.'

'We'll have half each, sure. Then I'll go up the town and get some milk and a loaf. Is there enough for biscuits?'

'There should be. Have a hoke in the tin.'

Ann finished her tea and put on her coat. She was back in no time. She knew Ma didn't like them shopping in Devlin's, but it was the closest shop, being just over the bridge. Ma didn't ask where she went and Ann didn't say.

'I just got one pint, Ma. That should do us till the milkman comes on Monday. We should think about getting a couple of pints on Saturdays as well. I saw Derek drive past while I was out. I thought they might be here before me.'

'No sign of them, love.'

The car pulled up a few minutes later and Ann and Ma went outside to watch them clamber out.

'Well, where did you go? Who did you see? Or more importantly, who saw you?' asked Ann.

Joe was ecstatic. 'We went all round the town twice. We passed you on Bridge Street coming out of Devlin's. Did you see us? Did the car look like something out of a film?'

Ma looked at Ann but said nothing.

'Yes, I did,' Ann said, 'and yes, the car looked like Cary Grant should have been driving it round London or New York or somewhere.'

Derek visibly grew in stature.

'I've got to go. Things to do, people to see,' he said, and he doffed his hat and got back into the car. Muriel went round to the driver's side and leaned in the window. She gave him a kiss on the cheek.

'Fancy a trip out to Lough Muck tomorrow?' he asked. 'It looks like it might be a nice day.'

'In the afternoon?'

'See you about two,' and off he zoomed.

* * *

Derek turned up on the dot of two. He was always bang on time, which Muriel found endearing and frustrating in equal measure. She often thought he needed a bit of chaos and spontaneity in his life. But Derek didn't do surprises ... until now.

Muriel knew straight away that something was wrong. It was the way he said, 'hello' and held the car door for her. It was normal, but it wasn't.

'What's wrong?' she asked as he pulled away from the kerb.

'Nothing. I have a surprise for you, that's all, but I want to wait till we get to the club, if that's all right. There's unlikely to be many there today. We'll probably have the clubhouse to ourselves.'

Muriel was on eggshells for the rest of the short journey to Lough Muck. This was the first time she had ever gone there without having to walk. On foot, it took an hour, but they were parking at the door of the swimming club within ten minutes – ten minutes spent in silence, listening to the car's engine and its wheels bouncing on the rough road.

Derek had a key, as he was the treasurer as well as their qualified swimming and lifesaving instructor.

'It's a lovely day. Do you mind if we sit outside?' he asked.

'Not at all. It's nice out here.'

There was no wind and the April sun was warm. They sat near the diving boards. Muriel felt as if she was going to wet herself. What if he proposes? What if he breaks it off? He did have a dance with Carol Dunn the other night and she's beautiful.

'Well, Derek? I'm bursting with suspense. What's the big surprise?'

'I've got something important to say.'

He took her hands in his.

Proposal! she thought. Oh God.

'You know that promotion I've been wittering on about and waiting for news about for ages?'

Work! Thank God. She nodded and gave him a little smile of relief.

'And you know I did the exams?'

'Yes, and you thought you might have done well but it was really hard to know.'

'Well, I got the results yesterday. The letter was there when I got home from your house. I passed!' He was grinning wider than she had ever seen him grin before.

Muriel was genuinely happy for him.

'I hadn't told you in case I didn't pass, but I'd already done the interview. The bank was just waiting on the exam results to confirm it.'

Her nodding encouraged him to go on.

'Well, to cut a long story short, I've got the promotion. I'm officially a branch manager of the Belfast Bank Company. Or I will be from tomorrow.'

'Oh, Derek, that's just wonderful. So well-deserved. You've worked so hard for this.' Muriel leaned over and kissed him on the cheek.

His big happy face suddenly became a big concerned face.

'What's wrong?' she asked. *Proposal*!

'The problem is, I have to go to Larne. It's the only vacancy and they want me to start two weeks from tomorrow. Anyway' – he paused to compose himself – 'this is the really important part.'

Proposal! It must be. Her mind reeled.

'I was wondering if after a few weeks, when I get settled, you might come up to Larne as well. We could get engaged, and then maybe married.'

Proposal! He'd said it. He'd asked her. Oh God.

Derek was still talking. 'If you'd like to, that is. I know it's a big decision, but I'll be on good money, and we'll be able to get a house with a proper bathroom, and there'll be lots of room for the weans.'

Weans! Weddings and weans!

Derek nattered on. 'My wages will only go up. I might even get a job in one of the big branches in Belfast in a few years' time. Then we'd be set for life.'

Weddings! Weans! Set for life! Oh, God. Please, what should I say?

'Are you asking me to marry you, Derek Clapton?'

'Yes, I suppose I am, but not straight away, obviously. Later, when we get settled.'

'It's a lot to think about. And so sudden. I'd have to give up my job. Where would I live before we got married? And Larne is so far away!'

Derek pointed to the shiny black car sitting a few yards away. 'Anytime you get homesick, it's just a short run. It's not as far as you think!'

'Oh, Derek. You are the loveliest man I've ever met!' In that moment Muriel believed this and her eyes moistened with tears.

'Is that a yes?'

'It's a … there's a lot to think about,' Muriel stammered. She could think of no other words.

'I appreciate that, what with the move and all. You have to be certain. It's a big decision. Best to wait. Best to think before making any big decisions. Best to be sure. No need to rush.' He was stammering too.

The slightest nod of her head indicated her agreement. Am I saying no? Does he think it's a no? She didn't want to hurt him.

* * *

'Where the hell is Larne?' Joe asked when Muriel got home and told them what had happened.

Ma cuffed his ear. 'Mind your language, Joe Brown.'

'Yes, Ma. Sorry, Ma. I didn't know Larne was a bad word! But seriously, where the eff is it?' Ma cuffed him on the ear again, and he feigned serious injury, rolling around on the floor, holding his ear with both hands.

'I think I've gone deaf,' he moaned.

'Good,' snapped Ann, 'we won't have to talk about you behind your back any more.'

'What?'

Ann ignored him and went on 'For your information, since you obviously slept through Geography in school, Larne is at the seaside. You can get a ferry across to Scotland from there. It's near the Glens of Antrim.'

'About as far as you can get from here and still be in Ulster,' Muriel added, then wailed, 'It's the arsehole of nowhere! What am I going to do in Larne? Do they even speak English?'

'But he's got a car,' Joe implored. 'I get one wee ride

around the town and then you dump him, just like you dump everyone.'

'I haven't dumped him. He's just moving away. I'm going to take some time to think and then we'll see what happens.'

Muriel saw mischief in Ann's grin.

'I think you should stop being so selfish and go with him. You said yourself he's a lovely man, and he's got a very good job and a car and a nice hat. What more do you want? And most importantly, I'd have our bedroom all to myself if you did the right thing and ran off to Larne and married Derek. How romantic would that be?'

Ma chipped in, grinning, 'I know you're very fond of Derek, and he has a very good job. He'll have a proper career and earn good steady money. He'll be able to keep you in fine style for the rest of your days. Your babies will be born safely and will grow up wanting for nothing. I've always said that you should never marry for money. But even if it's not true love, you can always pretend, for the sake of the weans. At least you'd be miserable in comfort.'

'Oh, Ma,' said Muriel, 'I know you're only joking, but you're right. I could have everything any girl could ever want if I married Derek and he is a lovely man. He'll always do the right thing and will always be there, but …' The 'but' said everything.

'Maybe he'll get promoted again and be sent back to Omagh and be an even bigger branch manager,' Joe suggested.

Muriel thought, please no, but said, 'Pigs might fly.'

'I saw a pig flying across Campsie once,' Joe began. 'Mrs McAleer had kicked it up the arse and whacked it with a broom when it tried to go into the pub. It was only a wee tiny pig, but it must have flew at least three feet in the air. You want to hear the squeals of it.'

They could all picture Mrs McAleer chasing the little pig out of the pub and the sombre mood was lifted.

'Plenty more fish in the sea, love.' Ma cupped Muriel's face in her hands, but she looked disappointed. Derek would probably earn more money in a year than she had earned in her entire life.

'But the tide's going out,' Ann said with a wicked grin, 'and you're not getting any younger.'

'It's certainly going out in Larne,' said Joe.

'Ha, ha, very funny,' Muriel said with a pout. 'My boyfriend's leaving me, I don't know what to do and all you can do is make jokes.'

'Sorry, Mu,' said Ann. 'I know you really like him, but in your heart of hearts, liking isn't really enough, is it?'

Muriel was quiet. She knew the answer to that question.

* * *

They were having dinner. Spuds, bacon and a small turnip from the garden that had been boiled beyond redemption and then fried in the bacon fat. Ma only ever bought two rashers of bacon for each of them, and they were sliced so thin they were virtually see-through.

'No news?' Ann said to no one in particular. 'No gossip, no scandal, no juicy murders to report? Is Mrs Chesney still the world's sickest person? A walking, talking, medical miracle?'

'Ma?'

Ma rarely had news or gossip, but when she had, it was usually significant. Now she shook her head and remained silent, mashing the last of her spuds into the last mush of turnip.

'Joe?'

Joe never told them anything about what he got up to, apart from how many goals he scored. He shook his head too and said nothing.

Muriel had been waiting patiently for her turn on Ann's list.

'Mu?'

She had wanted to go last so that her news would have maximum impact and couldn't be trumped.

'Al called today,' she said quietly and they all looked up.

'Is he coming over again?' asked Ma, who already knew the answer, as she'd met Louis in Reed's earlier.

'He says he needs to see Uncle Louis again. One last time before he starts his new job, but here's the most exciting bit. He wants to talk to me about a job in his new hospital. He wants to take a different approach to dealing with mental patients, sort of like what they do at the T&F.'

'You'll be well looked after then,' Joe said.

Muriel ignored him. 'They're setting up a brand-new telephone exchange in the hospital, and he wants me to help get it up and running. He said my way with people and communication skills would be a great asset.'

'What did you say?' Ann was all excited now. 'Are you going to go? London? Bloody hell! Sorry, Ma. How can you not go?'

'Is Lightnin Hopkins back in London playing for Spurs?' asked Joe, thinking ahead.

'That's an interesting thought, Joe. For you anyway.' Ann was suddenly very interested in all these new possibilities.

'You've got a good job here,' said Ma. 'What's wrong with Omagh? Hilda, and now you, thinking of galivanting off around the world. You know nobody in London. The grass isn't always greener.'

'I know that, but it's the chance of a lifetime – to have an adventure. I don't want to be wondering *what if* for the rest of my days.'

'Where will you live?' Ma, as always, focused on the practical. She had never benefitted from dreaming dreams. She'd only ever had one, once, and she vowed never to get caught up in that nonsense again. Dreams didn't pay the bills; you couldn't put them in the meter.

'That's something he wants to talk to me about. He said there was plenty of room in his house. I think it has seventeen bedrooms, but that can't be right, can it? I must have misheard him. Anyway, he said he knew this could be a bit awkward and people might talk. It seems like gossip is just the same in London as it is here.'

'Only bigger, and more of it,' said Ann. 'You'll be in heaven.'

'I know. Can you imagine!'

'I don't like the idea of you living at his house, even if it has a hundred bedrooms. It's not appropriate.' Ma was in full righteous flow. 'People will talk, and talk travels fast. How could I show my face at church if everyone here found out that you were living in sin with a stranger in London who just happened to be your boss? It doesn't bear thinking about.'

'Ma's right,' Ann said. 'Everyone here will know in no time, and two and two will become twenty-two. Can you imagine the craic Mrs Chesney would have if she was armed with that sort of gossip? She'd be calling Dr Bowles at least twice a day just to deal with the stress of it all.'

'So where will you live?' Ma asked again.

'The hospital has digs for nurses and other workers who might need them, and Al says I could get a room in there.

They're near the hospital, so I wouldn't have to travel, which will save some money. Al's house is out in the country, and he says it takes him over an hour to drive in every day in his car.'

'What sort of car has he got?' asked Joe.

'It's a black one,' said Muriel, never having seen or discussed it.

Joe rolled his eyes. 'What kind of black one?'

'A big shiny black one, with wheels and seats.'

'Stupid woman,' Joe mumbled. He wasn't quick enough this time to dodge Muriel's clip across his ear. 'That was sore!'

'Do you need a doctor?' she asked, the picture of innocence.

'Muriel knows a good doctor,' Ann said helpfully. 'He doesn't know much about sore ears, but he could have a go at your brain – if he can find it, that is.'

'My brain's too big even for Dr Al to fix. It would need a whole team of Dr Als to fix my brain – if it needed fixing, which it doesn't.'

'Enough,' Ma said. 'So what sort of money would this hospital job pay you? How much is the rent?' Instead of opportunity, Ma saw only problems, bills, uncertainty and worry.

'Al says people get paid better in London than anywhere else. He says it only makes sense to move if I will be better off and with better prospects for promotion.'

'He's very wise, our Al. Very thoughtful,' said Ann. 'Oh Mu, London! Real live shows. Big ballrooms with proper floors and proper big bands.'

'He is very thoughtful,' said Muriel looking all dreamy. 'He doesn't want me to move just for the sake of it. But London is even further than Larne.'

'But they speak English in London,' Ann said, her eyes shining like two big green marbles.

'Maybe he just wants to be close to you,' Joe said, theatrically clasping both hands over his heart like 'a girly girl', as he put it, and swooning.

'How are you going to be able to afford all those big shows? I hope you're not getting ideas above your station,' said Ma. 'And don't imagine Al will pay for everything. Get too dependent and he'll disappear off to his big house and posh friends and you'll be left on your own.'

'I'll have a job, Ma, and my own money. Besides, Al's not a snob. He likes normal things like music or going for a walk in the country. That's why he likes Omagh so much.'

'Do you know what his parents do? Does he know I'm a cleaner with three jobs?'

Muriel sighed with frustration. 'Seriously, Ma! He likes people for themselves. He and Uncle Louis got on like a house on fire and I know he will like you for you, not for what you do or don't do. He doesn't care about money.'

'That's because he has plenty. He'd care if there wasn't a bob for the meter on a Sunday night in December.'

'You could come over and get a job cleaning at his house, Ma. You could live in and you would only have one job and no rent to pay or anything.'

Ma looked at Muriel and said, 'I'm happy where I am, thank you.'

'I could go too,' Joe butted in. 'Sammy could get me a trial at Spurs.'

'Do you not have to be a good footballer to play for a team like Spurs?' asked Ann.

'I am a good footballer. Sammy says I'm good and Johnny Carey says I'm good, and he's played for Ireland.'

'Northern Ireland,' corrected Ma, even though she knew he'd played for the Free State as well.

'So what happens next?' asked Ann.

'We'll have a chat when he comes over so I can learn more about it, and then I'll have to have a serious think. I'm being realistic. It might be the best thing ever or it might just be pie in the sky.'

'You can have pie on your plate right here,' Ma said. 'Just settle for what you've got. Derek's a good man with a good job and good prospects. What's wrong with settling down with him?'

Muriel shivered inwardly as that prospect wandered across her mind again.

'How much does it cost to get to London?' Joe's curiosity was unlimited. 'Will you be able to go in an aeroplane?'

'No, it'll be by boat and train. But the hospital will pay my fare.'

'It sounds too good to be true. Getting all the way to London for nothing,' said Joe.

'Well, that's because Al has told them how good I am!'

'He only knows how good you are at chatting to him. He doesn't know how much time you spend gabbing to anyone who'll listen about the Mrs Chesneys of this world,' Ann put in.

'Whose side are you on?'

'Yours. Definitely yours! I can't believe I'll have the bed all to myself. Heaven.'

'Not much fun farting on your own,' quipped Joe.

'It's never stopped you,' Ann shot back. 'Your room smells like a cesspit.'

'Just think carefully, love – before you turn your life upside down,' Ma said. 'You need to take your time and I know you will. You're not as headstrong as Hilda. She just upped and ran off at the drop of a hat. Big cities can be lonely and dangerous if you don't know anybody. Nobody will be looking out for you.'

'I know Al. He'll look out for me and I'll meet people.'

'You could go out to his mansion for tea. There'll be proper cups with saucers and all. You know you drink from the cup?' Ann said.

'I'll tell them I like an old cracked mug and strong tea that you can stand a spoon in.'

'And you'll have to learn to stick your little finger out when you drink your tea,' said Joe.

'I know where I'll stick my little finger if you don't shut up!'

Muriel had had enough. 'All of you are doing my head in! Can we please put the radio on?'

Ma sighed. She looked very tired. 'Turn on the wireless, Joe. Tomorrow's another day and things will look different in the morning.'

'Yes, Ma.' Joe went over to the little table beside the fireplace and turned the knob on the radio.

They all sat silently, watching the radio's little panel begin to glow.

CHAPTER 16

Joe was convinced his brain was turning to mush in the tax office. Endless adding and subtracting; a nightmare of numbers that blurred into meaningless columns of pounds and pence. He started looking around for something else and Wilbur, who played in goal for the YMCA, put a word in for him at the Nestle factory, where he worked. After a cursory interview, Joe found himself in a new job. The factory was just outside the town on the Derry Road. That was its official name, not the *London*derry Road, so even Ma couldn't complain.

But to get there, Joe needed a bicycle. It was a very long walk, especially in the winter. He tried again to get his head round the concept of saving. He went to the cinema less often. He had fewer snowballs and minerals. This lasted about a week before he realised he would be older than Ma before he would have enough money. After a short negotiation, he borrowed a fiver from his sisters. The term of the loan was 'as soon as possible'. The interest rate wasn't even discussed.

So at sixteen and a half, Joe bought his first bike. It was red, a Humber Roadster, almost new, and it was beautiful. It even had a little canvas bag behind the saddle where he could put his piece box.

'It's lovely, son, but where did you get the money?' Ma interrogated him when he brought it home.

In order to avoid a sermon on the evils of debt, they couldn't let on to Ma the true nature of their financial arrangement.

Ann said, 'We bought it for him. He can't get to work without a bike. He's our wee brother and we love him and between us, we had the money.'

Muriel stood back looking angelic.

Ma was lost for words.

* * *

Harry was impressed by the bike. He had inherited his own from his older sister Doreen, so it was a girl's bike. And while Joe's was second hand, it was newer. But none of this mattered because they were free now. Joe would not have to sit precariously on the handlebars of Harry's bike as they wobbled their way to Lough Muck or the Leap Bridge.

'They work shifts,' Joe explained. 'I work from six in the morning to two o'clock, then somebody else takes over for the second shift to ten at night.'

'Is that how shifts work?' asked Harry sarcastically.

'Cheeky git.'

'Sounds great for the summertime, but what about winter when it's cold and wet and dark and slippery and horrible? Will you be able to get there in the floods?'

'We'll cross that bridge when we come to it,' Joe said with a grin. 'Get it? Bridge. Floods.'

'Yes, Joe. You're a very clever boy.' Harry patted him on the head like a child.

'Finishing at two – more time for football.' Joe rubbed his hands.

'But what if they put you on the two to ten shift? That will fuck things up.'

'If they try that, I'll invent an excuse to say I can't work late. My ma's bewildered and needs put to bed at six. Or I turn into a werewolf when the sun goes down.'

'It's vampires that hate the sun.' Harry shook his head.

'Vampires, werewolves, whatever. You'd not want one running around your factory howling at the moon.'

'That should work. You can do your best Bela Lugosi impressionation.'

'Impersonation.'

'Just testing.'

Joe began his first shift at the start of June. He felt all grown up as he cycled the two miles out to the factory. It was an imposing, intimidating building for someone who had never even seen a factory before, much less gone inside one. But go inside he did. He got new overalls, which were miles too big for him. He had to roll the legs up four turns so he wouldn't trip over himself. He also got a little white hat. There were three other new starts that Monday morning. All were led onto the factory floor by the shift supervisor, a large round man in a spotless white coat. His hat was a white fedora, not a cloth one with a net like the workers wore.

Training was brief. The fat white coat told them it was a milk factory, so everything had to be clean all the time. And not just clean – spotlessly clean. Hats and overalls had to be worn at all times on the factory floor. There was a ten-minute tea break at eight and a twenty-minute lunch break at twelve.

The rotund supervisor continued with his warnings. 'These machines are dangerous, so don't stick your hand or any other bits into them. They are noisy as well, so stick some of this in your ears until you get used to it.' He handed out little tufts of cotton wool.

The new starts were allocated to different machines and the white coat showed them how they worked.

'Any problems, shout as loud as you can. Any questions? No? Good. Off you go and try not to maim yourselves or break anything.'

So Joe became a factory worker and loved it. The banter was mighty during the breaks. He was clever enough not to fall for the obvious tricks some of his fellow workers tried to play on the new, green arrivals. Or so he told Harry. Best not to mention being sent out to the yard to find the head of the milking department. 'He'll be the man with the big red hands and the big, white bucket.'

It wasn't long before Harry got work with Nestle's as well. He was earning almost nothing at Torney's. He was good with his hands and got a job as a trainee engineer. His function was to fix the machines that Joe broke.

Harry and Joe suddenly felt very flush with their newfound, hard-earned wealth. Joe was on 19s 6d a week, Harry a bit less, as he was officially an apprentice. He would get a pay rise when he qualified.

'Shouldn't take too long,' he said after his first week. 'The lads seem to just hit things with hammers most of the time. The hardest bit is taking the machines apart for the cleaners.'

'We can afford to sit in the back of the flicks.' Joe stuck his thumbs in his belt. Swaggering like a swell.

'We could buy a Coke each.' Harry mimed glugging a glass.

'I'm not sure Nigel would like the company,' Joe said, looking thoughtful. 'He takes his flick-watching very seriously, and we wouldn't be able to talk or anything, even if the film was shit.'

'True. Better stick with the plebs down the front.'

'Better sport.'

'We won't need to sneak in anymore.'

'Joyce'll think we're not right in the head if we don't sneak in now and again. Catching us out makes her day."

'You're right, Joseph. Don't want to lose the old breaking and entering skills just in case Nestle's shuts or gets blown up – like if there's another war.'

'Nobody's going to bomb a milk factory.'

'What about ice creams at the interval?' Harry rubbed his belly. That was something they had only ever done once.

'No need to go mad just because we're rich.'

They dreamt of good things in a world where everything was possible, and a few bob in your pocket really was your best friend. They didn't talk about taking girls to the pictures, Harry, because he didn't have a girlfriend and he really fancied Ann; Joe, because he didn't have a girlfriend and he really fancied Doreen, though he might have a girlfriend soon. Dolores had kissed him at Lough Muck. Obviously, more kissing and going to the pictures and then sex was bound to follow. He didn't know how these things would happen, but that wasn't important.

'New boots,' Harry was still dreaming.

'New shoes.'

'New bike.'

'Hold on a minute. I haven't even paid for this one yet!' Joe was feeling so rich that he thought he might actually pay Muriel and Ann back.

'You'll have to cough up, once they know how much dosh you're earning. You should make a plan. So much a week, then you'll know where you are.' Harry tried to look serious.

'Just as skint as I was before will be where I'll be.'

'Only with a bike.'

'True, but there's no need to be so flippin' logical, Harry. A bike *and* extra dosh would be better. Why do things get more complicated as you get older? When we hadn't tuppence between us we didn't give a fuck about anything.'

'We couldn't afford to give a fuck about anything.'

'Or pay for one.'

'That's disgusting.' Harry screwed his face up.

'Have you not done it yet?'

'What? Paid for a fuck?'

'Had one. Ever?'

'No, have you?'

'No, but remember out at Lough Muck when wee Sean got in over his head and started to panic and I went in and saved him?' Joe said.

'You told me you pretended to save him – that he was only mucking about.'

'That doesn't matter. All that matters is that his big sister Dolores thought I saved his life. She showed me how grateful she was … and she was *very* grateful.' Joe winked.

'You mean she let you do it? You're having me on! Did you even know what to do? Maybe she knew what to do.' Harry was gobsmacked. 'What happened?'

Joe gave Harry a meaningful look. 'You know—' and his exaggerated hand movements left nothing to the imagination.

'Seriously? Was it sore?'

'No. It was great.'

'Better than doing it yourself?'

'No comparison.'

'Will she get pregnant?'

'Are you thick or what? You have to … you know.' Joe thrust his hips backwards and forwards very vigorously.

'Easy Joe. You'll dislocate yourself.'

'And then you have to marry her. After you've …' Harry thrust his hips backwards and forwards less enthusiastically.

'Aye. See, I told you. Life just gets more complicated as you get older. She's actually nice. Told me she's fancied me for ages. But she's got big teeth and laughs like a horse that's got its head stuck in a briar. I couldn't listen to that for the rest of my life. Imagine every time you told a joke, she'd bray like a scalded donkey. And she's a taig.'

'It does sound complicated and painful.'

'You can't be a grown-up until you've done it, so we'll have to try it sometime soon.'

'Me and you?' Harry backed off looking horrified. 'You're a beautiful human being, Joe Brown, but I think I'd prefer your sister. Hate to burst your bubble, but doing it with girls seems more appealing, even if the getting-up-the-duff bit is a pain in the arse.'

'You still fancy Ann?'

'Who wouldn't? She's like a film star. She looks like Hedy Lamar.

'Not first thing in the morning she doesn't.'

'I'd love to see her first thing in the morning.'

'Dirty bastard. That's my sister you're talking about.' Joe playfully slapped Harry on the head. 'She's too old for you and she's going steady with Walter Green.'

'Maybe she would like a proper man.' Harry straightened his scrawny shoulders. 'Anyway, you can talk about sisters.

Our Doreen says she can feel your eyes boring into her arse every Sunday at church.'

Joe went bright red. He thought his lustful gawping had been very discreet. Time to change the subject. Joe grabbed his bike. 'Last to the YM buys the Cokes,' and they disappeared in a swirling cloud of wheels and legs and dust.

CHAPTER 17

'Well, have you had a think?' asked Al, as he set down two Black Bush and a small jug of water on the little round table in the corner at the Royal Arms.

'The job and London and everything sound like heaven,' Muriel began, rotating her glass nervously.

'So you've decided?' Al took a sip of his whiskey.

'I've flip-flopped a hundred times. I've made up my mind and decided, then I've unmade it again. London sounds so exciting. All the big shows and the shops, but it's scary too. There are probably more people in one street in London than in the whole of Omagh and Omagh only has one decent dress shop.'

Al smiled. 'Yes, there are a few more in London, but you don't have to go to them all. Not all at once anyway. I'll look after you and you'll make friends quickly.'

'Ann says I could chat to the King and the Pope at the same time and not bat an eyelid, but it's different when it's on the telephone. It's maybe not so easy in real life.'

'The telephone *is* real life, and Ann's right, you're very good at it. The hospital needs someone good who shows an interest and says the right thing at the right time. Anyone can learn the technical side, but it's the people part. You either have it or you haven't. It's very special to have the ability to put people at their ease when they might be stressed to heaven and back.'

'That's a lot of stress.'

'It's the most stress ever in the history of stress.'

'So in your medical opinion, you think it takes the gift of the gab to reduce these sky-high stress levels to more normal heart-attack levels.'

'Yes. But it can't be just prattling, incoherent noise like a waterfall. It has to be focused, showing you're listening and understanding, distracting them from their troubles for a moment or two, all the while sounding calming. More like a babbling brook.'

'That's very poetic, but are you saying I babble?'

'The right sort of babbling is good and good babblers are as rare as hen's teeth.'

'All right then, I'll go! No, I need another wee think. I want to go but what if no one understands my special babbling because I speak like a country yokel? Everyone will have a posh accent like you.'

'You can be very well-spoken. They'll understand you. You just need to slow down at times and try not to use words that no one outside Omagh has ever heard of.'

'Like?'

'Like slabber or head buck cat.'

'Or sheugh or boggin'?'

'Exactly. Say girls and boys instead of cutties and cubs.'

Al listened patiently as Muriel continued to rehash the arguments for and against. All the cons came from Ma, all the pros from Ann.

'Mad if I go and mad if I stay.'

He ordered another round and they sipped their drinks and watched the room fill up with people and smoke. They talked about London. Muriel was bewitched as Al described the Underground. She was goggle-eyed at the huge number of cinemas, theatres and restaurants. London Bridge, the Tower of London, Buckingham Palace; she could see them all in real life and in colour, not just black-and-white pictures on *Pathé News*.

Afterwards, they walked the short distance to Sedan Avenue not saying much.

At her door, Al said, 'Would it help if I spoke to your mother?'

'God, no. I suggested she have a chat with you to put her mind at ease. That you're genuine, but she panicked at the thought of it.'

'Why? Am I that intimidating?'

'Don't take this the wrong way, but you are too grand. The poshest people she has ever met – that any of us has ever met – are the people she works for. It would be like meeting the King. Just too much. I told her that Uncle Louis would vouch for you and confirm you are who you say you are – a good man with only my best interests at heart.'

'Well, that's something. You need to take your time, Muriel. There's no point giving up everything you have here and coming to London if you're not a hundred per cent convinced that it'll be all you want it to be. But don't take too long. We'd love for you to start as soon as possible, as the new exchange must be installed by the end of August.'

'And you'll be thinking about my official job title?'

'Hmmm, yes. Top Telephonist? Communications Maestro? Super Slabberer? Head buck cat?'

'That'll do nicely.'

'Good night then. I'm sure you'll make the right decision, and I'm positive it'll be just the best thing ever.'

He gave her a peck on the cheek and once again she could hear him whistling the 'Missouri Waltz' as he wandered off up the street.

* * *

'I might never see any of you or my friends again,' Muriel confided to Ann. Ma had gone up to her room already. They all knew what she thought of this madcap idea and she had nothing more to add to the debate or the doubts swirling around Muriel's mind.

'It's London, not the moon. Or Larne. Other people from Omagh have gone there and returned alive – from London, I mean.

'Ma could die before I could get home again.'

'I could die before you get home again. You could get run over by a bus. Anything can happen, but you can't do nothing just in case something might possibly happen maybe somewhere sometime. Go to London, for God's sake. I'm so jealous. I don't know why you're still dithering.'

'Ma's chest has got worse.'

'It's a wee bit of a cough. I'll look after her. She's as hard as nails. You can come home for Christmas. If you don't like it, or it doesn't like you, just leave. Someone with your super-duper skills could get a job anywhere.'

'What skills have I got? At least you're a whizz at typing and shorthand. I can't do anything.'

'You're the best talker, know-it-all busybody, kindest, most generous person I know, and you can remember who said what to who forever. That's a lot of talents for someone who's not that old.' Ann grinned at her older sister.

'Your skills can be measured. Not like me.'

'Anyone can type faster than someone else or know how a telephone works. But the very reason Al wants you to go and work for him is because you're good with people and put folk at their ease. If there were championships for that you'd win every time.'

'Gosh!' Muriel blushed, unused to gushing compliments from her family.

'No more back and forth. Go to London, Mu. Maybe Al will ask you to marry him. Maybe that's why he wants you there – so he can get to know you better before popping the big question.'

Muriel had tried to blot out this impossible fantasy. 'Perhaps Ma is right and I shouldn't aim above my station. His family wouldn't be happy about him marrying a wee girl from Omagh who knows nothing about anything.'

'Don't do yourself down. Ma comes from a different generation. She wants the best for you. She's frightened of change. Maybe Al, being a genuine gentleman, not in the posh sense of the word, is waiting to make sure you feel the same way he does, and that's why he wants to get to know you better.'

'He's never even hinted at any sort of attraction. Yes, he walks me home, and we've had lovely conversations, but he hasn't tried to kiss me, other than tonight when we got to the house. And it was only a wee peck on the cheek.'

'Lady Muriel Tolleshunt-Darcy! It has a ring to it and you'll need a ring to make it come true. Imagine the diamonds he could afford. I can see the headlines in the *Conn*: "Lady Muriel Tolleshunt-Darcy, formerly of Omagh, was seen drinking her tea from a saucer, but she did have her little finger sticking out. She also slurped her soup in front of the King".'

Muriel laughed. 'Do you think he knows the King?'

'Them posh 'uns all know each other. He probably has the King round for dinner regularly. I bet the King likes Black Bush too. And he'll definitely invite him to open the new telephone exchange!'

'Do you think so?' Muriel's eyes were like saucers.

'Only one way to find out.'

'But I'm not as adventurous as you are.'

'If it was the other way around, you'd be pushing me out the door.'

'You could come over and visit.'

'Only if you're going to a ball and I get to dance with a film star and have a pint of Guinness with the King.'

They continued to get increasingly carried away in the fantasy. Then it was back to reality. 'I'm meeting Al tomorrow after work. I'll tell him then,' Muriel said. 'He needs to know as soon as possible.' Her face grew sombre. 'I so need Ma to be happy for me.'

'Joe will miss his big sister.'

'He'll only have you left to annoy.'

'He's growing up. He'll be fine.'

'I could get him a ticket to see Sammy play for Spurs. He'd like that.'

'See, you're, right? It just gets better and better.'

'Oh God, why did Derek have to be so boring?'

'If you don't go, you'll spend forever wondering. And I'll get blamed for not pushing you hard enough.'

And so the sisters went round and round until Ann had enough. 'You're doing my head in. I need my sleep!' She turned towards the wall. 'In case you're wondering, I'll be dreaming of dancing with the King and living in a place where you don't have to eat liver and onions every Thursday.' And she fell asleep.

Muriel was more restless. All her decisions in life so far had been easy: what dress to wear, who to go out with, what to tell whom. Normal life required no big decisions. Clothes had to be washed, put through the mangle and hung up. The fire and the gas had to be lit. Coins had to be put in the meter. Life was predictable. Safe. But it didn't have to be.

CHAPTER 18

The next day, Muriel met Al in the Café Rex. They ordered fish suppers with tea, bread and butter.

Al picked up a chip with his fingers, blew on it and bit the end off. 'These are good. Best chips I've had all day.'

Muriel smiled nervously at his nervous little joke. 'Did you see the bands today?

'I heard them long before I saw them, but they were quite a sight. The big drums make a frightful din.'

'They're called Lambeg Drums and there'll be even more bands on the twelfth of July. That's the day of the big parade.'

'So this was just a warm-up?'

'Aye. Any excuse to bang their drums and annoy the Catholics.'

'Very impressive, I must say.'

'I've decided to go,' she blurted out, just as another big chip entered Al's mouth. He immediately spat it back out onto his plate.

'Sorry about that.' He dabbed his mouth with the paper napkin. Once he'd recovered, he said, 'Oh, Muriel, do you mean it? That's wonderful news. I think you're making the right decision. You won't regret it. But what about your mother? Is she happy?'

'I don't think the words "Ma" and "happy" have ever been said in the same sentence. She thinks it'll all end in disaster, destruction and probably death. Seriously, though, we've talked about it up and down and round and round and she only wants the best for me. But I know she'll just add my absence to her already huge worry pile. She'll still have Ann and Joe for local day-to-day fretting. Hilda and I will make up her international worrying department, so she'll be fine.'

'How do they feel? Don't let your chips get cold.'

'You sound like Ma! Ann has her job at Black's and is getting on well there. She's the smartest of us by a mile, and the prettiest. All she wants to do is dance and she has Walter. They just have to realise they are made for each other. As for Joe, he thinks of nothing but playing football. He says he's met a couple of soldiers at the Army Training Corps who are professional footballers in real life. They've told him and his mate Harry that they could be good enough to make it and they should go for trials. But he's got a good job at Nestle's to fall back on if his wee bubble gets burst. God love him, he's so enthusiastic. The same boy will survive without his big sister.'

'No girlfriend yet to badger him?'

'Badger? Girlfriends don't "badger" – they provide insight and guidance, but no is the answer. All he talks about is football.'

As Al sprinkled more vinegar on his fish, she asked, 'Can you even make a living playing football? It seems a bit far-fetched to get paid to kick a ball about.'

'Many people do and even more want to. It's got to be more fun than working in a factory.'

'Enough about them!' Muriel blew on a piece of cod.

'Too right. Let's talk about you. But eat up first,' and Al forked a big battered bite into his mouth.

'Yes, Ma.'

Decision confirmed at last, the pair made chip butties, the melting butter running down their chins and over their fingers.

'Happy days! What a mess,' said Al, licking his fingers.

'Magnificently messy,' Muriel said, rubbing butter off her chin with her napkin.

They sat on and discussed the practicalities of it all. The hospital would confirm her appointment in writing and provide further details and her new job title. They agreed that she would definitely be the Super Slabber, but this title perhaps didn't properly reflect the dignity and responsibility of the role. With the letter would come tickets for the journey and information about where she would be staying. Oh, and her salary, which he estimated at five hundred pounds per year.

'Are you having me on? I know people get paid more in London, but isn't that the sort of money people get when they've been working for years and years and know what they're doing?'

'People like you, you mean? Being in charge of the new exchange is a serious job with serious responsibilities.'

'I've never had responsibilities before. Are they painful?' Muriel joked but she was worried and felt a weight landing on her shoulders.

Al laughed. 'Bracing is a better word, but I knew from that first call that you were the person we were looking for. Yes, I could hire someone else, had you decided not to accept, but I really believe you'll be brilliant at it. Trust me. Don't worry.'

'I promise. I'll let Ma do all the worrying. Instead, I am going to do "excited anticipation".' She put on her most exuberant face.

'I'm terrified already!'

* * *

Muriel left a fortnight later, after the by now familiar farewells and hugs and tears aplenty at the station. Soon after, a letter arrived to say she had got there safely.

> *Al met me off the train at Euston Station, which is huge. Not like Omagh, with only two platforms. Euston has hundreds. The noise of the trains and the people was deafening. There were millions of people, all going at a hundred miles an hour in every direction, all at the same time.*
>
> *Joe would be very envious of Al's car. It's very big. Al says it's a Bentley. A Mark Six, to be exact. Joe will know what that is. It's dark green with white doors and white tyres.*
>
> *It took ages to drive to the hospital. Al said there was a quicker way, but he wanted to show me the sights. We went past the Houses of Parliament and Big Ben and drove across the Tower Bridge. They all looked huge. London is so vast it's impossible to describe it properly and I have only seen a tiny part of it so far.*
>
> *My lodgings are very small, but I have my own room and my own wee bed (just like you now, Ann.) I have a wee table, a washstand and a wee wardrobe. It has two drawers underneath it, so I have an extra drawer! No clothes to put in it yet though.*

Work is very busy. Lots to learn. Everyone is very friendly, but like everyone here, they all go at a hundred miles an hour all the time.

It's a bit lonely at night. No one to chat to. No wireless. I'll have to get one when I get my first pay.

Al is one of the head buck cats in the department. His boss is a professor of psychiatry. How impressive is that?

Anyway, I hope you are all well and I will be in touch again soon, but write anytime with news. If there is any news.

'So far so good, eh, Ma?' Ann said.

'She says she's lonely.' Ma nodded as if this was confirmation of her worst fears. She looked old and tired in the flickering firelight.

'She won't be lonely for long, the same girl.' Ann tried to sound upbeat. 'Would you like a cup of tea?'

'That would be lovely.'

'Joe can read the letter when he gets back from football. He'll like the bit about the swanky car.'

They had tea and digestive biscuits buttered together.

CHAPTER 19

The three remaining Browns looked down at another letter that the postman had stuck through the letterbox. It lay face down on the tattered old mat. It was brown and mysterious looking.

Ann broke the tension. 'It looks important. They always use brown envelopes for important stuff.' She poked it with her foot.

'It must be bad news,' Ma said. 'Muriel's only been away a couple of months. Maybe she's coming home.'

'Well, it's not from Hilda,' Joe said. 'Hers are blue.'

'You open it, Ma, if it's important,' Ann said.

Ma sighed. 'Well, it's not going to open itself.' Her knees cracked and her back creaked as she bent down to lift the letter. Her back cracked and her knees creaked as she stood up again. She turned it over and held it up so all three of them could read the address.

Mr Joseph Brown,
12 Sedan Avenue,
Omagh,

Co Tyrone,
Northern Ireland.

'A letter for me! I can't believe it,' Joe exclaimed. He was hopping with excitement.

'Open it, for God's sake,' urged Ann.

Joe took the letter from Ma. He noticed that her hands were trembling. His own hands were shaking as he stuck a finger into one end of the stuck-down bit and tried to prise it open. The envelope ripped down towards the address and he stopped just in time.

'I'll get a knife.' He disappeared into the kitchen and returned with the little sharp knife they used for peeling the spuds. He slipped it into the top of the envelope and neatly sliced it open. Inside the envelope was a single piece of paper. Joe unfolded it and stared in shock.

'What is it, son? Have you been sacked?'

'Let's see.' Ann tried to grab it from Joe.

'What does it say?'

'It's from Matt Busby,' Joe said breathlessly.

'Who?' asked Ma.

'Matt Busby. The manager of Manchester United. I told youse about Johnny Carey when he said he was going to put a word in for me and Harry to Matt Busby about maybe going over for trials. He's been acting as a scout for the club while he's over here. Keeping an eye out for talent. He said he thought we were good enough. So he must have put a word in, 'cause they want us to go over. Bloody hell, I can't believe it.'

'Calm down son. You're wriggling and shakin' like I don't know what. Read it out. Slowly.'

'Do you want me to read it? Maybe there's big words in it.' Ann grinned at her wee brother and tousled his hair.

'I think I can manage, thank you,' Joe said, regaining some sense of composure. He cleared his throat, theatrically. '*Dear Joseph* ... Even you don't call me Joseph,' he said, looking at Ma. '*Dear Joseph, You have been recommended to me by Mr Johnny Carey, who has seen you play and train during his recent visit to the Army Training Corps in Omagh. He says you have considerable potential. I would like to invite you to attend trials here in Manchester so we can assess this potential more fully.*'

He looked up and beamed at Ma and Ann. 'Trials!'

'You look like a wee boy whose Christmases have all come at once.' Ann was beaming too as she put her arm around Joe's shoulder.

Joe shrugged free and read on. 'These initial trials will last for four days and will take place in the first week of September.'

'That's less than a fortnight away!' Ma was indignant. 'They could have given you a bit more warning.'

'They must be desperate.' Ann put her arm round Joe's shoulder again

'There's more.' He shushed them. '*I hope you will accept my apologies for the short notice, but I trust you will be able to attend. Please contact Monica at the telephone number at the top of this letter and she will arrange your transportation and accommodation. Yours sincerely, Matt Busby.*'

'Does this mean they actually think you might be good?' Ann was trying to remain calm.

Joe whooped so loud that Ma had to cover her ears. He hopped up and down clenching his fists. 'Yes, yes, yes,' he hissed through clenched teeth.

'Joe! The neighbours'll think someone's been killed.' Ma put her hands on his shoulders to steady him.

'Sorry Ma, but this is bigger than the biggest thing that's ever happened in the history of the world.'

Ann said, 'I vaguely remember you rabbiting on about Johnny Carey being over and working with you and Harry at the ATC, but were you expecting this?'

Ma, ever sceptical, was studying the letter to be sure it was genuine and not a practical joke.

Joe took a deep breath and began to explain. 'Remember ages ago when you met Sammy Hopkins at the Starr?'

'Yes. Very fit. Nice man. Decent dancer.'

'Well, he's very fit because he plays football for Spurs. He was here with the ATC, and when me and Harry found out, we joined the ATC so we could play for them and train with Sammy. We still played for the YMCA too 'cause the ATC only play on Wednesday evenings. Anyway, Sammy taught us heaps of stuff about football and how we could get fitter and smarter.'

Ann was about to say something, but the exchanged looks were enough.

'He showed us how professionals train. Then earlier this summer, Johnny Carey appeared. He's in the ATC as well and was posted to Omagh for a while. He came to the training and watched us play. He plays for Man United and he's played for Northern Ireland too. And the Free State. Anyway, before he left, he said he would mention us to his old friend Matt Busby, who was in the ATC at one time himself.'

Joe paused for breath and ran his fingers through his tossed hair.' I told you I was a good footballer. Remember when I said to Mu about going over to London as well and Sammy could get me a trial with Spurs, you thought I was speaking out of my arse. But I was serious. This is serious. I can't believe it!' He pumped a fist in the air again.

'What does this mean exactly?' Ma asked. 'Are you going to play football for a living?'

'Twelve pounds a week, Ma. That's what Johnny Carey gets every week. I could buy a car. We could have a proper house with a toilet. One that doesn't get flooded.'

'This house has done us rightly. What would you want to buy a house for?'

'You wouldn't get twelve pounds a week,' Ann said. 'Not starting off.'

'Okay so, maybe four pounds a week. That's still a lot more than I get at Nestle's.'

'What's wrong with Omagh? Why does everybody want to go somewhere else? You can play football here.' Ma looked genuinely confused and upset.

'It's only a trial,' said Ann. 'Nothing is for sure yet.'

Suddenly Joe seemed more grown up. 'I know I might not get picked. There are loads of talented players out there, but they wouldn't go to all the trouble of bringing us over if they didn't think we were good enough. They're not stupid. They can spot a good player when they see one. Harry and me think we're good enough and that's half the battle, or so Johnny Carey says. He says you need to have confidence in yourself.'

'I suppose it's worth a try, son,' said Ma and she hugged him.

Ann and Joe looked at her open-mouthed.

'Nothing ventured, nothing gained,' she added. 'But you'll need to be prepared for disappointment. The odd setback or two just makes you stronger. Life can be harsh, but you need to learn this for yourself.'

'Ma!' Ann exclaimed. 'Just let him go and enjoy playing football. This is his dream. I think it's brilliant and I couldn't be happier. I know you worry about us, but I for one, am going nowhere. I like my job and I like Walter, so you're stuck with me at least.'

'Poor old Ma!' Joe beamed at his now favourite sister. 'I have to go and see Harry!' He pulled on his gutties.

'You need to be careful, son. What if Harry didn't get a letter?'

'Never thought of that … Of course he got a letter. No show without Punch. I can't go on my own.'

Joe went out to the yard and wheeled his bike through to the front door. As he opened the door, they heard Harry before they saw him. He was racing down Sedan Avenue whooping at the top of his voice.

Joe's face split from ear to ear.

'Man United, Joe. Bloody Man United. Can you believe it?' Harry dropped his bike with a clatter and hugged Joe.

Eventually Harry released his mate from the bear hug, and when Joe got his breath back, he wheezed, 'I jumped up and down and clapped my hands like a toy monkey when I read it. Couldn't believe it. Still can't believe it. It's like a dream.'

'I kissed it. Front and back. All over. Even the envelope. Hello, Mrs Brown.' Harry's cherubic cheeks were redder than ever. He looked like he was about to burst.

'Hello, Harry. Looks like you got good news as well.'

'Maybe we should read it again,' Joe suggested.

They read the letter again, jabbing fingers at it, hopping from foot to foot.

'You two need to calm down or you'll blow a gasket,' Ann said. She went over and gave Harry a hug. Joe saw him go bright red and chuckled. 'You don't want to pull a muscle that you might need, Joe,' she added. 'Like the wee one in your head.'

'Ignore my very jealous sister, Harry.' The boys went outside. 'What did your ma say? I'm sure your da thinks it's great.'

'Da never says much and he's an Arsenal supporter for some unknown reason. He just said that I should play for a good team, but I saw him smile. He doesn't smile often, so that's something! He thinks I'll be able to get him tickets for the FA Cup Final, even if United isn't in it. He's tried to let on that's all he cares about, but I know he's excited. And proud. Ma is all for it. Glad to get rid of me. One less mouth to feed and all that. But seriously, she wants me to get on in life, although she doesn't understand why I want to go away. She thinks football is just a game and not a job, but she knows this is a brilliant opportunity. If I'm happy, she's happy What about yours?'

'Much the same. Ma thought my sisters were mad when they left – what's wrong with Omagh, don't try and get above your station, the grass isn't always greener, dreaming only leads to heartache, etcetera, etcetera, etcetera. She must be getting used to the idea by now, or maybe she's happy to get rid of me too. No muddy kit to wash. Anyway, she understands I have to give it a go. She probably thinks I won't make it. Then I'll settle down and everything will be normal. For Ma, nothing beats normal and settling down.'

'So let's show them all. We'll become famous footballers and everybody will be happy.'

'Is your da really an Arsenal supporter? He's nearly as thick as you are.'

'Nobody is that thick. I'm the thickest person I know – apart from you, of course.'

'We need to tell Nigel and the lads. Can't wait to see their faces. Man United, here we come!'

Nigel didn't look surprised. 'It must be a mistake,' he speculated calmly. 'They must have sent you the wrong letters. It's obvious they don't require any level of intelligence in their potential recruits.'

'Don't be daft. Of course, there's an intelligence test,' objected Harry. 'They ask you your name, and if you get that right, they ask you to put on your boots. And if you get those on the right feet first time, you're in.'

'So, if you practise putting on your boots before you go, you might have a chance,' Nigel said, laughing.

Sadness flickered across Nigel's face before he spoke again. 'Now who am I going to explain things to? Like what a film is really about? The deeper meaning of it all – the social nuances, the references and comments and all that stuff? I'll be Nigel-no-mates at the Cake Shop! You can't leave me. Don't be so bloody selfish.' Desperation entered his voice, 'Please think about someone else for a change. You should give up this crazy notion of becoming rich and famous and stay here, so I'll have someone to be smarter than.'

Joe laughed, 'You're smarter than everybody, so don't give us that.'

'But you're my favourite mental minnows. No one else comes close.'

'When we're famous, you can come over to Manchester to watch a match,' Joe promised. 'We'll get you tickets in the royal box, even though you'll probably be a millionaire by then. You won't have to pay, 'cause the top players all get free tickets. It'll be brilliant.'

The rest of the gang were beyond excited and said it wouldn't be long before Joe and Harry would be playing for Northern Ireland because they only had a couple of good players and even two eejits like them couldn't be any worse. Eyeball even asked for their autographs, and they scribbled their names on the top of his *Beano*.

The time to go came round very quickly. At the station, Nigel waited until the families had done all their goodbyes and issued all their instructions about how to behave, which was mostly a list of things *not* to do. He approached Harry and Joe as they were just about to board the train and gave them a box each.

'People will talk if I give you a hug and I'd probably break your skinny ribs, so I hope these will do instead. Don't open them until the train pulls out 'cause I haven't brought a hanky.'

Harry and Joe stepped up to get on board.

'Aw, fuck it,' said Nigel, and he grabbed them both in one big bear hug.

'Jesus, Nigel, if I'd known you felt so strongly, I'd have stayed,' said Harry.

'You know you've always been my favourite.'

'Bastard.' Joe tried to look nonchalant and got onto the train.

They found two seats facing the front and pulled down the window to wave as the train pulled away from the platform, but quickly pulled it up again when the compartment was filled with sooty smoke and small lumps of hot ash.

Their excitement could not be contained and it took them a little while to realise this was the first time they had ever been away anywhere on their own. Then they opened the boxes. Inside was a new pair of boots each.

'Are you blubbing?' asked Joe.

'Flippin' heck, these must have cost a bob or two.' Harry whistled, held a boot up and smelled the leather. 'I hope we've time to get them soaked. Remember, Johnny said to put new boots on and then soak them in the bath for at least an hour.'

'Our old boots may have to do for the first day. Have you got any dubbin?' Joe asked.

'I "found" a tin of Cherry Blossom at the ATC last week.' Harry was the picture of innocence.

'Poor old Nigel.' Joe was holding both boots out at arm's length.

'He'll be all right.'

'How could he be all right without us? Be honest.'

'True, but he'll manage somehow.'

They looked out the window at the world racing by, a world of limitless, wondrous possibilities.

CHAPTER 20

Life was quiet, too quiet, in their little house. The anticipated joy of having the bed all to herself had quickly given way to a strange feeling of too much space. Ann had never been able to wriggle about before, and now, two months later, it was still odd and disconcerting. She and Ma also hadn't realised just how much noise Joe managed to make, seemingly without any effort – going to bed, getting up and pretending to wash, dressing, devouring breakfast, or crashing his bike through the house before shouting, 'see you later,' and blasting out a fart as he pushed off, always on his right foot, to cycle to the factory.

Fred had called on the Monday evening after Muriel left. That was very unusual. He thought they might need a wee bit of company. He always seemed to judge these things well – when to call and what to say; when not to call and what not to say. Ma was glad to see him.

They all had a little sip of the Jameson's that Fred brought. Again, that was unheard of, having a wee drink on a weeknight, but it helped lighten the mood. So much had happened in the last two years.

After the happy memories came the unspoken sadness, the vast void that was Da. Fred and Ann knew Ma was thinking about him. She looked vacant as she sat staring at the fire. Fred asked quietly, 'Do you miss him, Kathleen?'

'Joe?'

'You know who I mean.'

'No,' she replied, with a little less conviction than she intended. Her eyes got glassy and she looked like she was about to cry. But she didn't; the mask was firmly back in place and they knew not to probe any further.

But Ann wanted to know more about Da. What happened? What had he done? She hoped the right time would come. Maybe it would be easier to talk now that there were just the two of them.

They had another wee drink. On the radio, the Ray McKinley Band was playing, and the conversation slowed. Then it became a comfortable silence, each of them lost in their own thoughts.

Ann went up to bed with a jar, even though it was a balmy night. The warmth might help her sleep in the vast, empty space. She rolled over just because she could, and rolled back again. She lay on her back and extended her hands and feet towards each corner, star-shaped, then curled up into a tight ball. She was about to lie face down when she heard an unfamiliar noise downstairs. She crept out onto the landing and looked down.

She could only see a small square of floor just inside the front door but it was enough. She watched the vague flickering shadows as Fred and Ma danced.

Her heart leapt and then she heard Ma whisper, a little loudly, maybe because of the whiskey, 'What if Ann hears us?'

Fred's response was inaudible.

Ann felt like shouting down, 'Don't worry, Ma, I'm asleep!' Instead, she crept back into bed, smiling. Wait till Hilda and Mu heard about this, she thought.

* * *

Never a dull moment in this house,' Ann said as she closed the front door.

'What?' Ma screeched from the scullery.

Ann shouted, 'I said there's never a dull moment in this house!'

'There's no need to shout. I'm not deaf.' Ma had crept up behind her in the living room.

They were both laughing as Ann bent down to pick up the letter. Letters were becoming commonplace. They knew it was from Hilda because it was flimsy and blue.

'That dozy milkman has left two pints again.' Ma held them up as evidence. 'You did put a note out for him, didn't you, love?'

'I did. Don't know what happened to it. Maybe he can't read.'

'Surely every milkman can tell a number one from a number two?'

'You taught us that when we were potty training!'

Ma was actually laughing.

'He'll be calling for his money tomorrow,' Ann said, 'so I'll explain the maths to him as best I can'.

'Don't be too sharp with the lad. He's only new. And Joe will be back soon, so we'll have to go back to getting two pints.'

'See? Never a dull moment. All these milk shenanigans and a letter from Hilda. I hope your heart can take it, Ma.'

'I'll put the kettle on. We can read the letter later.'

'Good idea.' Ann put her arm around her ma's shoulders and gave her a little squeeze. Just bones; a clothes rack with clothes on.

'We'll be okay,' Ann said as much to herself as to Ma, who had disappeared to light the hob.

'You need to put a penny in the meter,' she shouted.

'No need to shout,' Ann whispered, having followed her into the kitchen.

Someone banged loudly on the front door. Ann looked out the window. 'It's the coal man!' she shouted. Then she held the back of her hand up to her forehead in a theatrical faint. 'This is all too much for a girl.'

'Tell him just one,' Ma shouted.

'I can hear you, Mrs Brown. No need to shout,' said the coal man.

He carried the bag of coal through the house to the yard and dumped it in the coal shed. Ma gave him five bob.

The letter had to wait until after dinner and all the washing up was done and the pot of tea made. Ann got a couple of Rich Teas from the biscuit tin while Ma retrieved the letter from the mantelpiece.

'You read it, love.'

> *Dan has been posted to Winnipeg. His ma and da still live there, which is great. They have a store that sells guns and fishing rods and all sorts of hunting and camping stuff, as well as her woolly jumpers. They are really nice people. Very down to earth. You will love them when you meet them.*

'You can buy a gun in a shop? Like a pint of milk? I hope they never bring that idea over here!'

'They'd be sold out in no time,' Ann said. 'Imagine if everybody had a gun.' She shivered at the thought.

Before it gets really cold in late October or early November, we will be going on the train way up north to a place called Churchill, which is on the shore of Hudson Bay in the Arctic.

'That must be near the North Pole,' said Ann before reading on:

Dan says that this is the time of year when you are virtually guaranteed to see a polar bear and maybe even the Northern Lights. It will be very exciting but it will be extremely cold – Dan reckons maybe as cold as minus fifty. Can anywhere get that cold? Maybe he is just trying to frighten me. There is a navy base there called Fort Churchill. Dan will work there through the winter. The trains can't get through because the snow can be ten feet deep, so we will be stuck there until the springtime.

'I don't like the sound of this Churchill place,' said Ma. 'It sounds desperate. I hope they have plenty of coal. Ten feet deep! How could you go anywhere? You wouldn't be able to open the door or see out. How would you get to the bog? You'd have to use the po all winter.'

'And where would you empty it?' Ann said. 'You'd be able to see everything in the snow! Doesn't bear thinking about. Maybe they have inside toilets.'

'Oh aye, maybe. Never thought of that.'

Ann kept reading: '*Dan is very well. I hope all of you are as well. Is Muriel still going out with Derek?*'

'God love her.' Ma gently shook her head. 'She doesn't even know what's going on with her own sister.'

'And Joe. There's a lot to tell her in our next letter.'

The rest consisted of questions about Joe, Fred, Ann and Walter and wondering if there was any chance of wedding bells soon.

'No chance,' said Ann, blushing furiously.

'Why not? He's a lovely boy. So well-mannered and you've been going out with him for a long time now.'

'There's a difference between going out and going dancing. We dance, we go home, that's it.'

Ann went back to the letter.

> *I have a wee job in the camp working in the shop. I've taken up knitting and knit a lot of stuff for the soldiers. They seem to love it. I can hardly keep up.*

Ma was about to comment when Ann jumped in. 'Ma, wait till you hear this last bit!'

> *Finally, I have saved the best news for last. I am pregnant and the baby is due in March next year. I am feeling very well and all is going well. Dan is beside himself with excitement and I am sure you all will be too!*

'You're going to be a granny!'

Ma was like a child getting a ninety-nine with an extra flake in it. A moment of genuine joy crossed her weary face. 'That means she's gone about twelve weeks. Who's there to look after her?'

'The army will have proper doctors. I bet they have midwives and everything. Hilda won't be the first soldier's wife to get pregnant. She'll be well looked after.'

'That's true,' Ma said wistfully. 'Will this wean be born at home, do you think? Is there a hospital in this Churchill place, if anything goes wrong?'

‘Ma, Ma, Ma, she’ll be fine. Army doctors are the best in the world. She’ll have Dan, and his parents will be around once they get back to Winnipeg. They probably mean to be back there before the wean’s due.’

Ma’s joy quickly dissipated, replaced by her normal pessimism. ‘She’s so far away. I might never get to see my own grandchild.’

‘Be happy for them. It’s great news.’ She gave Ma a gentle hug, but Ann knew her ma would fret and worry from now until the baby was born. Then she would fret and worry about how it was getting on, and then she would fret and worry if Hilda was coping. Nothing she could do or say would change that.

‘We’ll have to get a telephone,’ Ann said. ‘Then you could speak to Hilda and listen to the baby cooing and gurgling. Wouldn’t that be brilliant?’

‘How can we afford a telephone? It must cost a fortune to ring faraway places like Canada. Do they even have telephones in Canada?’

‘Of course they do, and it’ll cost us nothing if they ring us. You’ll be able to tell how she is when you speak to her.’

‘We’d still have to pay to have the phone, and then you’d be on it all the time gabbing to Iris and Walter and God knows who else.’

Ann tried not to show her irritation. ‘I’ll put phone money in a separate tin, or maybe you can get one with a slot where you pay for the calls when you make them, like a phone box. We could call Muriel and Joe too. Will you at least think about it?’

‘We’ve done all right till now without one. Nothing wrong with letters.’

‘Except that letters from Canada take a month to get here. Imagine being able to talk to her right now. A letter’s not the same. You wouldn't end a chat with *That's all for now, yours sincerely*.'

Ma smiled wearily, too tired for debate.

'I wonder how many she's going to have?' Ann mused.

'Two is plenty. One of each.'

'Which two of us are surplus then, unwanted and unloved? Joe must be safe as he's a boy – well, sort of. So it means you have to pick one of us girls.'

'You're the only one here, so you're my favourite. At the minute anyway. And when Joe comes back everything will be perfect. One of each.'

'You're dodging the question.'

'It's a silly question. I love you all equally, all the time.'

'I know. I'm only talking nonsense.' She put her arms around Ma and pecked her cheek. 'You deserve to be happy.'

'I *am* happy.'

'I'd hate to see you unhappy if that's the case. You've a face on ye that would curdle milk.'

'That's enough cheek!'

'After tea, why don't we go up to the phone box and call Muriel. She'll never forgive us if we don't tell her the good news right away.'

'Do you know how to work it? We don't know her number. How much will it cost?'

'No idea, but we'll bring plenty, just in case. You drop in one or two pence at a time during the phone call, so we won't waste any.'

Ma's face registered alarm.

Ann reassured her. 'It's only England. It shouldn't cost that much.' She crossed her fingers behind her back as she said it.

'It's gone six. She might not be in work this late.' But Ma already had her coat on.

'Still worth a try and it's cheaper after six.'

They squeezed into the phone box outside the post office and Ann lifted the black Bakelite handset. She heard buzzing in her ear. 'It's working. I think we dial nought for the operator.'

'It says it there.' Ma indicated the box.

'You do it, Ma.'

Ma stuck her index finger into the hole marked zero, pulled it round to the metal clip at the end and then let go. There was a satisfying whirry, clicking sound as the dial returned to its starting position.

'Number please?' said a voice on the other end. Ann didn't recognise it.

'I don't know the number,' she said, 'but it's the telephone exchange at the Maudsley Hospital in London that we want to get through to.'

'Hold the line please, while I try and connect you.'

Heads together, mother and daughter listened as the line clicked and buzzed. The phone box steamed up. They couldn't see out. Ma wiped the glass. Ann realised Ma wouldn't have been disappointed if someone she knew walked past and saw her.

'Open the door a crack, Ma.'

'Everyone will be able to hear what we're saying.'

'There's nobody about and we can close it again when we get connected. I need to breathe.'

After a short wait, the operator came back. 'I'm connecting you now. Please put one and six in the slot and press Button A.'

Ma looked horrified and mouthed, 'One and six!'

Ann pushed a shilling and six pennies into the slot. They clanked their way down into the innards of the machine.

'Push the button, Ma.'

Ma pushed Button A and hunched her shoulders like an excited child.

'Maudsley Hospital. How can I help you?' said someone with an English accent.

'May I speak to Muriel Brown, please?' Ann asked.

'Whose calling?'

'It's her sister, Ann.'

The hand over the mouthpiece did little to conceal the switch to broad cockney. 'Mew Mew, it's your skin and blister!'

A second later, Muriel came on the line. 'Ann? Ann?' She was breathless. 'What's wrong? Is Ma okay?'

'We're all grand. We've some great news. Hilda's expecting! The baby's due in March. She's going up to the North Pole for the winter with Dan.'

'Crikey! Slow down! Let me speak to Ma.'

Ann handed the handset to Ma, who cleared her throat and whispered tentatively, 'Hello?'

'Hello, Ma. How're ye keepin'?'

'Working away as usual, nothing else for it.'

'It's great to hear your voice!' Muriel sounded emotional.

'Does Hilda know I'm in London?' Muriel asked.

'Not yet. She asked if you were still going out with Derek.'

'Oh, dear. Poor old Derek. I wonder how he's getting on.'

'How is London, love, and work? Are they treating you well?'

'Yes, everybody is very kind and helpful and the job is going well. What do you think of the phone? Isn't it great being able to have a chat? And it's so clear, it's like you're here beside me.'

'Ann wants a word.' Ma passed the handset over as if it were made of glass.

'Hello, Auntie Muriel!

'And Auntie Annie and Granny Ma,' Muriel said, laughing. 'That doesn't sound quite right.'

'Nana will do for me.'

Muriel bombarded them with more questions about Churchill before they got a chance to get more details about her new life in London.

'Lovely people here. But I can't understand a word they say half the time. You were talking to Di just then. She's a cockney from east London. "Skin and blister" means "sister". They don't half talk some rubbish,' she said, knowing Di could hear her.

'And Al?' Ann wanted gossip.

'Hardly ever see him. He's very busy. We saw him a lot at the start when we were getting the exchange set up, but now it's just my wee team left to crack on with it.'

'How many are in your *wee team*?'

'Di, Flo, Agnes and me. All best mates. But what about you? Still seeing Walter?'

'Still dancing if that's what you mean.'

'Nothing more? I know he's easy-going, but you've been "just dancing" with him for ever. Maybe he needs a wee bit of encouragement.' Both girls laughed.

'That's enough of that kind of talk, ladies,' said Ma loudly so Muriel was sure to hear. 'Men don't need *encouragement*.'

'Yes, Ma,' replied Ann and Muriel simultaneously, still laughing.

'I'll be ancient at the rate Walter goes at.'

'Hello, caller. You will need to put in more money if you want to continue your call.'

‘Do you want to continue?’ asked Muriel.

Ma was shaking her head.

‘I don’t think so,’ Ann replied. ‘Ma’s exhausted by all the excitement.’

‘It was lovely to talk to you, Ma. Please call again soon.’

After the goodbyes, Muriel realised she had forgotten to tell Ma that Al had invited her out for a fancy meal. Ann and Ma realised they’d forgotten to tell her about Joe.

‘We can save it for next time,’ Ann said. ‘Joe might have his own big news by then. We should call on the ninth. It’ll be her twentieth birthday. Can you believe it?’

Then Mrs Chesney walked past, just as they left the phone box. Things couldn’t have got any better! Ma was blissfully smug as the women exchanged pleasantries. Tongues would wag and questions would be asked. Perfect.

CHAPTER 21

The train hissed and chuffed into Omagh station. Clouds of steam enveloped the huge black engine. Acrid smoke billowed into the compartment after the conductor opened the window in the door.

Joe and Harry were in a fitful sleep, exhausted after travelling overnight on the Liverpool boat.

The conductor came down the carriage and stopped where they were curled uncomfortably. 'Omagh, lads. Omagh station,' he barked in the loud voice that seemed to be reserved for train conductors and army sergeant majors.

They blinked awake, yawned, stretched and sat up. They were stiff from trying to sleep on the hard seats.

'My arse is numb.' Harry said, massaging his left buttock.

'My leg's still asleep, and I've pins and needles in my arm,' moaned Joe.

'The train's great, but I think I've travelled enough.'

Gently flexing their limbs, they reached up to the rack for their duffle bags.

'I'm mingin'. I need a bath,' Harry said, sniffing his armpit.

'Calm down. It's only September, but you might be right.' Joe held his nose.

They got off and walked up James Street, then veered right down John Street. They stopped at the top of the Courthouse Hill and looked down the straight line of High Street and Market Street.

'Good to be home.' Harry yawned and stretched.

'Have you any money left? I have …' – Joe counted – 'sixpence and one, two, three pennies.'

Harry jiggled his coat pockets and trousers and pulled out two thruppenny bits and a ha'penny.

'Enough for a coke before we go home.'

They went down to the Café Rex and shuffled stiffly into a booth. The Cokes disappeared in two quick gulps, followed by two very loud, sour, burps.

'Sorry, ladies,' Joe said to the two old dears sipping tea at the table next to them.

Outside, Harry said, 'Did you see the look on those two auld dolls' faces?'

'It was very rude.' Joe sighed. 'Anyway, back to porridge on Monday.'

'Only for a while, Joe. Only for a while. United will be in touch soon and we'll be back on the train to Manchester to sign up.'

'I hope you're right,' said Joe. 'Wouldn't it be just … I can't even think about it anymore.'

They'd talked of nothing else the whole way home. Their analysis veered from completely optimistic to completely pessimistic in the same sentence. The running was easy, but they'd never done any training in a gym before. The weights took some getting used to.

As far as their ability went, they were as good as any and better than most. Some were too slow on their feet or too slow in their heads. Others were not as good as they thought they were. A few were too timid and nervous.

The boys learned that top-level football wasn't just about being a good player. You had to hold your position, mark your man, go back for corners, but not always. There were tactics to learn, as well as free-kick and corner routines. Their minds were as tired as their bodies.

'Will you be at church tomorrow?' asked Harry.

'Probably. Ma will make me go. She won't believe me when I tell her I'm knackered. *You were only playing football*' – Joe put on a fair impersonation of Ma's quiet lilt – '*And you're always playing football, so get out of your scratcher*. And I'll say, "Yes, Ma" as always. So the short answer is, I'll be at church, but don't blame me if I start snoring in the middle of the sermon.'

'Nothing new there then. See you tomorrow.'

They went their separate ways, Joe down Bridge Street, Harry down Market Street and across the bridge into Campsie.

Joe was greeted like a hero returning from the war. Ma heaved herself up and gave him a hug that nearly squeezed the breath out of him.

'Ann, Ann! Joe's back!'

Ann was in the yard filling the coal scuttle. She came in and looked him up and down.

'You look terrible – worse than normal.'

'So do you, but we've been up all night travelling. What's your excuse?' Joe said with a cheeky grin. 'Harry was sick on the boat again and the train seemed to take forever. You don't get much sleep on it.'

'But you're back now safe and sound, and that's the main thing. You look different – bigger, more grown up.' Ma's face shone with delight.

'I've only been away a week.'

'Could you not sleep on the boat?' asked Ann.

'We only had chairs. Harry could get sick on a frozen pond and his boking kept me awake.'

'How did you get on? Did you get picked?' Ann asked.

Ma's ears pricked up. 'I'll wet the tea and you can tell us everything. We have a fresh soda.'

'Is there jam?'

'Lemon curd.'

'Now you're talking, Ma. They don't have proper bread in England, or lemon curd.'

Ma and Ann listened intently as Joe told them everything. A man called Dave met them and drove them to Manchester in an old pale green Morris Cowley. It took ages. Harry had to stop the car twice to boke in the ditch. They stayed with Dave and his wife, Edith, who was a lovely woman. They had a dog called Blackie. They were mad United supporters. Edith worked in the laundry at Old Trafford and Dave drove people around in his car. He didn't seem to do anything else.

Joe described the training, the practice sessions and the gym work. 'There was even classroom stuff. With blackboards and chalk. Like being back at school, only not as boring.'

They were disappointed that the trials took place at City's ground at Maine Road, as Old Trafford still wasn't rebuilt after being bombed in the war.

'You look as though they fed you properly,' Ma noted.

'We had lunch at the ground. Soup and sandwiches. Breakfast and dinner were at Edith's house. Her food was good, Ma, but not as good as yours.' Ma beamed at him. 'They still have proper rationing over there, not like here.'

'Was it a big house?' Ann asked. 'They had room for you two big lumps?'

'Harry and I had to share a room, but there were two beds in it, so that was good. Dave and Edith had two boys killed in the war and we had their room. It was a wee bit spooky at times. We could hear Edith crying sometimes at night, but she told us all about them. She said she liked to talk about them.'

'That's desperate,' Ma said. But after a respectful pause, she quickly moved on to enquiring if there was an inside WC and a proper bath with real taps.

'The loo was inside – downstairs and the stairs creaked like mad, so you couldn't sneak down – and there was a proper bath.'

Joe wanted to get back to the football. 'Players came from all over England, Scotland, Wales, even the Free State. But we were up with the best of them.'

Now he looked smug. 'There were lots of pretty girls always hanging around too. They loved the way we talked. They said we sounded funny. They'd never even heard of Omagh.'

'I hope you didn't get up to any mischief.' Ma looked as if she was going into Worried Ma state.

'Don't know what you mean, Ma.'

'Don't worry, son. If you don't know what I mean, then there's nothing to worry about.'

Ann and Joe exchanged knowing grins.

'So, you think you did well then?' Ann said, changing the subject.

'As well as anyone.'

'But they didn't ask you to stay or anything?' Mas said.

'They'll write to everybody to tell us who's been picked and who hasn't.'

'When will that be?'

Joe shrugged. 'Don't know. Soon I hope.'

'What'll you do if you get through and Harry doesn't?' asked Ann.

'It'll be even worse if he gets through and I don't. I'll never hear the end of it.'

'Would you go on your own?'

Ma sat up at Ann's question.

'Never even thought about it, but I'd have to go, wouldn't I? Harry would tell me to go, just like I'd tell him. It's not like I'm married to him.'

'Joe!' Ma was horrified. 'You're not one of those, are you? Tell me you're not.'

Joe sighed heavily. 'No, Ma. It's just a saying!'

'Mr Lee's brother was one, or so everyone says, but he got killed in the war, so it was all right.'

'That's an awful thing to say,' objected Ann.

'I didn't mean it was good he got killed. I mean it was … I don't know what I mean. Forget I ever said anything. We have a chicken. I'll go and stick it in the oven.' Ma shuffled off and shouted from the kitchen, 'There's a letter from Hilda on the mantelpiece. She's expecting.'

'Are they calling him Joe?' Joe shouted back.

'It might be a wee girl.'

Joe hadn't thought of that. Ann looked happier to see him than he expected. He was happier to be home than he expected too. It was good to be the centre of attention for a change.

CHAPTER 22

Sunday morning and Joe's church trousers finally died. He held his belly in as best he could to get them buttoned, but as soon as he exhaled, the button flew off and disappeared under the bed. He bent down and heard cloth tearing.

He was still searching for the button, head under the bed, arse in the air, when Ann looked in to see if he was up and ready for breakfast.

'What a sight first thing on a Sunday morning. That's going to put me right off my breakfast.'

'I bet you wish Walter had an arse as good as mine.' Joe stood up, button in hand, and patted his bum.

'Leave Walter out of this.'

'Oooh, I think you like him a lot more than you let on.'

'Put some trousers on. If you have any that fit that is. You'll soon be as big as Nigel.'

Joe threw the button at her as she disappeared out the door.

Even Ma couldn't work a miracle with the dead trousers. 'I told you you'd got bigger.'

'It's all muscle from the training.' Joe held his arms up and squeezed his biceps. Ann burst out laughing.

'Two Brussel sprouts on a stick.'

Joe blushed and put his arms down again.

'Don't listen to her, son. You look very grown up. I think you look lovely.'

'Ma!'

'What a lovely boy.' Ann stroked his hair teasingly.

'Now now, children. Not on the Sabbath.'

'Yes, Ma,' they said together.

'Anyway, you're not the only girl who thinks I'm lovely. I'll tell you that for nothing.'

'Ooooh, tell us more, Casanova Joe.'

'Is there anything to eat in this house?' Joe ignored her and went to make toast.

It was deemed unseemly for Joe to wear his everyday trousers to church. They only remotely resembled trousers, being shapeless and shiny. They were what he wore to work every day. The only other pair he owned were ancient corduroys that Da had left behind. They had always been far too big for him, until now. They had patches on both knees and a button missing at the fly.

'I'll put a button on, but those are only fit for the garden.'

So Joe got to stay at home for the first time ever, apart from when he was genuinely sick. He'd found a copy of *The Hotspur* on the boat and while they were at church, he read it for the umpteenth time. He loved the Shadowman story. It started like it was about football but took a dark twist at the end. He was dreaming about being the hero, Tommy Hamilton, when Ma and Ann got back from church.

'Was Harry there?' he asked.

'Yes, and looking very smart. He asked where you were. I

couldn't say you had no trousers, so I told a wee fib and said you were feeling poorly and were very tired,' said Ma.

'Doreen was looking well,' said Ann, giving him an exaggerated knowing look.

'She always looks well. You wouldn't think her and Harry were brother and sister.'

'What do you mean?'

'Well, she's very pretty, is all I'm saying.'

'That's cruel. Harry is a very handsome boy.'

'But not as handsome as me, eh, Ma?'

'No one could be as handsome as you, son, and you've lit the fire, so you're not only good-looking but you're useful as well. You'd be a great catch for any woman.'

'Thank you, Ma. You're the best Ma I've ever had and you're obviously a lady of great discernment and intelligence. It's a pity those admirable qualities haven't been inherited by your daughter.'

'Have you been working on that wee speech all morning?' asked Ann.

'I just made it up there now.'

'Ha, there were at least three big words in it. You must have spent hours on it.'

'You're just jealous 'cause the biggest word you know is jitterbug.'

'Children, children, please, you'll give me a headache. Can one of you start the spuds?'

'Yes, Ma. Sorry, Ma.'

Joe vowed to buy himself a new pair of Sunday trousers. He was earning more than Ma now, so it was only right he started to look after himself. He would need Ma with him though, to make sure he bought the right ones, and she was good at haggling.

He'd never bought clothes before, but when he was a famous footballer over in Manchester, he would have to know how to buy suits and other fancy stuff. Apart from his bike, the only things he'd ever bought were tickets for the flicks, minerals and snowballs. Time to grow up.

They went to Bloomfield's, Nigel's father's shop, on Tuesday afternoon when Joe got home from work. Ma didn't work on Tuesdays and Ann decided she had to be involved in this momentous transaction as well, so she got the afternoon off. She said she would add a young lady's perspective to the purchase. Joe wasn't sure what that meant. She explained that she knew the latest style for men from going to dances. Ma might choose something old-fashioned, or even worse, culchie-looking.

Joe hoped Nigel wasn't going to be there as they entered the large, quiet cathedral of clothes and cloth. The wooden floor shone, smelled of lavender polish and creaked gently. The whole shop smelled of new. But he *was* there, the floor creaking a little less gently as he approached.

'I wasn't expecting you,' said Joe.

'I work here, you eejit. Hello, Mrs Brown. Ann. To what do we owe the pleasure of your company this fine day?'

Joe pretended to be sick and Nigel laughed. Ma preened at the courtesy.

'You can cut the fancy chat, you big goat. I'm here to buy a pair of good trousers.'

'We only sell good trousers. What happened to your old good trousers?' Nigel asked, knowing full well what had happened – Joe had told Harry and Harry had told Nigel.

'I just need a new pair, that's all,' answered Joe. 'So, wind your neck in.'

'Joe Brown! Where are your manners?'

'Sorry, Ma, but he's trying to be smart.'

'He is smart,' interjected Ann. 'You said so yourself. Nigel is the smartest person you've ever met.'

'Aw, Joe.' Nigel ruffled Joe's hair. 'That's the nicest thing anybody's ever said about me.'

'Let's just get this over with,' Joe said gruffly, now they had successfully embarrassed him. 'Have you any decent trousers that might suit me?'

'That last bit might be difficult. Mr Nesbitt is our trousers expert. I'll call him over. Just to warn you – he might have to measure your inside leg! I'll tell him to wear gloves.'

Ann covered her mouth to suppress a cackle.

'I'd get less abuse if I'd gone to Swan's.'

'But you wouldn't get Mr Nesbitt's expertise in that area.' Nigel looked down. 'He's a genius with the old tape measure.'

Mr Nesbitt was called. He was wearing an extremely dapper suit with a tape measure draped around his neck. He was very professional. Joe thought he seemed to be enjoying himself a bit too much.

'Twenty-eight waist, thirty-one inside leg,' Mr Nesbitt announced. 'What colour and fabric was sir thinking of?'

'Sir doesn't do much thinking, but he wants a grey pair. Dark grey, not black. Must be hard-wearing,' said Ann.

'Corduroy,' said Joe.

'Catch yourself on! Nobody wears corduroy trousers to church,' said Ann.

When Ma repeated Ann's request, adding that they should not be too dear but good quality, Joe felt like a little boy again and wished he'd come on his own.

'Worsted wool might be the best,' recommended Mr Nesbitt. 'The rayon wool blend is cheaper but doesn't last as well or have the quality. If they're only for church, they should last for years.'

Mr Nesbitt brought out the trousers and everyone had a feel of the material. Ma and Ann nodded and muttered their approval.

'We'll need to take them up an inch, unless you want a tailor-made pair. Would you like to try them on?'

Joe panicked at the thought of taking his trousers off in the shop. 'No, I trust your fastidious measuring, Mr Nesbitt. How much will that be?'

'What? The trousers, the taking up or the tailoring?'

'The first two. I don't need tailor-made. These are fine.'

'Relax, Joe,' said Nigel. 'Taking up is included. Alterations are all part of the service for our best customers.'

'I've never been a customer before, so how can I be a best customer?'

'Thinking ahead. You'll become a best customer when you're a famous footballer and people in Manchester and all round the world ask you where you get all your fancy clothes and you'll say "Bloomfield's of Omagh is the place to go".' But Nigel's smile said: *I won't hold my breath.*

Joe looked at him as if to say: *Dream on, my big fat friend.*

Ma looked at Ann as if to say: *Nothing beats a trier.*

What Joe did say was, 'Good thinking, big man, but how much do I owe you?'

'You can pay me later when you collect the trousers, if you want,' Nigel replied with a wink.

Ma quickly interrupted. 'He will pay you now. Neither a borrower nor a lender be.'

'Sorry, Mrs Brown. I wasn't implying that he buys them on tick. I just meant they will be ready tomorrow. I agree that

Polonius's advice to Laertes is still as valid and prudent today as it ever was.'

Ann and Joe both knew Ma had no idea what Nigel was talking about.

Joe got there first. 'He's showing off again, Ma. They're in *Hamlet*. We did it at school. Polonius is trying to give advice to his eejit of a son. "Neither a borrower nor a lender be, for loan doth oft lose both itself and friend, and borrowing dulls the edge of husbandry." Isn't that, right?' He looked at Nigel.

'Correct. You obviously work hard at appearing to be a completely uneducated ignoramus.'

'It takes a lot of talent to look this thick.'

'Mr Polonius was right. Now how much for the trousers?' Ma interjected.

'Fifteen and six to you, Mrs Brown.'

'I'm paying for them,' said Joe.

'That'll be fifteen bob then, seeing as you're about to become one of our best customers.'

Joe shot his mother a questioning look.

'If you're happy, it sounds fair to me. Have you enough money?'

Joe fumbled in his worn, baggy old trousers and pulled out a small wad of dirty crumpled notes and a few coins.

He handed a ten-bob note to Mr Nesbitt who held it between two fingers as if it were a soiled hanky. 'And one, two, three, four, five bob,' he said, counting out the coins.

'Thank you, sir. Your trousers will be ready tomorrow afternoon,' Mr Nesbitt said, bowing his head slightly

'Thank you. You at least have been very helpful,' Joe said.

The two friends exchanged winks.

'All's well that ends well, eh? Flicks tomorrow night?'

'What's on?' Joe was relieved his ordeal was over.

'A western. *The Doolins of Oklahoma*. Randolph Scott, if I'm not mistaken.'

'Is there a six o'clock?'

'Yessiree.'

'See you there.'

CHAPTER 23

The trees were celebrating the end of their season with a glorious display of colour. Winter was waiting. The pale shades of grey turned to charcoal as the light of the day faded to black, broken only by the little circles of light of the gas lamps. The lamplighter came round earlier and earlier and those with a vested interest started watching the rivers.

The letter from Manchester United came ten days after Joe arrived back. It was on the mantelpiece when he got home from work.

'Is that it, Ma?'

'Calm down, son. Put your bike out the back first.'

Despite his apprehension, Joe carefully leaned his bike against the yard wall before racing back into the front room. He lifted the envelope and looked at it from both sides, his heart thudding. His stomach churned. The best, worst, biggest, most exciting, most important exam result ever was inside.

'I'm scared, Ma.'

'You did your best son. That's all you can do.'

'Oh, Ma. Fingers crossed, here goes.'

Joe took a deep breath and opened the envelope. He unfolded the single page and scanned it. He turned it over to see if there was anything more on the back, but there wasn't. He read it again and started to shake. Tears filled his eyes. One trickled down his cheek.

'Oh, Joe.' Ma took the letter from his trembling hand and wrapped an arm around his heaving shoulders. 'Let's see it.'

It was short and direct. They thanked him for his time and his enthusiastic participation in their trials programme. His fitness and enthusiasm weren't in doubt and he obviously had talent, but just not enough to make it at the highest level. They wished him all the best for the future.

'Oh, Ma, I thought we'd made it.'

She hugged her son. He was shaking in her arms, and she felt the back of her blouse getting damp. All of a sudden Joe was a little boy again, upset beyond consolation, like when the wheels came off his little tin train.

'I was going to be a footballer. I want to be a footballer. I think I'm going to be sick.'

'You're only young, son. Maybe you can try again. There must be other teams.' Then she asked quietly, 'Do you think Harry got the same letter?'

Joe straightened up, wiped his nose on his sleeve and stuck his knuckles into his eyes. 'I'll have to go see him.'

'Do you need a clean hanky?'

'No, Ma. I'm fine.' He sniffed, took a deep breath and composed himself. Then he trudged out to the yard to get his bike, shoulders slumped.

Joe sped round to Campsie. Usually Harry or his Ma would spy him out the window and the door would be open before he got to it, but he had to knock that day. He knew this meant Harry had got the same news.

He was sitting in a chair in the corner of the tiny front room, clutching his letter. Harry looked up and his eyes were red. He'd been crying.

'You got the letter then?' Joe asked and Harry waved it like a white flag.

Joe had never seen Harry looking so deflated, defeated.

'I thought we'd made it, Joe. I really did. All the things they said when we were there …'

'I was sure we'd done it too. I thought we were as good as anyone.'

'It's a pity they didn't think the same.'

'What the f—,' and Joe remembered that Mrs Johnston was out in the scullery and could hear them. 'What do we do now?'

'We need Nigel.' Harry sniffed and wiped his eyes.

'Yep, let's go and annoy the big gobshite. He'll know what to do.'

Nigel was in the shop. He knew as soon as they walked in that something was wrong and what that something was.

'Not good news, I take it?' He knew it would be unmanly, but he wanted to give them both a hug. They looked so beaten, like their worlds had ended.

Harry showed him the letter.

'I think we should get some beer, go out to the Lovers Retreat and drown your sorrows. No, *our* sorrows,' Nigel said calmly.

'Don't know if I want a beer or not,' said Joe. 'We had a few in Manchester. Flat brown stuff that looked like flood water and tasted like shit.'

'We can get some Harp somewhere,' said Nigel. 'It's nice and fizzy. Very windy.'

'An exploding Joe is the last thing we need.' Nobody smiled. 'Mrs McAleer will sell us some, and it's on the way.'

'Let's go, troops. Sharpen your sabres,' ordered Nigel.

Nigel's da gave Nigel the afternoon off and the boys left the shop. They bought six bottles of Harp from the side door of McAleer's. Harry said they were for his da, who was well known to them as it was only fifty yards from his house.

Molly, the barmaid, just smiled. 'That'll be three and six, boys.'

Nigel counted out the money and Molly put the beer in a brown paper bag. They cycled slowly, silently out to the Lovers Retreat. The only sound was the clanking and clinking of the bottles in Nigel's saddle bag.

They sat on a bench near the waterfall.

'It's fuckin' freezing out here,' whinged Joe.

They had to slap the bottle tops off on the corner of the bench. They sipped their beer and Nigel tried to cheer them up, but he could get no craic out of them at all. The mood didn't lighten. The pair were lost in their thoughts. Instead of money, girls, adventures and playing football all day for vast amounts of money, they would be stuck with Nestle's and the YMCA. In silence, the boys watched the river cascade over the low falls.

'It's not exactly Niagara Falls, is it?' Harry mumbled.

'More like Niagara stumbles,' Nigel said. This got a grunt from Harry. 'Would it have helped if you'd got the new boots earlier? You'd have had time to soften them up properly.'

'Don't think so, Nige. Can't blame the boots.' Joe patted his friend on the shoulder.

'If we could blame you or the boots or anything else, we

would. We just weren't good enough is all.' Harry took a slug of his beer and burped.

It started to drizzle. It felt like they were sitting inside a cloud that had no silver lining.

'Do you want my second one?' Joe asked them both. 'I'm going home. Thanks for this, Nige.' He held up his unfinished bottle.

'Naw,' said Harry. 'It's Baltic out here.'

'Just leave them,' Nigel suggested. 'The winos'll find them and think Christmas has come early.'

They cycled back in silence. Joe was at the back behind Nigel. He watched his friend's enormous backside shift slowly from one side to the other and couldn't think of anything funny to say.

* * *

'We'll have to be gentle with him for a while,' Ma told Ann when she got home from work and found out what had happened. 'He's gone over to see Harry. I've a feeling he'll have got the same news.'

'I can't believe Joe was crying,' said Ann.

'The last time he cried, he was six. Remember when the wheels came off that wee train Fred got him the Christmas your da died?'

'I remember. He was inconsolable, until Fred brought him a Kit Kat.'

'I don't think a Kit Kat will do it this time, love,'

'We should make liver and onions for dinner. He loves that. I'll go up to Kenwell's.'

'Do you have enough money? There's a few bob in the tin.'

'I'm grand, Ma. A wee sliver of liver won't be too dear.'

Ann put her coat back on and went up the street to the

butchers. Oliver Kenwell wasn't just a butcher; he also played saxophone in the eponymous OK Swing Band, who were virtually resident in the Starr. Oliver was behind the counter when she went in.

'Och Ann! How are you keeping?

'Not too bad.'

'What can I get you?'

'Can I have three thin strips of liver, please, with no tubes?'

'There are no tubes in this shop, apart from Andy.'

Andy looked up from the board where he was trimming ribs.

'Watch your fingers.' Oliver smiled.

He got an entire cow's liver from the back and sliced three wafer-thin pieces. He held them up on a piece of brown paper for Ann to inspect.

'Will these do?"

'They look lovely. How much do I owe you?'

'That'll be nine pence to you.' He wrapped them in the paper and tied the package with a bit of brown string.

'You playing on Saturday night?' Ann asked.

'Aye. Looking forward to it. It might be one of my last nights at the Starr, though. I'm thinking seriously of going over to America. See if I'm really any good or not.'

'Gosh! New York?'

'Maybe New Orleans. The music down there is just out of this world.'

'Will the band keep going without you?'

'Don't see why not. It's up to them. They could find another sax player easy enough.'

'He'd need to be good to replace you.'

'That's very kind of you. *Especially* you. You and young Walter are easily the best hoofers in the place.'

'Now it's you being kind.'

'I'm serious. You should enter some competitions. You two stand out every night.'

Ann's cheeks went a little pink and she looked down at her feet. 'I'd better get back. Good luck in America.'

'I'm not going just yet. I'll see you on Saturday night.'

* * *

Joe could smell one of his favourite smells in the whole world as he got off his bike outside the house. He had to stop himself blubbing again, as he knew Ma and Ann had made liver and onions especially for him to try and cheer him up. It would be very odd if they were too nice, he thought, especially Ann, but he'd make the best of it – it didn't happen too often.

'How's Harry,' Ann asked, looking concerned.

Joe attempted humour. 'I've never seen him so flat. He looked like a big ugly pancake with red cheeks.'

'Have you been drinking?' Ma came over and sniffed his face.

'We had one beer. Nigel thought it might cheer us up, but it didn't work, and our sorrows remain undrowned.'

'Can something be *undrowned*?' Ann asked, but Joe didn't respond

'Drink rarely works, son. Your da …' but Ma changed the subject. 'I better go and check on the spuds.'

Ann commiserated with Joe and felt genuinely sorry for him.

'All I've ever wanted to be was a footballer.' He shrugged his shoulders and Ann could see his eyes glistening again

Ann hugged her wee brother properly for the first time since they were children. He was a big strong lump, but at that moment, he was a wee boy again, confused by life's random unfairness.

'What are you after?'

'Nothing, I'm just trying to be nice.'

'You've never been nice before. You must be after something,' he said, trying to joke.

'Not true! I remember being nice when McGartland's dog ran off with your teddy.'

'I was three!'

'See, you still remember it.' She squeezed him tighter.

'Dinner's ready,' Ma called.

Joe ate every pick of his dinner but without his usual speed or noisy enthusiasm. Ann and Ma exchanged trivia in an attempt to avoid discussion of the letter. Joe cleared away his plate in silence, boiled a kettle, filled his jar and went to bed.

He was gone the next morning before Ma and Ann rose.

'I thought I heard him clattering about, trying to be quiet,' said Ann.

'That boy doesn't know the meaning of the word quiet,' said Ma. 'I hope he's gone to work. He needs to forget about playing football for a living and get back to normal. He's got a good job, and if he works hard, he might get a promotion. A lot of people would be happy to have a job like that. Indoors, safe, warm and dry. All he needs is a girlfriend, then he can get married and settle down.'

* * *

Joe did go to work, and everyone noticed the change in him.

Harry stopped by his machine on his way to fix some other machine. 'How's it going?"

'Nothing for it but to get back to porridge. You?'

Harry sighed. 'I've felt better. It's like when I found out there was no Santa, only worse.'

'What do you mean there's no Santa? You're supposed to be cheering me up!' Joe gave his friend a weak flicker of a smile.

'And you're supposed to be cheering me up! See you at lunchtime.'

When Joe got home, Ma was at Jimmy Reed's house and Ann was at Black's. He cleaned out the grate, brought in a bucket of coal and a few sticks and lit the fire. It was just beginning to draw nicely when there was a huge downdraft and the room filled with soot and smoke.

'Fuck, fuck, fuck!' He hissed through grated teeth. This happened regularly, like the floods or the toilet freezing. Normally it didn't annoy him too much. Today it made him want to cry again.

Everything would need to be cleaned. He opened the window and a chilly blast howled in. He closed it again. He sat down in Ma's chair. He didn't know what to do next, so he just sat staring at the floor.

A car horn beeped outside and he glanced out the window to see who it was. Must be for next door, although the McGartlands didn't know anybody with a car. He looked again. A little green car was at their door, completely filled with Nigel. In disbelief, Joe stepped outside.

Nigel leaned over and pushed open the little fan window in the door. 'Hop in. We'll go for a spin.'

'Whose car is this?'

'It's mine. Da bought it for me when you and empty-head were over in Manchester. He said I'd been working hard and seemed down in the dumps. I think he got it cheap, 'cause there's a new model coming out soon. I've never driven it on my own before.'

'Well, you may get used to it 'cause there's no room for anyone else in there. It's perfectly Nigel-sized.'

'Get in.'

Joe was hesitant. Had Nigel ever driven anything before? 'Have you done the test?'

'I've applied for it. It's expensive – seven and six. We'll go and pick up the idiot. Maybe go out to Lough Muck?'

'If you really want to cheer me up, you'd just give me the car.'

'Why would I want to cheer you up? Your sullen self-pitying silence is a pleasant change. Easier on the ears. Let's go!'

'I can't. I've just lit the fire and smoke has gone all over the show. I've got to clean everything before Ma gets home.'

'Tell you what, I'll collect empty-head first and come back.' And Nigel drove off with a few judders and jolts.

Twenty minutes later the horn beeped again. Joe had managed to clean the place and damp down the sparking fire. The passenger side door opened and Harry spilled out onto the pavement.

'I'll go in the back,' he stammered. 'It's safer.'

'I don't feel like going anywhere.' Joe said, leaning against the doorframe.

'It's a great wee car.' Harry tried to sound excited but failed.

'Lovely, I know, but I'd rather be on my own.'

'You're such poor company you'll bore yourself to death in no time,' said Nigel. 'This moping and wallowing is not doing you any good. Or any of us. Let's hit the road!'

Joe tried to smile. He loved Nigel for coming to see him in his new car and the fact that he was breaking the law. Having neither licence, insurance nor experience made it even more noble.

He hoped he didn't look as miserable as Harry.

'Just take me home again, Nige,' said Harry. 'We can go another day when we're in better form and you know what you're doing.'

'I *do* know what I'm doing. You just have to keep it between the hedges and try not to kill anyone or hit any other vehicles. How hard can it be? Anyway, I'll practise diligently and we can try again next week when you might have stopped feeling so sorry for yourselves.'

'Piss off,' said Joe.

'But take me home first,' Harry said.

'I've a good mind to make you walk, seeing as you think I'm a threat to life and limb.'

'It'll be practice for you, even if there's no hedges. You'll need to add another rule – keep off the footpaths.'

'Sounds sensible. I'll learn that one tonight. Get in and close the door, Harry. See you next week,' he said to Joe and with a few shudders and jumps, they were away.

Nigel was true to his word and called back the following Wednesday. It was half-day closing in the shop and he had the afternoon free. He tooted the horn of the little car that looked as though it had been built around him

'He's improved since last week,' Harry piped up from the back seat.

'That wouldn't be hard.'

'As promised, I've been practising diligently. Da has given me a few lessons and I've learned the footpath rule off by heart. I think your experience today should be a joy and one you'll want to repeat on a regular basis.'

Joe slipped into the passenger seat and closed the door with a satisfying clunk. He swivelled round towards Harry. 'Are you sure you won't be sick in the back?'

Nigel looked horrified.

'Aye, just steer round the potholes,' Harry said.

'Another rule!' Nigel shook his head.

'And we haven't even got to "stay out of the sheughs yet",' Joe joined in, feeling his mood lift despite himself.

The car inched forward smoothly, much to Joe's amazement.

'The trick is that you have to press in the clutch, then move the gear stick into the middle. This is known to us professional drivers as "neutral". Then you press the clutch again and move the gear stick to the required position to engage the next gear. It's called double clutching, but that might be a bit too technical for you two dopes.'

They went out the Derry Road, past Nestle's. After a few minutes Harry said, 'You're actually not a bad driver for a giant.'

'Thank you, but I think size is relative. You two are just incredibly small. Like this car. It's like being in Lilliput.'

'The laundry?' Joe said, all innocence.

'The ocean of your stupidity really is bottomless,' Nigel said, laughing.

'How come your da lets you out in a brand-new car on your own when you haven't even done the test or anything?'

'I told you, I've applied for the test, which is the next best thing to actually doing it. More importantly, he's in Belfast today looking at new things for the shop.'

'Whale meat is a new thing,' said Joe out of the blue. 'I hope he's not getting any of that.'

'Butchers do meat. We do trousers, as you know. And where did that come from – *whale meat*? You can't get whale meat.'

'They live in the depths of my ocean of stupidity – whales,

I mean – and when we were in Manchester, they were talking about eating whale meat 'cause they still have proper rationing over there. Isn't that right, Harold?'

'That's right, Joseph.' Harry had no idea where Joe was going with this. 'You'd love it, Nigel. The portions are enormous.'

Nigel laughed. 'Do you get a whole whale each? Imagine eating Moby Dick.'

'One rib could feed a family of six for a fortnight.' Harry was giggling

'I suppose it tastes like fish,' Nigel said.

Joe looked disgusted. 'Do you remember nothing from school? They aren't fish and they eat plankton, which is particularly delicious on toast with Marmite. Seriously though, they said over there that the taste depends on the type of whale.'

'What do you mean?' asked Nigel with a feeling he'd regret it.

'Well, humpback whales taste humpy, blue whales, sort of blue, a grey whale tastes a bit grey and as for sperm whales – well, best not to ask.'

Nigel spluttered as he tried to stop laughing, 'That's disgusting. How could anyone know what *that* tastes like?'

'I know someone who knows.'

'Who?' Harry and Nigel said simultaneously.

'Dolores Mullan.'

Nigel slammed on the brakes. Joe's head hit the windscreen. Harry fell in between the front seats. 'Jesus, Joe. I can't even see the hedges,' Nigel said. 'The tears are trippin' me.'

'Yep, she says it tastes like sweaty, fishy feet. If fish had sweaty feet, that's what it tastes like.'

'So she's tasted sweaty feet? Good God!' Nigel was aghast.

'She probably has. Who knows. But what she actually said was, *it* tastes like the *smell* of sweaty feet and fish.'

'How could she possibly know that?' asked Nigel, and this time he knew he'd regret it.

'Can't say,' said Joe smugly.

Harry was shaking with laughter. 'Does this mean you have to marry her?'

'I hope not. She's a taig for a start. Anyway, I think the unique biology of the event should mitigate against any potential pregnancy unless there's something that Father Mullan hasn't told her, but she does seem to know a lot about these things.'

'Is Father Mullan her da?' Harry could hardly speak for laughing.

'You know her real da, Paddy Mullan, is an IRA man,' said Nigel. 'You don't want him finding out what you've been up to with his beloved daughter.'

'So they say,' said Joe, 'but he's always been nice enough to me in the shop.'

'That's 'cause you're buying something off him,' Harry said.

'You're very cynical for one so young,' Nigel said, 'but you're probably right.'

'If he knew what we know, he might not be so pleasant,' Harry said.

'Have *you* done this … this perversion?' Nigel looked at Harry.

'No, I'm waiting for Dolores to realise that Joe is completely inadequate, both physically and emotionally, and what she needs is a real man.' Harry grabbed his own crotch.

'She'll not find one in this car, that's for sure,' Nigel

said and he let out a massive fart that led to rapid window opening. 'We should get going.'

He pulled out the choke, turned the key and the engine spluttered and died.

'Too much petrol, I think.' He pushed the choke back in and tried again. The engine fired into life.

'It was literally choked,' Harry said.

'Just like Dolores,' Joe said.

Nigel and Harry just shook their heads.

A few miles farther on, when they had recovered, Harry said, 'Seriously Joe, what if Paddy Mullan finds out that you and Dolores have … well, you know?'

'He won't find out, and anyway, he thinks I'm a hero.'

'Because you dived in and saved that wee lad?' Harry said. 'You've told us this before. He wasn't in any real danger, but you made it look all dramatic with lots of splashing and waving of arms and stuff.'

'Exactly. Mr Mullan thinks I'm a hero and that's all that matters.

'I seem to remember she showed her gratitude differently the last time you told us this story. Was she grateful more than once?' Harry asked.

'That would be telling,' Joe said coyly.

Nigel stopped the car again. He looked serious. 'I think young Dolores might be suffering from a condition called Spineosa Nervyosa Trappidoidees.'

'Eh?' The other two spluttered together.

'It means she has a trapped nerve in her spine; so every time she lies down, her legs fly open.' Nigel could hardly finish for laughing. 'And it's untreatable.'

When the laughter died down a bit Joe said, 'She's not like that. She's actually very nice.'

'Are you saying you fancy her? More than you fancy Doreen?' Harry looked like he was enjoying Joe's discomfort.

'No chance and I don't fancy Doreen either. I can't help it if her glorious backside is in my face every Sunday. I'm just saying Dolores is not like people think.'

'Maybe people should stop telling wild tales about her,' Nigel said.

'It was only a bit of craic.' Joe looked contrite.

Harry slapped him on the back of the head. 'Liar, liar, pants on fire. But it was a good story.'

'Time to head home,' Nigel announced. 'I'll drop you two goats off, then I'll go and get the car fumigated.'

A few weeks later Nigel passed his test and began trying to teach Harry and Joe to drive. Joe stalled the car repeatedly. He slapped the steering wheel with both hands in frustration. 'I don't know why I'm bothering. I'll never have enough money for a car. Driving is just another thing I'm useless at.'

Nigel had had enough. 'If I hear any more self-pity, I'm turfing you out. You might be able to get a better job if you have a licence.'

'And you could borrow the car to impress the girls,' added Harry. 'I'm sure Dolores would love to go for a ride in a car, if you pardon the expression.'

'No fuckin' way,' said Nigel. 'Not in my car. I don't want it smelling of fish and feet or whatever. Smelling of sweaty gobshite is bad enough.'

'It's not your fault, Nige. You should just try and wash more often.' Harry sat back quickly to avoid an elbow in the face.

'Flicks on Saturday?' Joe asked as he got out at the house.

'What's on?' Harry asked Nigel.

'*Pursued*, with Robert Mitchum.'

‘I’m not in the mood for a comedy.’

‘It’s not a comedy.’

‘Is it sad?’

‘It’s very sad.’

‘And all moody and mournful?’

‘It’s very moody and mournful.’

‘Sounds like shite to me. See you there.’ Joe fell out of the car and was gone.

CHAPTER 24

Ma thought Joe had settled down well as autumn faded into winter – without any floods this time – but he wasn't the same exuberant boy. She and Ann both noticed he was unusually subdued.

He was working hard and playing football, but not as much. He still went to the pictures and he and Harry went out regularly in Nigel's car.

One evening they were listening to the radio after dinner. Ann was reading *Moby Dick*, which made Joe smile and Ma was knitting a pair of socks, the needles clicking and clacking in time to the music. Joe was just sitting staring into the red glow of the fire. Ma looked up at him.

'Penny for them, son. Are you frettin' about something?' she said.

'I'm all right. I can't stop thinking about Manchester, that's all.'

'It's not good to dwell on things you can't change. What's done is done. I know it's hard, but you have to forget it and move on. You've a decent job, which you like. You just need to settle, work hard and do the best you can. You'll find the right girl someday and when you get married and have children, you'll wonder what all the fuss was about. Football isn't real life, son.'

'I know that now. I do have a future with Nestle's. I got an awful ribbing about Manchester from them, but it was harmless. They all lined up for free tickets for the cup final! But my supervisor says I'm in line for training and promotion, maybe into the office. More money can't be a bad thing.'

'There you go, and you know what I always say …'

'A shilling in your pocket is your best friend,' Ann and Joe recited in sing-song voices.

'It's true. I don't care what anyone says. You'll be running the place in no time.' Ma looked proudly at her son.

'That'll be the end of Nestle's then,' said Ann. 'For your information, I'm doing a test myself on Monday week. The Pitman's one hundred words per minute shorthand and typing test. Mr Black says that when – not if – I pass, it'll mean an extra five bob a week.'

'We'll not know what to do with all this money,' said Ma.

'We'll have a best friend in both pockets,' chimed in Joe.

'Maybe you could stop work, Ma,' Ann suggested. 'Or at least cut down a bit. You're not getting any younger and you've been working for about a hundred years. Maybe it's time to take a wee rest.'

'What would I do all day? I've never not worked. What would I do for money? I'd have to ask you two and I wouldn't like that.'

'We've been asking you for long enough.'

'That's different. It's a mother's duty to look after her children.'

'And it's a child's duty to look after their ma. Maybe just cut back is all I'm saying.'

'Plenty of time to worry about that. There's life in the old dog yet.' She coughed a harsh hacking cough and spat into her hanky.

Joe and Ann looked at each other, concern written on their faces.

* * *

Not long after Christmas, a few raggedy snowdrops appeared in the back garden. Nobody remembered ever planting these hardy harbingers of spring. When the children were young, they used to compete to be first to spot a wee green shoot, then a wee white bud. Signs of better days ahead – or longer days anyway.

Ann had passed her Pitman's test and left Black's to take up a new position with the Ministry of Food. The office was in Cookstown, about thirty miles from Omagh. She had to get the bus, which meant very early starts. The bus stopped at every hole in the hedge, so it took over an hour each way. That meant she wasn't home until after six, but her pay had increased and she was now in the Civil Service – a job for life, a clear career path, a good pension. The kind of job Ma definitely approved of. Ann was clever, ambitious and would do well.

For Joe, everything was much the same, except he was beginning to take girls to the pictures, rather than going with Harry and Nigel. Nigel still went on his own and sat where he always sat. He didn't need quite as much space as he used to. Despite owning a car, he was still running regularly and it was beginning to show.

Harry had started going out with a lovely wee girl from

Spillars Place. They had met at Christmas when he offered to help her blow up some balloons in the Reform Stores for their festive display.

Ma still worked one day a week for each of her three gentlemen, but her cough was slowly getting worse and she was beginning to fall asleep in her chair in the evenings, often with her sewing or knitting on her lap.

Fred called more often than he used to. Ann still heard them quietly dancing some evenings. They didn't talk much, just gently waltzed around the tiny room. She wondered if Joe heard them as well.

Ann and Walter were dancing as often as they could. Although Ann had always said she was happy that they just danced together, her worry about his lack of initiative in the romance department was increasing. He was still driving his bread van, still polite, considerate and funny, and Ann still enjoyed his company, even if he had curly blond hair. But she couldn't help dreaming of being swept off her feet by a tall dark handsome stranger who looked like a film star and could dance like Fred Astaire.

Life was good – dull, but good. Dull was safe, predictable, and Ann and Joe knew Ma liked it that way.

Muriel hadn't come home for Christmas. Al had invited her to join his family at their house out in the country and she couldn't resist the experience of Christmas in such a grand mansion, though it terrified her too. She justified it to herself by reminding herself that she would also earn overtime staying and working over the holidays. Instead, she sent a long newsy letter and a parcel with gifts and some money. Life was anything but dull for Muriel. She went out for drives with Al in his big fancy car. They were getting on very well and had gone to a posh restaurant called The Criterion for her birthday back in September. They had champagne, which was lovely. She now had four staff. The new girl was from Glasgow, so nobody understood a word she said.

Hilda and Dan returned safely from Churchill before the winter set in. She wrote in her Christmas card that she'd seen a real live polar bear and nearly had a heart attack when it appeared from nowhere. It was the size of a car and just wandered down the Main Street. Its feet were a foot wide. The locals had a rule: never lock any doors, because if a bear appeared, you had to get out of its way into the nearest building as quickly as you could. There was no point trying to run away. It would just catch you and eat you, head first. They were now back in Winnipeg, but Dan said they would be moving again soon – hopefully after the baby arrived. Not long now!

So life was dull but good all round. But then one Friday evening, everything changed.

The Browns had just had their dinner – smoked fish off the van that came round every week; Ann had poached it in milk and used some of the fishy, milky juice to mash the spuds – and Ma was knitting a new jumper for Joe. Ann was reading *Frankenstein*. Joe was just sitting listening to the wireless. Then out of the blue, he straightened up, cleared his throat and announced, 'I'm joining the navy.'

Ann's mouth dropped open. She set her book on the floor and gawped at her wee brother. She hadn't realised he was that upset about the football trials.

Ma put her knitting down and pushed her glasses up off the end of her nose. 'Where did this come from, son? The navy? Why now?'

Joe started to explain. 'I was in the Cake Shop when this bloke in a navy uniform came in and sat down beside another man in civvies who was already there. He was wearing a smart dark blue suit. Worsted wool if I'm not mistaken.'

Ma and Ann couldn't help smiling.

'The navy lad looked my age and the suit man a few years older. They sounded local. They ordered barmbrack with butter and the sailor closed his eyes when he took his first bite, like he'd really missed it. Then the suit said, "Welcome home. How was it?" And then the sailor told him the best story I've ever heard.

'He was just back from his first trip on a battleship called HMS *Vanguard*. He'd been all over everywhere. Places I've never heard of. They'd sailed from Portsmouth to Gibraltar. He saw dolphins jumping in front of the ship. They went across the Mediterranean to the Black Sea, up through the Bosphorus and into Crimea. The charge of the light brigade and all that. They stopped at a city called Sevastopol, and on the way back, they called into Cairo, Rome and Malta.

'He'd been seasick at the start, but then he got used to it and loved the rolling and swaying. He was very brown. He didn't look like he was from Omagh at all. He'd eaten all sorts of strange things, like prawns and octopus. He'd seen whales and sharks and flying fish, and he'd even swimmed … swam … swum in the sea. Imagine that!

'He said he must have fallen in love at least four times, but they never stayed anywhere long enough for anything to happen. He saved nearly all his wages 'cause there was nothing to spend it on. On his next trip they're going to a place called Trinkomalinco, or something like that, in Ceylon and then on to Singapore and Japan.'

Ma and Ann listened as the words poured out and Joe quivered with excitement. This was the most alive he'd been since Manchester.

'I could end up in Canada and see a polar bear, or America

and see the Rio Grande and real live Indians. I could shoot a moose and eat it. Imagine that! I could go anywhere and do anything.'

Not knowing what else to say, Ann offered to make tea. She knew what Ma would say.

Ann brought in the teapot just as Joe was saying, 'I've thought of nothing else since, Ma. I know you think I'm mad and you only want me settled down. But the only girl who would have me here is Dolores Mullan.'

Ma looked horrified.

'Thats not going to happen, Ma.' Joe smiled.

'Don't let her da know that you're even thinking of joining the navy.' Ma stood up unsteadily. 'I think I'll skip the tea. I'll be up all night.' Ann knew she would be anyway.

'He's always been okay with me.'

'He's not a good person son. He's done some terrible things.'

'I know. I'll say nothing.'

But Ma couldn't leave without a few parting words. 'Sleep on it, son. See how you feel about it in the morning. And stay away from that girl and her da.'

'It's too late to sleep on it. I've already joined.'

Ma fell back down into her seat.

'What?' Ann burst out. 'You can't join the navy just like that. Surely you have to do an interview?'

'I spoke to the sailor in the café and he told me what to do. I've been accepted into the Administration and Wages Department. I told a wee fib when the forms arrived. Remember I said that package I got in the post was study stuff for work, for my promotion? It was actually navy forms, and the letter I got today was to say I've been accepted.'

'You've been busy.' Ma's face fell. 'What will Harry

think … and Nigel?'

'Harry won't join the navy, that's for sure. He'll understand. He's got Sandra now. Nigel will survive.'

The conversation took the predictable course, but Joe was determined. He said it wasn't just about Manchester and it wasn't another daft notion.

'You don't need to be good at anything to join the navy,' he explained, 'but I'll know a lot more when I come out, and that'll help me get an even better job.'

He didn't want to stay at Nestle's and go to the pub on Saturdays. He didn't want to get married and he certainly didn't want children, at least not yet – and then only with someone he really wanted to have a family with.

He saw Ma purse her lips at that. 'Sorry Ma, but I just want to make sure I'm properly in love and grown up before I even think about all that stuff.'

Ma's face betrayed what she was thinking – true love was for fairy tales. Disappointment and compromise were what everyone had to settle for.

'Don't think too big and you won't be disappointed,' was all she said.

But Joe turned it round and said he would be disappointed if he didn't think big. All her old cliches – a bird in the hand, better safe than sorry, marry for money – were wheeled out, and it slowly dawned on Joe that what Ma really feared was everybody leaving her. Da, Hilda, Muriel, and now him. Her 'safe' world wasn't safe. It was fragile. She'd never thought big, but had still ended up disappointed and now she was scared. He wanted to wrap her up and hold her forever.

He caught a look from Ann. She knew it too.

They finished their tea and Joe went off to fill his jar.

Ann knelt on the floor in front of Ma and put her hands

on her bony knees. 'I'm not going anywhere, Ma. I'm staying here with you.'

Ma pursed her lips to say a silent thank you. She looked tired and older than her years.

'I don't understand why nobody wants to stay at home and live a normal life. What if he gets sick in Trinkobalinko, or whatever it's called? What if there's another war and he gets caught up in it on the other side of the world?'

'You must agree, he hasn't been the same since he got that letter from Manchester,' Ann said softly.

'Aye, and I just want him to be happy, but *normal* seems to make him unhappy. So maybe he has to try this or he'll never be content. Perhaps then he can come home and settle down.'

Joe came back into the room just as Ma was going upstairs. When she was out of earshot, he whispered to Ann, 'God love her. I think she's terrified of being left on her own.'

'Aye. It probably goes back to when Da left, but you need to live your life, Joe. I'll stay with her.'

'But that's not fair. You want to be a dancer. You want to be in shows and marry a film star. How are you going to do that if you stay here?'

'Never mind me. That's all just stuff and nonsense. I want to stay.' She broke eye contact and looked at the fire.

'I'll never forget this,' Joe said and squeezed her shoulder.

'Get off. You stink of fish.'

They could hear Ma coughing as she came back downstairs to fetch her jar. 'Have you two been talking about me behind my back?'

'Of course! Anyway, I'm off to bed. Football tomorrow.' He gave her a little kiss.

Ma attempted a smile. She had already decided that in the morning she would tell him he must go, though the hope lingered that maybe he'd have second thoughts.

Joe didn't change his mind.

* * *

'I knew you were thick, but I didn't think you were that thick!' was Nigel's verdict. 'The navy! That's the most hare-brained idea I've ever heard?'

Joe told them about overhearing the sailor in the Cake Shop.

'So this is really our fault,' Harry observed. 'If we'd been at the Cake Shop, you wouldn't have been able to earwig other people's conversations, as our rapid wit and repartee would have required your complete attention, as it always does. And then you wouldn't know about Trinkobinko or prawns or dolphins and you'd still be normal boring Joe.'

Nigel chipped in, 'This proves we obviously can't leave him on his own for more than a few minutes. It's too dangerous. But what has the navy ever done to deserve this?'

'It's my best idea ever,' enthused Joe. 'In a couple of weeks, I'll be off to see the world and have adventures in strange and foreign lands.'

'But you won't be on land,' Harry pointed out helpfully.

'And you aren't allowed to fart in the navy, did you know that? Aboard ship anyway,' said Nigel.

'Even up on deck?' asked Harry.

'Even up on deck. Apparently, it goes back to Nelson's day when somebody let off a huge one on the gun deck just as they lit the touchpaper to fire their biggest cannon. Very messy.' They laughed hysterically. 'They called it the poop deck after that,' Nigel added. Further explosions of laughter got the other customers in the Cake Shop staring.

'You can't put me off. It's too late,' Joe spluttered.

Just before Joe left to join up, they went to the flicks to see *Dick Barton Strikes Back*. Afterwards, they wondered about the fancy sports car Dick drove and why he didn't wear the protective headphones that were lying about everywhere. And they wondered again what had possessed Joe to join the navy.

'Maybe somehow your brain got dehydrated, like Dick's did,' Harry suggested to Joe.

'Good theory,' Nigel concurred. 'It would explain this totally irrational notion to go off with a gang of strange men in a giant tin bath.'

'Nice try.'

They finished their Cokes and snowballs and Harry and Nigel wished their crazy friend all the best.

He didn't want any fanfares or tearful farewells at the station. He said his final goodbyes to Harry and Nigel in the Cake Shop two weeks later. The next morning he embraced Ma and Ann at their front door and was gone, off to HMS *Royal Arthur* in Wiltshire to do his initial training.

CHAPTER 25

The next few weeks were almost surreal for Ma and Ann, but they tried to carry on as normal. The chores still needed to be done, and Ann quickly realised just how much Joe had done around the house. She also hadn't realised how much Ma had gradually delegated and how little she was capable of now, especially on the days that she worked. Ann did all the shopping, but Ma still issued detailed instructions on what to buy, how much to buy, where to buy it and how much to pay for it. Ann largely ignored these instructions, but in her post-shopping debriefing, they were followed to the letter, and Ma was happy if there were a few bob left over to put back in the tin.

The evenings were getting longer and the garden needed attention. As soon as Joe had been old enough, he had taken on the digging, weeding and planting. He knew how to chit the spuds and bank them up and when and how best to plant the few other things they grew in their little back garden – onions, turnips, a few cabbages – he had even started to grow lettuce and scallions.

Now that Joe had gone, Fred said he would get his nephew Denis to call round. He worked for the Council and was a keen gardener without a garden. So the beds got dug and planted; he even scrubbed the yard with chemicals that he got from work. One smelled like Jeyes Fluid, but Denis said it was ten times better and it removed years of green slime and dirt. The yard looked like new… almost. Denis was a good worker, and he refused to take any money. He said he liked the work and was happy just to take a few spuds and carrots in return.

This was a mutually agreeable arrangement. Soon Denis was taking on other tasks around the house. At one stage, Ann even contemplated asking Walter to help, but then she thought he would probably be useless at hard work, as he just sat in a van all day. She was amazed he wasn't getting fat.

Ma refused to cut down on her jobs. The long days left them both so tired that Ann couldn't go dancing during the week and Ma often fell asleep in her chair with whatever she was footering at lying in her lap.

But the Saturday dance was sacred, and following her chat with Oliver Kenwell, she was beginning to look at entering competitions, though she hadn't discussed this with Walter yet. She saw an advert for one in the *Conn*, but it was in the Crofton Ballroom in Bangor in three weeks' time. That might be too far and too soon. From a technical perspective, they were ready, but not mentally. Walter would panic at the very thought of it and he worked on Saturdays. As for Ann, she hadn't the energy. Saturday was the only day to get things done, especially the shopping. But she knew these were just excuses. Bottom line – she and Walter weren't ready.

Another letter came from Hilda. She and Dan had a little boy. Eight pounds seven ounces and all well. They were calling him James, but he would be known as Jimmy after Dan's da. They were still in Winnipeg but would be going somewhere else soon. Everything else was good.

Ma and Ann replied to say how much this news had cheered them up, filling them in on Joe's football adventures and his sudden departure. They mentioned Ann's job, which was bringing in extra money, and Fred and Denis being saviours. Ma would have given anything to meet wee Jimmy in person.

A few days later, they were amazed to get a letter from Joe.

'That was quick. He's learned to write already,' Ann said with a smile.

'Ann! There's no need for that. What does he say?'

'You read it, Ma.'

'He's passed his training. Second in his class! He'll be joining a ship called the HMS *Duke of York*. It's a famous battleship.' Ma pushed her glasses up. 'He's still working in administration and wages 'cause he's good at sums. They're sailing to Singapore. It will take them weeks. The food's good and the rest of the lads are good craic. He's enjoying the training and learning loads.'

'Well, that's all very reassuring!' concluded Ann. 'A lot of letter on one page. I must look up Singapore the next time I'm in the library. I think it's away over near Japan.'

'I don't like Japan.'

Ann didn't ask why. Probably to do with the war.

Fred popped in more frequently. Most nights Ann went to bed early and left them to it.

She knew Fred and Ma still had the odd little burl round the living room, and one night she heard them whispering. She crept to the landing.

Fred's voice drifted up. 'She'll be okay. She's a good girl.'

'But she's all on her own now and has it all to do. I can't do half the things I used to. She's too tired to even go dancing.'

'Shush, you've done more than your share. Everything's fine.'

Silence then, and Ann went back to bed. She tossed and turned for a long time. The front door opened and closed quietly and the stairs creaked as Ma came up to bed.

'What time do you call this?' Ann called out.

'Cheeky! Go to sleep!'

Ann could hear the smile in Ma's voice. 'Yes, Ma.'

CHAPTER 26

Ann had always lived in the here and now, but the recent past and present reality had brought the future into sharper focus. She was beginning to wonder what, if any, Walter's intentions were towards her. She thought of all the possible suitors she had turned away. But Walter had always been The One. She had no idea why.

Mostly she believed she could do worse than settle down with him. The dancing dream was just that – a dream. Walter was gentle, caring, funny and good-looking, in a soft sort of way. They were very relaxed when they were alone together, but she was beginning to think they weren't alone together often enough.

She knew this was partly her fault, as she'd always given the impression that all she wanted to do with him was go dancing, but now it might be good to spend more time with him and find out what made him tick. They went to the pictures the odd time, but he always watched in silence. At the start, she had liked that because she wanted to concentrate on the film, especially if it was Fred and Ginger.

It was her fantasy to be able to dance like them, on a stage, in a film, in a gorgeous gown. She hadn't been interested in the kind of noisy gymnastics that the other couples got up to in the back seats, possibly because of Ma's many dire warnings about reputations being lost and boys only being interested in 'one thing'. But now Ann was getting worried that Walter was genuinely only interested in the film.

What was wrong with him? What was wrong with her? Maybe he needed a not-so-gentle push. Maybe she should go out with someone else. But she liked Walter. The question was, did he really like her?

If only her sisters were still around to confide in.

* * *

The truth was that Walter *did* like Ann, so much so that he was almost paralysed with fear. Fear of pushing too hard, saying the wrong thing, asking the wrong question. Like her, he loved dancing and the pictures, but mainly because it was time spent with her. She was still full of chat about everything and great fun and she still wound him up all the time. He had got used to that 'cause he knew it wasn't malicious in any way. She must be fond of him because a gorgeous girl like her would have gone off with anyone she wanted.

He'd noticed she was more tired since Joe left, with longer days and more responsibility, but she never complained about anything – at least, not in a serious way. She seemed content and happy, but they never really talked about the future – nothing further than the next dance or the next movie. Walter didn't know how to start this conversation. He was frightened of scaring her off. She always said she wanted to marry a film star and he was no film star. In so many ways she was out of his league – brainy, ambitious, gorgeous, confident.

All he knew was that he adored being with her, being close to her, dancing with her. He had known she was The One the very first time he set eyes on her. They had been together for three years now. They couldn't continue like this forever. He was nineteen and he still hadn't done 'it'.

This last thing bothered him the most. All his friends were constantly going on about sex and asking if he and Ann had done it yet. They'd never even had a quick grope in the cinema, let alone a full-on kiss. Walter knew his friends knew. They'd tease him about it, ask him if maybe he wasn't a ponce after all, what with his love of dancing and all.

He remembered Ann had made the first move back at the Starr and asked him what he was waiting for. So what *was* he waiting for? They should be thinking about their future – sex, marriage, a house and a family, hopefully in that order.

* * *

Ann was thinking the same, but she had become increasingly sure that it be up to her to take the relationship to the next level, or at least find out if something was wrong. She was almost certain Walter was cracked about her, but for some reason, he didn't strike back when she teased him.

Ann realised, maybe for the first time, that she was thinking about the future realistically. She was no longer dreaming about being a dancer or a movie star. Or married to Gregory Peck. She wasn't frightened about what this more down-to-earth future might bring, but she definitely didn't want to just drift into it. It had to be on her terms.

To start with, she needed a job back in Omagh. Running up and down to Cookstown every day on the bus made the days too long, even if the job itself was great and the other girls were good fun. She would talk to Walter about her thoughts and plans. Did either of them even have a plan? Did Walter even have a thought? It would be good if Walter was having these same thoughts but was just reluctant to be the first to say anything. Just like she was.

They could be stuck in this stalemate for ever if someone didn't take the initiative. The time had come to find out, Ann decided, where they were and where they were going.

She started looking for a job in Omagh. She asked Ma to bring home a copy of the *Ulster Herald* and the *Conn* from her gentlemen when they had finished with them, in case they had different job adverts. Both papers came out on a Thursday. The *Herald* was 'them uns' paper and was full of Gaelic football reports and ads for ceilidhs, as well as stuff like masses, novenas and confirmations. The *Tyrone Constitution*, or *Conn*, was the Unionist paper, full of *proper* football, rugby, cricket and royal news.

Ma said none of her gentlemen took the *Herald*, but she always brought home a copy of the *Conn* from Albert Lee on a Friday. Ann had to call into the library every Saturday morning to view the *Herald*. It only took her a couple of weeks to realise that both newspapers listed the same jobs, except for the ones she had no chance of landing.

* * *

'Walter Green,' Ann said to start the conversation.

'Ann Brown,' Walter replied.

'We need to talk.'

'Oh dear, what have I done?'

'Nothing, and that's the problem.'

Walter looked perplexed, but Ann could see that he sort of knew what she was on about. 'What exactly do you mean by nothing?'

'I'm not sure, but what I think I mean is that we have been going out together for nearly three years.'

'Three years and twenty days,' corrected Walter, smiling.

Ann laughed. 'Are you keeping a diary? Is that right?

'No, but it must be close.'

'The thing is …' She put her hands on her knees and took a deep breath. 'I think we get on very well together, maybe better than well and I know I'm always winding you up, but you know I only do it because I really like you. That film-star talk is just spoofing. I think you really like me as well. But I don't know for sure because you never say, just like I never say. So I was wondering, are we both not saying in case if we do, it'll be the wrong thing and it'll spoil everything and you'll run a mile?'

Walter put his forefinger gently on her lips. 'Woah, where did all that come from? But I know what you mean. I've fancied you – actually more than fancied you – since that day in Black's.'

Ann smiled at the memory.

Walter went on. 'You're the smartest, most beautiful girl I've ever met.'

'How many girls have you met then?'

'Two, and you are the best by a country mile.'

'Two. Go on.' Ann put on her concerned face.

'I never dreamed in a million years you'd want to go out with me. I always thought you just liked dancing with me and you were just waiting for Mr Right to come along. I know I'm a better person because of you. I can tell a rumba from a foxtrot and do both without falling on my arse. I read books now that don't have pictures in them. I watch films that don't have John Wayne in them and I nearly always understand them. I just love being with you.'

'But? It sounds like there's a but coming.' Ann was genuinely concerned now.

'You already mentioned it.'

'Meaning?'

'I didn't want to scare you off. The truth is, you'd need a Thompson machine gun to scare me off. Maybe we've been frozen with fear because we like each other so much and it means getting serious about our future. And that's scary!'

He'd said it – *the future.* Plans, responsibilities, lifetime commitments, all wrapped up in a single little word.

'All of a sudden that sounds very grown up and serious. I didn't think you had it in you.'

'Had what?'

'Serious thoughts. In your blondie, bubbly head.'

'My other girlfriend thinks I'm very grown up and very handsome.'

'She's not completely thick then.'

'So what do we do now then?' Walter asked. 'Now that we've suddenly got all serious and grown up.'

'A good way to begin would be to spend more time together, doing different things … as a couple.'

Walter looked very coy. 'Things like what?'

'Like this,' and she put a hand on each side of his head and kissed him hard on the lips. He responded until they had to come up for air.

'And what else?' Walter was blushing bright red, not sure what to expect next.

She guessed what he meant, but she said, 'There's an excursion to Portrush coming up on the fourteenth of August.'

Walter's face fell in exaggerated disappointment. 'That's two months away!'

'We should go. Spend the day together. I'm sure we'll do other things before that.'

'Is it a church outing?' Walter looked worried.

'No, just one of Willie McGettigan's wee trips.'

'That'll be a long time together on the train, with no dancing and no flicks.'

'Oh, dear, I never thought of that. What will we talk about? You could tell me all about bread rolls and bread vans and all things bready.'

'And you can tell me all about how short shorthand can be and what life is like in a typing pool full of gossipy girls.'

'It'll be a race to see who gets bored the quickest. Work talk should get us the length of Newtownstewart. Then we'll have to think of something else.'

'Seriously, I can't think of anything nicer than spending the day with you, talking about bread and typing.'

Ann thought Walter looked relieved and happy. She sighed and it felt like the weight of the world had been lifted off her shoulders.

'We could go swimming – in the sea! Can you swim?'

'I've never tried, but I like the thought of you in a swimsuit! Can *you* swim?'

'You dirty brute, and yes, I can. One of Muriel's ex-boyfriends was a good swimmer, and he taught us all out at Lough Muck.'

'*Ex*-boyfriends? Swimming might not be good for a long-term relationship, by the sound of it.'

'I think she saw his big hairy legs and took fright.'

'You'll be okay then,' Walter said, flushing.

'I didn't think you'd be hairy. Have you any hairy bits?'

Walter blushed again. 'Ann Brown! You're a terrible woman, but maybe you'll find out someday.'

'I'm only messing as usual.' She gave him a proper hug and a kiss.

'But we need to stop messing now and get all grown up and serious. There's more to life than having fun.'

Ann put on her sad, crestfallen face. 'Something to look forward to, being all grown up and serious and sad.'

'Yes, we need to get a lot sadder. Too much fun isn't good for you.'

'I agree, but can we wait until after Portrush to get all serious?'

'Absolutely. No need to hurry the onset of sadness. There'll be plenty of it soon enough.' Ann shivered as if someone had walked on her grave.

'Good. See you tonight then for more boring old dancing.'

'Should be a good one. The OKs are playing.'

'I'll try and look happy. I promise.'

Ann smiled as she watched Walter stride off down Market Street on his wee white legs. She skipped up the street to do the shopping.

CHAPTER 27

The July weather was good enough for them to take a walk out to Lough Muck one Saturday afternoon. They passed the orchard where the friendly farmer had caught Ann and her sisters stealing apples when they were very young. A bit farther and they turned down the road to the lough.

It was a beautiful day and it turned out that lots of people had had the same idea. Crowds of walkers and cars full of noisy families passed them. Walter suggested this might be a good time to begin his swimming lessons as there would be loads of people splashing about and he wouldn't stand out and look stupid.

Ann changed and waited for Walter outside the gents' changing hut. He emerged from the dark interior into the sunlight looking like a church candle with a black band round its middle. His trunks were too big and he was pulling the strings to tighten them around his waist. He looked very self-conscious and didn't know where to put his hands. Then he saw Ann. She was wearing a bright red swimsuit that clung to her in all the places that needed clinging to.

'Ann Brown!'

'Walter Green.'

'You look like a film star out of a magazine!'

'You shouldn't be looking at those magazines. You'll do yourself a mischief.'

Her auburn hair hung loosely around her shoulders. He knew she had beautiful green eyes, but today they shone like emeralds.

'You don't look too bad yourself,' Ann said, noticing he looked lean rather than skinny. There were muscles where there should be muscles. Wee ones, mind you, but at least they were there. 'Have those legs ever seen the sun?'

'Not since I was in short trousers.'

'Not that long ago then.'

Ann wasn't tanned either, but her skin was naturally sallow and went brown easily.

'You'll need to be careful you don't get sunburnt. Let's get in the water.'

Ann took his hand and they tiptoed across the warm worn grass to the water's edge.

She pointed to the diving boards and said, 'I don't suppose you want to just take a buck leap off one of those and see what happens? Sink or swim – best way to learn apparently.'

Walter smiled nervously. 'I'll save that for later. I'll just wade in and you can do the rest.'

'Like I taught you how to dance?'

'Exactly. How hard can it be?'

'Not very, when you get into that cold water. I mean … you have to start paddling for your life to stay warm!' She blushed, then gave him a push.

Walter gave her a push back. 'Ann Brown! You're a wile woman.'

'Let's go,' and she took his hand and led him out into the freezing water.

Walter's face screwed up with the cold. 'They're all looking at you,' he said.

'Don't be silly. They probably can't believe it – a milk bottle with black trunks on.'

'It's not just the boys either. You're the most beautiful girl here by a mile.'

'You like the attention?'

Walter nodded and his face said *most definitely, yes.* He squeezed her hand and she squeezed back.

He looks pretty good in his swimmers, she thought, not the scarecrow I was expecting. And he's got lovely blue eyes. Am I in love?

'The easiest stroke is the breaststroke, so I'll show you that first. Then you can have a go.'

'I like the sound of that.'

'Grow up and be serious, please.'

'Yes miss, sorry miss. I forgot.' Walter folded his arms like a schoolboy.

Ann effortlessly swam round in a circle. Walter made sure his feet could touch the bottom before he went for it. After a few minutes of flailing, he stood up. His curly hair had gone lank and was flattened to his head.

'You're doing well.'

'I thought I was half fit, but muscles I didn't know I had are starting to hurt already.'

'Do you want to stop?'

'No. If you want me to learn to swim, I'll learn to swim.'

They splashed and thrashed about until Walter was exhausted and a fair proportion of the lough was inside him. They were shivering as they got out of the water and were still shivering as they walked home. Walter put his jacket around their shoulders. This brought them close. Ann smelled clean and fresh. She put her arm around Walter's waist. He felt lean and hard and strong.

* * *

The day of the excursion to Portrush arrived and they dressed up for it. Walter wore his dark grey Sunday suit with a white shirt and a blue tie. Ann wore a blue dress in the latest style that showed off her slender waist.

'You look as stunning as ever, Ann Brown,' Walter said as they walked round to the train station.

'You don't look so bad yourself, Walter Green.'

'I've been going to the YM a few times in the evenings. Trying to get fit for ... well, anything that might come up. If you know what I mean.'

Ann laughed and hoped he meant to make the little double entendre, but he was such a dope that he probably hadn't.

They boarded the train and Walter asked her if she wanted to sit at the window.

'I don't mind as long as I'm facing the way we're going. I think I'd be sick if I had to sit backwards.'

'Me too,' said Walter.

They sat and watched the throngs on the platform gradually dwindle as the train filled up. Most of the day-trippers seemed to be families with small, very noisy children and there seemed to be about a million of them in their carriage.

'I have a headache already.' Ann put the back of her hand to her forehead.

'Do you think we were that noisy when we were wee?'

'We never went anywhere when we were wee. No money, so Ma bore the brunt of the noise. But I'm sure we were perfect angels, at least some of the time. How she was able to give us a few pence now and again to go to the flicks and get a few sweets, I'll never know.'

'It's hard enough making ends meet when you've just yourself to look after. Imagine having a whole pile of weans to feed and clothe as well.'

'Do you ever think about having children?' Ann asked, looking straight at Walter. 'Not right now of course. It would make an awful mess of the carriage. When we're older?'

'I don't think I'll ever be old enough. Hard to imagine being somebodies da.' Walter took her hand in his.

'No more dancing, no more flicks, no more romantic walks in the moonlight at the Lovers Retreat.' She looked wistfully at him and fluttered her eyelids. He burst out laughing.

'We've never done that.'

'What?' She was still fluttering.

'A romantic walk in the moonlight at the Lovers Retreat.'

'It's still romantic, even on a wet afternoon. Anyway, I didn't think you were the romantic type. I thought you liked bread vans and trains and engines and manly things like that.'

'Like dancing?' Walter seemed a little uneasy at the direction the conversation was taking.

'Dancing is manly. Are you suggesting Fred Astaire isn't manly?'

'He is man-shaped I suppose,' Walter admitted.

'You mean thin and bony with no arse?'

'Ann Brown! I know you're a great admirer of my arse.'

'I'd be a bigger admirer if there was a bit more of it to admire.'

'Well, I'm not complaining.'

'About the size of your arse?'

'No, I'm not complaining about the bum that *I* admire.'

Ann blushed slightly. 'Have you been looking at my bum behind my back?'

'Well, it *is* behind your back. That's why it's called your backside.'

Ann laughed and clasped both his hands in hers. 'That's very childish. If we can't say serious grown-up things, we should say nothing.'

They held hands, sat back and watched Northern Ireland flash by.

The day was perfect, hot and sunny. When they got off the train, they headed for the East Strand and walked all the way to the white rocks. They hadn't brought their swimming togs, but Walter rolled his trousers up. They paddled in the cold sea, skipping about trying to avoid stepping on painful stones, slippery seaweed and odd-looking jellyfish.

They went to Barry's and admired the views of the coast from the Ferris wheel. They screamed like children on the roller coaster and held hands on the little boats in the boating lake. The sounds and the smell of the place were overwhelming – clanking machines, dropping pennies, people of all ages screaming and laughing, burning sugar from the candyfloss machines and static electricity from the cars on the race track. Their money disappeared very quickly.

As they were leaving, Ann asked, 'Do you think we have enough money for an ice cream?'

'I believe so, Madam. Your wish is my command.'

'I'll have a ninety-nine then, please, my good man.'

'Certainly. Would Madam like sprinkles?'

'Can't have a ninety-nine without sprinkles.'

'True. Chocolate or red?'

'Too many choices! Chocolate. No, red. No, both. Surprise me.'

They walked the short distance to the building on the South Pier with 'Teas and Ices' in large letters on its green roof and sat on the harbour wall outside the Harbour Bar. Feet dangling over the water, they watched the little fish darting about aimlessly below them. They licked the lavishly sprinkled pokes like two kids and commented on the day-trippers strolling along Kerr Street. It was a magical moment. Time seemed to stand still. They didn't speak, just leaned together in a comfortable silence.

'We'll have to think about dandering back up to the station soon.' Walter sighed sadly, breaking the spell.

'What time is it?'

'I'll go into the pub and have a look.'

'Do you fancy a pint before we go?'

'I'm not sure if we have enough.' Walter hoked a handful of coins out of his trouser pocket along with a very well-used hanky.

'Jesus, look at that,' Ann said, horrified.

'I think that's been in these trousers since I got them.' Walter held it out at arm's length.

'When you were ten?'

'Probably, but that's not that long ago, remember. I have a shilling and three thruppenny bits. Oh, and a farthing.' He held the coins out in the palm of his hand. 'That should be enough.'

Ann rooted in her handbag. 'I have the princely sum of two bob.'

'Plenty. We can go mad and have a half each. Wouldn't it be lovely if we could drink them out here?'

The pub was packed, but Walter fought his way to the bar, saw the price list, ordered a couple of shandies and fought his way back out into the sunshine.

'We've an hour before the train.' Walter handed her down her glass. 'It's like a madhouse in there.'

'People enjoying themselves, I suppose.'

'I know, it's ridiculous. They should act like proper grown-ups.'

'All worried and sad.'

'Exactly.'

Ann took a large slug. 'If we'd not spent so much in Barry's, we could have had another one.'

'This is enough.' He held his glass up to the sun. 'Right now, this is everything I need in the world.'

'Walter, you're getting older and wiser by the day.'

'But not sadder, I hope.'

'No, not today.'

They clinked their glasses and drank to the postponement of care and responsibility.

'Here's to the future.' Ann raised her glass and took a sip.

'Our future,' said Walter. Ann didn't contradict him.

Walter took the empty glasses back into the madhouse and they set off for the station, arm in arm. Ann slept with her head on his shoulder on the journey back. Walter looked like the cat that got the cream.

The rest of their summer was idyllic. They went for romantic walks in the moonlight at the Lovers Retreat. They went swimming on the sunnier weekends and they continued dancing and going to the pictures. They were a proper 'going out' couple at last.

CHAPTER 28

One Saturday night at the end of October, as they got their coats from the ballroom cloakroom, Ann said, 'Mary's having a party next Saturday night at her house after the dance. It's for her twentieth. It'll be Oliver's last night with the band as well, before he heads off to America.'

'Are we invited?'

'Well, I am. Not sure about you. She didn't actually say "and Walter".'

'So you're going on your own then?'

'I could, I suppose, but where's the fun in that? Their house is enormous. Her da must be making a fortune from the Starr. In fact, I was thinking …'

'Oh dear. I don't like it when you do *thinking*.'

'I was thinking that we never really get the chance to be properly alone together. So perhaps with their house being so big and all, maybe we could find a wee quiet room somewhere. Just the two of us.'

'What for?' Walter looked all innocent.

'Are you thick or what? You know what for. Being alone.'

'What?' Walter started to grasp where this was going and he wasn't sure how to respond. He gulped, buying time. His wildest dream could be about to come true and it terrified him.

'Just us. Being romantic.'

Disbelief and doubt flickered across Walter's face, but then it flooded with joy.

'You look a bit … faint. I don't know. Are you okay?' Ann peered at him as they left the building.

'Bowled over is more like it,' Walter finally managed to say. 'Are you sure? I mean are you *sure*? We don't want to rush things before we're ready.'

'Walter, nobody could accuse us of rushing things. We can't just be *going out together* forever, can we?'

'I know, but if it's not broke and all that. It might spoil things.'

Ann was getting exasperated. 'It's anything but broke.' She sighed. 'But we won't know until we try, will we? I think – well, I hope – that you want to try as much as I do.'

'You know I do. I think you're the most beautiful girl in Omagh, maybe in the whole world, so of course I do, but I'm afraid of ruining what we have. I'm afraid of disappointing you.'

'What are you going on about, you daft idiot?'

Ann had no idea how terrified Walter was feeling in that moment. What if he couldn't perform? He knew it worked, but he'd never tried it in combat yet.

'This is all new to me.'

'That makes two of us.'

Walter let out a huge sigh of relief.

'Seriously, Walter, I've thought about this and there's nobody I'd rather do this with than you. There's nobody I've ever wanted to do this with but you.'

‘Oh God.’ Walter flushed beetroot.

‘You’ll be fine. We’ll have a wee drink to help us relax and it’ll be lovely. Just make sure you wear your best clean pants and bring some *you-know-whats* with you.’

Walter looked confused, then realised what she meant. He smiled, but he was anything but fine.

CHAPTER 29

Ann left the Starr Ballroom by the side door. She was glowing and had a light sheen of sweat on her face. The last dance was always a slow one, but she had only just got her breath back from the jiving. On Monday she was starting her new job back in Omagh. Almost giddy with joy, she decided to have a quick fag in the alleyway before they went on to Mary's party.

Walter followed her out. 'That was fantastic!'

'Aye. The band were brilliant tonight.'

'*We* were brilliant tonight,' Walter said. 'We should enter the next competition, no matter where it is.'

'You've changed your tune. It'll be a while till I can afford a new dress and I'll need new shoes.'

Walter smiled at her. 'You're beautiful and talented enough. You don't need anything new. You could win wearing a coal sack.' He looked down at his own shiny shoes and fidgeted.

'I'm not so sure about that,' Ann said. 'But keep going. What are you after?'

'A drag of your fag would be good.'

She handed him the half-smoked Woodbine.

'Woodbines? Bloody hell!' Walter hacked as the harsh smoke seared his throat.

'Ma calls them coffin sticks … or is it *coughin*?' Smiling, Ann took the fag from him. 'We should head up to the party.' She inhaled and passed it back to Walker.

'When we finish the fag,' Walter said, inhaling and choking.

'When we finish the fag.' She took it back from him and took another shallow drag.

They'd agreed they might need a few wee drinks to help them relax and Ann thought Walter was as happy as she'd ever seen him. She leaned forward and gave him a peck on the cheek. 'Thanks for a great night, Walter.'

'My pleasure. It's not over yet.'

'The best is yet to come,' Ann said, smiling naughtily at him.

'I love you, Ann Brown.'

'I love you too, Walter Green.'

Walter leaned forward and his lips brushed her cheek. He closed his eyes and inhaled deeply, her perfume filling the air between them.

He kissed her harder, passionately. She responded. He brushed a wisp of her hair back from her face and gently stroked her ear. She laid her hands on his shoulders.

Suddenly Walter was pushing his body against her, pressing her back into the wall. His hands slid up under her dress and cupped her bum. So she grabbed his bum as well. But now as he pushed into her more tightly, any jokey thoughts about Walter's bony bum, turned into alarm.

'What's got into you?' She could feel his 'excitement' as he squeezed against her. 'Stop it, Walter.' She tried to push him away. 'Not now.'

She gasped for breath as Walter broke off from the frenzied kissing. 'Why not? Tonight's the night.' His eyes were wide and wild.

'At the party, all romantic and private. Not here, you bloody dope. You've no thingy on and anyone could see us!'

Soup Bowles says his da told him you can't get up the duff if you do it standing up. So why wait if we're in the mood now.'

'I'm not *in the mood* now and Dr Bowles doesn't know his arse from his elbow.'

Walter squeezed against her again. He was fumbling with his trouser buttons with one hand and her knickers with the other.

Ann was panicking now and struggled to free herself. 'Walter! Please! You're hurting me. Stop it!' She tried again to push him away but soon realised he was beyond hearing.

'Stop it, Walter!' She slapped his face, desperately hoping someone would emerge from the dance hall but it was too late.

He didn't stop.

At least it didn't last long.

Afterwards, she slapped his face again, leaving red welts on his cheek.

'Fuck you, Walter. That was really sore. You hurt me! Look at the state of me. I can't go to the party like this.'

'Jesus, Ann,' he said, panting and rubbing his cheek. 'You'll be all right. We'll get cleaned up. Does this mean we have to get married?'

'God, you're clueless,' she spat out bitterly. 'I want to marry a grown-up.'

He began to laugh nervously.

'It's not funny,' she said and started to cry. 'You've ruined it. Destroyed everything. What the hell got into you?'

Walter tried to put his arms around her, but she pushed him away. 'I'm sorry,' he whispered, and tears welled up in his eyes. 'I don't know. You're so beautiful. I couldn't help myself. I don't know … I … I'm sorry.'

'Everything's ruined,' her face was streaked with tears. 'I'm going home.' She picked up her bag.

Silent tears trickled down his face as he watched her walk away. He didn't move. He didn't go after her. He shouted 'I love you, Ann Brown.'

But she didn't turn round.

Walter watched her walk away from him. She was crying and still fixing her clothes and hair. He was numb. Shaking. He couldn't believe what had just happened, what he had just done. Things had spiralled out of control. It was supposed to be their special night and he'd ruined it. He knew Ann had been really looking forward to it. They both had, and now it looked like their first time might be their last. He'd actually hurt her! Should he go after her? She was already at her door. What if she never spoke to him again? What would he do? He wiped his nose on his sleeve and buttoned up his trousers. His legs were trembling. He felt sick.

It started to rain. The cigarette lay on the ground, soggy and unfinished.

CHAPTER 30

Ann crossed the street and opened her front door as quietly as the rusty hinges would allow. The creaking stairs gave away her arrival as they had always done.

'Is that you, Ann?'

'No, it's Fred.' Ann tried to sound normal, but Ma knew something was wrong.

'What's wrong, love? Are you not going to the party?'

'I don't feel very well. I've got a pounding headache. I'm just going to bed.'

'Is Walter all right?'

'I don't care if he's all right or not. I don't care if I never see him again.'

'You can't mean that. What's he done?'

'Nothing, Ma. He's just … an eejit. We had a row. I don't want to talk about it.'

'You'll feel better in the morning. A good night's sleep and you'll be as right as rain.'

'Yes, Ma.'

'Will you be all right for church?'

Fuck church, she thought. *Sorry, Jesus*, didn't mean that. She knew Ma couldn't go on her own. 'Yes, Ma. I'll be fine in the morning.'

'Good girl. Just remember, all men are idiots, even the good ones. Whatever he did, I'm sure he didn't mean it. It'll sort itself out, just wait and see.'

If only you knew what he'd done, Ann thought. 'Goodnight Ma.'

'Goodnight, love.'

Ma was up with the light as usual. She knocked lightly on Ann's door. 'Are you awake?'

Ann dried her eyes on the sheet. She'd eventually cried herself into a fitful sleep, but had been awake in time to see the daylight appear through the gaps in the curtains that didn't quite meet in the middle. Fuck Walter for being so stupid, for being so uselessly Walter, for having too much to drink. He'd ruined their perfect fairytale evening. She hoped he felt as bad as she did. No, she hoped he felt worse, like the complete stupid bastard that he is. What on earth got into him?

She brushed her hair, cleaned her teeth, put on her Sunday dress and was ready. Ma had made tea and toasted soda.

'What happened last night, love? You look like you haven't slept.'

'Thanks, Ma.' She took the plate and a mug of tea. 'We had a row. We fell out, that's all.'

'It must have been serious.'

'I thought I knew how dopey he was, but he surpassed himself last night.'

'You'll be okay. I'm sure you can make it up. I know how fond you are of him.'

'What makes you think that? I never want to see or speak to him ever again.'

'You wouldn't be so upset if you weren't fond of him.'

'I don't want to talk about him, Ma,' Ann said, but she knew Ma was right.

In church, the Johnstons settled into their pew in front of Ann and Ma. It wasn't lost on Ann that all five of them were still there, the whole family still together. She ached for her sisters.

Harry asked if they'd heard anything more from Joe.

Ann was struggling with the pleasantries 'No, but we'll tell him you were asking about him, if we ever hear from him again that is.'

Harry's only news was that Nigel was thinking of taking up rugby. He had to be good at something.

Ann was glad that nobody from the party was in church. It must have been a great night and everyone would have bad hangovers. The service was a blur. She felt uncomfortable sitting on the hard pew.

She armed Ma back home and the rest of the day was spent on the usual Sunday chores. She hoped Walter didn't come round and try to apologise. How could she face him? Her mind slowly turned to the next day when she started her new job. She put the slug in the fire to heat it up, then lifted it with the tongs and put it into the old iron. She dampened her best blouse a little, ironed it carefully and hung it on the rail in her room. 'Please God,' she prayed, 'let me be in good form tomorrow. I can't be droopy on my first day.'

She went to bed early, the new job being all the reason she needed. There were no great objections from Ma or Fred. They liked being with each other, she thought. Could she and Walter have ended up as old and as happy? Now she would never know.

Monday morning was wet and windy as she walked to the

Ministry of Agriculture offices on the Dublin Road. She felt flat and worn out, but as she entered the building, she put on her party face and gave a cheery 'Good morning' to the friendly receptionist who greeted her.

The excitement and adrenaline rush of the new environment distracted her for the entire day. Her desk in the typing pool was in the back corner of a large room that had four big windows down the opposite side. She had a desk in the darkest corner of the room, but she was just in the door. She'd be at the front beside a window in no time.

There were twelve girls in the typing pool and Ann knew a few of them. They were all very friendly and chatty. None of them had been to the party and for a few hours, Ann didn't even think about Walter.

That evening Ma asked how it went.

'It was good, Ma. Dorothy, Janet and Florence all work there, so it should be good craic. It's much the same job as I was doing in Cookstown.'

'How many of them have the Pitman's 100 Words certificate, I wonder?'

'I don't know, Ma. Quite a few probably, but I'm going to do every test I can. Onward and upward.'

'Good for you. Are you going to see Walter?'

'Not yet. It's too soon. He needs to stew for a while. If he comes here, I'll go out the back and you can tell him I'm out.'

'I couldn't just lie to his face.'

'That's not a proper lie. I *will* be out – out the back, so it wouldn't be a lie at all, would it?'

'He's probably even more upset than you are.'

'Good! I hope he feels like shit.'

'Oh, Ann. He's really upset you, hasn't he. What did he do?'

'He behaved like a culchie from the bog. I'd rather not talk about it?'

'I'll say no more. I'm sure you'll sort it out. I'll clear these dishes.' The deep furrows on Ma's brow indicated the severity of her worry.

Fred rarely visited on a Monday and very few people ever called at all, unless they were looking for money. So it was a surprise when there was a loud rap on the door after tea.

'That's not Fred's knock,' said Ann as she got up to see who it was, hoping it wasn't Walter.

It was Walter's da and his face was ashen grey. He was visibly upset.

'Mr Green, come in. It's bucketing.'

He stepped inside and removed his sodden coat and equally drowned duncher. Ann took them and hung them up on the hook behind the door.

'Thanks, Ann. It's about Walter.'

Her stomach clenched. 'Is he okay? You know we had a row?'

Mr Green slumped into a chair.

'He's in hospital. They took him up to Belfast today. I didn't want to bother you yesterday, being Sunday and all. All I know is he got knocked down by a van in the Back Market on Saturday night. It was Bertie Roulston. I didn't believe him at first because Walter had told us he was going to a party with you and it was still only eleven.

'Apparently, Bertie was just starting off in his van, when Walter turned the corner into the Back Market. He seemed to be staggering a bit, head down, he wasn't looking where he was going and he walked straight into the van. He fell backwards, arms whirling and his head hit the corner of the wall. There was a lot of blood. Bertie drove him straight out to the County. They patched him up, but they said they couldn't do any more for him, so he's away to the Royal today.'

'Oh God! Did he say anything? How bad is it?'

'Would you take a drop of tea, Mr Green?' Ma said, hovering.

'I'll not stay. He's been unconscious the whole time. His head is badly bruised and cut. They're worried about a skull fracture. He might have brain damage. That's why they need the experts in Belfast to have a look at him. He's no other injuries. Just a bruised leg from the van.'

Ann thought her heart was going to jump out of her chest. She put her face in her hands and burst into tears. Ma held out her hanky before putting her arms around her quivering daughter.

Mr Green reached for his coat and cap. He didn't know what else to say or do, so he put them on and turned towards the door. Ma stood up to see him out. She thanked him for letting them know.

Ann's brain was in turmoil. So that's why he never came to apologise. God love him. I hope he's okay, she thought. She caught her breath and blew her nose. 'Can I go and see him, Mr Green?'

'I think he'd love to see you, Ann. He talks about nothing else. Ann this and Ann that. He was very excited about the party.'

'We didn't go to the party. We had a row and I came straight home.'

'Was he drunk?'

'No, not really, maybe a wee bit. It doesn't take much.'

'I know. I don't think he's ever been drunk, but Bertie said ...' he shrugged his shoulders.

Ann's head was swirling with what ifs, could haves, and maybes. He'd ruined their big night, but now he was in hospital with his head in a sling!

'Are there visiting times?' she asked.

'I don't know. I called the ward from work today and they said he's stable. I never thought about visiting times.'

Ann felt a compulsion to go right away. 'I'd like to go as soon as possible. Tomorrow.'

'You've only just started your new job, love. They won't let you take a day off so soon, especially if he's not a relative. You've only done one day.' Ma was trying to calm Ann down without success.

'I'll go and see Mrs Crammond first thing. I'll explain. She'll understand. She'll have to.' Ann was wringing her hands in agitation.

'I'm going on Thursday. It's my day off, if that's any good to you. You could come with me. I'll get you free on the train.'

'Thanks, Mr Green, but Mrs Green will want to be there with you on Thursday. What time's the first train? No, I need to go in and see Mrs Crammond first. Is there one about half nine? I'll get that.'

'Calm down, love.' Ma put her hands on Ann's shoulders. 'You'll make yourself sick and then where will you be? No use to anyone, much less Walter.'

Mr Green said, 'There's a train at 9:35. Our Walter's in the right place now. This new National Health Service thing is great. We don't have to pay a penny.'

'I can't see how that can work,' Ma said. 'You get nothing for nothing I say, but thanks again for coming round to tell us and in that weather. You never even had a drop of tea.'

'That's all right. I'll be at work in the morning, Ann, if you do manage to get the day off.' He pulled his duncher down tight. 'I'll leave you in peace.' He left, closing the door quietly behind him.

'It's a good thing he didn't stay for a cuppa,' Ma said, trying to lighten the mood. 'We'd nothing in to have with it. You can't give anyone a barefoot cup of tea. We'd be the talk of the town.' Even in a crisis, etiquette had to be followed and appearances maintained.

Ann didn't smile back.

She couldn't sleep, and dawn broke making the cold, wet greyness, more visible, which just made it worse.

CHAPTER 31

Mrs Crammond was less than impressed at first, but she caved under a relentless onslaught from Ann who explained how bad Walter's injury was, how he might have brain damage and how they had just got engaged. He hadn't even had time to get a ring. She was so beside herself with worry that she wouldn't be able to work anyway. She would make up the time, she promised. And it was only one day after all.

When Mrs Crammond put her hands up in surrender, Ann asked, 'Are you sure?'

'Yes, you'd be about as useful as a chocolate teapot today anyway. At least if you see him, it'll put your mind at ease and I might get a day's work out of you tomorrow.'

'You will, Mrs Crammond, you will. I can't say how much this means. Thank you. Thank you!' She went to clasp Mrs Crammond's hands in hers, but the woman pulled them away.

Ann raced round to the station and found Mr Green looking very smart in his Head Porter's uniform, but his eyes betrayed a sleepless night.

'I got the day off,' she gasped.

'Good for you.' He handed Ann a tin lunch box. 'The wife made this for him, in case you were going up today. Dunno what the food's like in these places but that's egg and onion with salad cream, his favourite.'

As Ann took the box, she realised she hadn't even known what his favourite sandwiches were.

'I'll call over when I get back tonight, if it's not too late,' she said.

'The last train is at half six, so you need to get that. It gets in here at half eight.'

'I'll call then, if that's okay.'

'We'll not be able to sleep until we find out how he is. I hope he's come round by now.'

'Me too. I'll see you tonight then,' and she ran to get her ticket.

The train moved in slow motion compared to the Portrush trip. The journey seemed to take forever. She shuffled and fidgeted. She looked but saw nothing out the window. The other passengers were ghosts. The few young children were in a silent movie. The conductor came and spoke to her and punched her ticket like he was a mime artist.

Eventually, the train dragged itself into Great Victoria Street station. Ann was first off and asked the man checking the tickets at the barrier for directions. She hardly glanced at the Grand Opera House before she turned left into the Grosvenor Road and the rain hit her in the face. She felt nothing as she bent forward into the gale.

The Grosvenor Road entrance was not the main one, and the hospital was huge, so she had to ask three different people before she found the reception desk. Then she had to wait behind a big round woman with a squawking infant hanging from her arm. Ann couldn't understand a word she or the receptionist said, but then something was 'stickin' out' and the woman seemed very happy and proceeded down a corridor, trailing the child behind her like a teddy bear.

Ann stepped up to the desk and said she wanted to see Walter Green, brought up from Omagh yesterday.

'Visiting is from half ten to half eleven. You've just missed it, I'm afraid. Afternoon visiting is from three to four. You can come back then.'

The poor receptionist got the full Mrs Crammond barrage, with extras. 'I've come all the way from Omagh in a hurricane and I got the day off and it's only my second day and nobody told me about special visiting times. He might have brain damage and we just got engaged and his parents are waiting on me to tell them how he is and …'

'Slow down, slow down.' The girl was smiling kindly. 'What's his name again?'

'Walter Green.'

The girl lifted the handset of her big black phone and dialled three numbers. She spoke quietly to someone for a minute. Ann couldn't hear the conversation, even though her ears were out on stalks.

'Matron says it's okay. You can go up to see him.'

'Thank you. Thank you so much.'

'It's all right. You've come a long way. In a hurricane and all! Good Luck.' The receptionist gave her directions to Ward 21, which involved lots of stairs and long corridors.

Emotions spun and collided in Ann's brain as she navigated the maze. Anger, fear, sadness, love …

What would she say to him? What would he say to her?

A nurse met her at the double doors. 'You're here to see Walter Green?'

'Yes. How is he?'

'The doctor will be round later. They have to do more tests. He's down here,' and she led Ann between the lines of identical white beds with anonymous faces sticking out the top. Some looked awake, most didn't; it was hard to tell.

'Has he woken up yet?'

'No, but he's stable.'

That meant nothing to Ann. At first, she didn't recognise him. His head was wrapped in a bandage. His ghostly white face looked very young. His eyes were shut. His lips were blue. He looked like a corpse. Ann stood at the bedside and couldn't stop the tears.

'Oh, Walter,' she whispered and she knew for certain that she loved him. Her other emotions merged into an overwhelming sadness.

'I'll get you a chair.'

'Can I hold his hand?'

'Yes, it might help. You should talk to him. He'll hear you.' The nurse reached under the sheets, brought Walter's right arm out and gently laid it on the covers.

Ann cupped his hand in hers. He was cold and his hand was soft and floppy. She put her forehead on the bed and more tears flowed.

'He's being well looked after,' the nurse said. 'Dr Healy is one of the top neurologists in the whole country. He'll know more after they do the X-ray.'

'X-ray?' Ann looked up, drying her eyes with her hanky.

'It's like a photograph, but it shows the inside of his head. It'll reveal if there's any damage or swelling of his brain. I'll pull the curtains round. Would you like a cup of tea?'

'Thank you. Thank you very much. You're very kind.'

'There's a ladies' back down the corridor,' the nurse added, pointing, and then she left them alone.

Ann gazed at Walter for a long time. He looked asleep. Peaceful. Very still. The only movement was the almost imperceptible rise and fall of the covers as he breathed in and out.

'Not much craic out of you today, blondie,' she whispered, her face close to his ear. 'You know I had to throw my knickers away. My best party knickers – ruined, thanks to you. What got into you, Walter? You hurt me. You know that? I wasn't sure what I was going to say to you if you'd been awake, but that doesn't matter now.'

She tried to get comfortable on the hard seat. 'Your da called round at our house last night to tell us you were here. I had to get a day off work and I only started yesterday. I came up on the train. It seemed like the slowest train in the world ever and then they weren't going to let me in 'cause visiting time is over. But I'm here now. The nurse said you can hear me, so shut up and listen.'

She shifted around on the seat. 'They're going to try and find your brain, which won't be easy, and then they're going to try and fix it, which will be even harder, but you might actually end up being quite smart. Smarter than you were before, which isn't saying much. Then, when you're all fixed and clever, you'll come home and we'll get engaged and we'll get married. You won't have to ask me. I'm telling you that's what's happening. No need to say anything.' She shook him gently. 'Wake up, Walter. Please wake up.'

She squeezed his hand. Nothing.

It was so quiet she could hear the drip, drip of clear liquid in a bottle hooked up to a pole beside his bed that travelled down a tube and into his arm. A nurse brought her a cup of tea. Ann asked her what the fluid was and she explained that it contained vitamins, minerals and other things the body needed. The purpose was to keep Walter hydrated and fed, as he couldn't eat or drink anything until he woke up which, she said, was only a matter of time.

'Your da is coming up to see you on Thursday,' Ann said, opening the lunch box. 'He gave me an egg and onion sandwich for you. I didn't know they were your favourite. Do you want it? No? You won't mind if I have it then. I'm famished.'

She ate the sandwich. Perhaps the smell would rouse him. 'Lovely fresh bread, so it is. From your place, of course. It's a bit too salty, but maybe that's the way you like them. I started my new job yesterday. I'm going to do more tests, get more certificates. I could be the boss someday. Maybe you could get a certificate in van driving or something when you're better.'

She talked herself to a standstill and then just sat holding his hand.

The nurse came back. She said Ann would have to leave as they had to get Mr Green ready for his X-ray. It was still bucketing outside, so she said she'd sit in the corridor and wait for him to come back, if that was allowed. An hour passed. Someone brought more tea. Walter didn't come back. The nurse sat down on the chair beside her.

'You're not a relative are you, Ann?'

'I'm his fiancé.' The lie came easily to her. 'We got engaged on Saturday. We haven't even chosen a ring or told anybody yet, apart from my boss. So please don't tell anyone, will you? Not even his da.'

'No, of course not. But if you're not family, it means I can't tell you very much.' The nurse looked at Ann's face and caved in. 'They've completed the X-ray and Mr Healy says he needs an operation straight away. There's swelling on his brain and it's pushing against his skull. The surgery should ease the pressure, then Walter can start to heal. He's being prepared for the operation now. Mr Butcher will be doing it, so he's in very good hands.'

'An operation? It sounds serious. Will he wake up afterwards?'

'That's the idea and we'll also be able to assess if there's any damage.'

'What sort of damage could there be?'

'He might have fractured his skull or have a bleed on his brain.' When Ann looked alarmed, the nurse added soothingly. 'It's a very successful surgery and Mr Butcher has performed hundreds of them. But I've told you too much already. Although you are his fiancée, after all.'

'Mr Butcher? Is that really his name?'

The nurse smiled. 'Yes. It's a bit unfortunate, isn't it.'

'Poor Walter, he'll be scared out of his wits. He doesn't like blood and stuff.'

'He won't feel a thing, and when he wakes up, he won't know what happened.'

'Nothing new there then! So, he's going into surgery right now?'

'Yes. You may as well go home because he won't be back up on this ward today and they won't let anyone see him down in the recovery ward.'

Ann found herself asking, 'Can I visit on Saturday? If he's not home by then?'

'Yes, just come up anytime. Ask for me. My name's Sinead. And his family can ring the ward for an update.'

'Saturday would be best for me. His da is coming up on Thursday.'

'Let's hope Walter is awake by then. Tell his da he's getting the best of care.'

Ann believed the nurse. She believed they knew what they were doing. He would recover. She knew it.

The rain had eased as she walked back through gloomy streets to the station, where she caught the late afternoon train.

This time the journey progressed at a normal speed. She felt more relaxed. She watched the countryside unfold as they trundled along and the people getting on and off when they stopped. She even smiled at the conductor as he punched her ticket.

Mr Green was on the platform when they pulled into Omagh.

'You're early love,' he said as he helped her step down from the carriage into a rainy evening. 'I'm doing a bit of overtime so I'd be here when you got back.'

'That's awful good of you, Mr Green.'

'How is he? Was he awake?'

'No, he wasn't. They decided they had to do an operation straight away. That's why I was able to get the earlier train. Walter might not be back in the regular ward. He's in Ward 21 for a day or so. He has to stay in the recovery ward until he's recovered, I suppose.'

'An operation? On his brain? That doesn't sound too good.'

Ann explained about the X-ray as best she could, but could provide no details. When Mr Green looked alarmed, she assured him that the doctors had done the operation many times before.

'Whatever this X-ray thing showed made them decide they had to do the operation right there and then?' Mr Green's brow creased.

'Yes, they said they had to be quick, but the surgery will help him regain consciousness. Then he can start to recover.'

'I see,' Mr Green stared vacantly across the station.

Ann realised she had to stay positive. Mr Green was shaking.

'They'll know how serious it is after the operation and they said to ring anytime for news. I told the nurse – her name's Sinead – that you were coming on Thursday. She is lovely and said you needn't worry about the visiting times either. You can go anytime and stay as long as you like. But ring ahead in case he's still in recovery.'

'That's a good idea.'

'She said the doctors looking after him are the best there is.'

'Good. That's good,' he whispered almost to himself.

'I hope you don't mind, but I ate your sandwich. I was starving when I got there. It was lovely. I asked Walter, but he didn't want it.'

Mr Green smiled. 'No problem, love. I'll bring another one on Thursday. He'll be ready for it by then. You've had a long day Ann. Mrs Green and I are really grateful. You get on home and get dried.'

'Will you let me know how he is as soon as you get back on Thursday?'

'Of course. You'll be the first to know whatever there is to know.'

She walked home, and as she dried her hair in front of the fire, she told Ma all about her day. Steam rose from her coat that was draped over a kitchen chair. It was lovely to be home. Bacon and cabbage for dinner. A warm fire and her own bed.

* * *

Mr Green knocked their door on Thursday evening. He looked as tired as Ann had been after her trip. He entered under a hail of questions.

'Well? How was he? Is he up?'

'No change. They believe the operation went well, but they'll know more in another day or two. He's still on a drip because he's not eating or drinking yet. He's as well as can be expected, is what Dr Healy said.'

'What's he like?' Ma asked.

'Nice man. Very quietly spoken, but he knows his stuff. You're still going up on Saturday?' he asked Ann.

'Yes. First train.'

After thank yous, goodbyes and reassurances, Ann watched Mr Green walk up the street, pulling his duncher down against the cold. He looked old, tired and like he had the weight of the world on his shoulders.

CHAPTER 32

It was dry on Saturday. The train journey was a blur. Suddenly Ann was in Ward 21 again. There was a different nurse on duty. Ann sat at Walter's bedside and held his hand. The nurse, Sonia, made her tea.

Ann sat for hours. She talked herself round in circles. She prayed for him to wake up, but he didn't and then it was time to go.

When she got back to Omagh, she walked out to Walter's house and reported that nothing had changed. She had had to eat the sandwich again. Mr Green invited her in, but she said no thanks, she was too tired. Mrs Green came to the door and started to cry. She thanked Ann for going to see him.

'He's only a boy. What did he do to deserve this? What if he never wakes up?'

Ann and Mr Green tried to reassure her that it would all be fine, but as Ann walked home, she wondered, what if Mrs Green was right?

Mr and Mrs Green travelled up to see him that Thursday. There was no change.

And so life settled into a routine. Ann went back the next Saturday and Sinead met her at the entrance to Ward 21, smiling as usual.

'Well, Sinead, any change?' Ann asked.

'What about ye, Ann. Not so far. They've done more X-rays and the swelling has gone down a bit, so the operation has been effective. We just have to wait for your man to decide to wake up and join us again.'

Ann parked herself beside Walter. She clasped his hand in hers and told him every little detail about everything that had happened over the last week.

'Are you bored yet?' she asked after an hour of non-stop trivial information. 'What do you think of Iris buying red shoes? I mean even *you'd* agree they won't match anything else she has, but there was no talking to her. She had to have them.'

Sinead brought her a cup of tea. She ate her cheese sandwich. Other people came and visited other patients and left. Eventually she said, 'If I go now, Walter, I can get the earlier train home. Do you mind? It means I can get a few things done for tomorrow. I still have to take Ma to church. She's praying for you. If she was one of them, I think she would light a candle. I'm sure it all helps – somehow. It makes *her* feel better anyway and what else can she do? I'll see you next week. Same time, same place. In the meantime, try and behave yourself and do what Sinead says.'

She squeezed his hand and was about to stand up when she sat straight back down. He had squeezed back!

'Walter?' she squeezed his hand again. 'Walter. Wake up, Walter. Speak to me.'

She was sure his eyelids flickered, just for a second. She ran to the nurse's station. 'Sinead! Sinead! He squeezed my hand. I'm sure he did, and his eyelids are moving. I think he's waking up.'

The two of them stood at Walter's bed and gazed at the silent, barely breathing body. Ann's eyes welled up with emotion.

She sat down and squeezed his hand again. 'Walter. Walter. It's me, Ann. Open your eyes. Please.'

Sinead gave her a hanky to dry her eyes. 'It might have been an involuntary twitch. That's quite common in these cases. We'll keep a close eye on him.'

'Can you get the doctor? He might be waking up.'

'Dr Healy's not back until Monday. If Walter wakes up before then, we'll call his da at the station. You may as well go home and try to get some rest.' She patted Ann on the shoulder and went to see another patient, who was crying like a child.

Ann leaned in and whispered in Walter's ear. 'I love you, Walter Green.'

There was no more movement. She sat on a while longer and left in time to get the last train. She was *certain* she'd felt him squeeze her hand, seen his eyes flutter, but it was over in a flash. What if that's all there was? What if he never woke up like Mrs Green said? She scolded herself. Be positive. It would take time. Walter was young. He had plenty of time. As Ma always said, when God made time, he made lots of it.

The cold of December set in and the routine became more tiring. Then one Thursday evening Walter's parents called round. Mr Green looked happier than Ann thought she'd ever seen him. Even Mrs Green looked slightly happy.

'Has he woken up? Did he speak to you?'

'Let the poor folk over the door, Ann,' Ma said.

'Oh, yes, sorry. Come in.'

Mr Green delivered his report: 'He still hasn't woken up properly, but today we felt his fingers move a bit, just like you did, and then his eyelids began flickering. Next thing we knew, he'd opened his eyes! Only for a second or two, but then, he did it again an hour later and this time it was for longer. He still seems out of it, but he made noises – sort of moaning, gurgling noises. Sinead even managed to get a wee drop of water down his neck. They're delighted and say he's making real progress.'

Ann clapped her hands like a child. 'That's wonderful news. He'll be up and walking about in no time, just you wait and see. I'll bring him egg and onion on Saturday. He must be starving.'

They chatted for a while about the trains, the weather and the crowds in Belfast. Ma had gotten used to the Greens calling and always had a barmbrack or something in to give them with a cup of tea. They'd become friends.

When they left, Ma said, 'God love them, but maybe he's turning the corner, eh?'

Ann knew that Ma wanted this over almost more than she did. Ma was worried about her, about how stressed she was getting by the whole thing. The trips to Belfast left her very tired, but she still did all the chores and the shopping without complaining. She tried to be her normal cheerful self, but she had become more irritable. She would be all right when Walter was all right.

She knew a lot of people were praying for her and Walter, and that's all they could do. She was so glad she had Ma to lean on.

CHAPTER 33

Ann raced along the unusually pleasant Grosvenor Road. She didn't even mind the nip of winter in the air. She skipped down the seemingly endless central corridor to Ward 21.

'Sinead! I heard he's woken up.'

'I don't know about "woken up" so much, but he's certainly making progress. It's slow, but progress nonetheless.'

There was a hint of colour in Walter's cheeks – a shade up from parchment white – and he was sitting propped up so he looked less like a corpse. But his eyes were shut.

'Hi Walter. It's me,' Ann said, clasping his hand in hers as she always did. 'The big New Year's Eve ball is coming up again soon. 1950 – can you believe it! I got two tickets, but I don't know who to take. Your friend Ronnie is always asking about you and he's not a bad looker. I know he's not blond, but if you don't get up soon and give yourself a shake, I'll have to take somebody else. So what do you think? Everyone's asking if you're going to be there. No need to make your mind up right now. You can let me know the next time I'm up.'

She brushed a wisp of hair off his temple. 'Your hair's getting long. You'll have to get it cut if you're going to go to the ball. It's Baltic out there, so you're not missing much. Not long to Christmas. What do you want from Santa? I've got an egg and onion sandwich here for you, not for Christmas, of course, I mean for now. If you want it, that is.' Ann thought the quality of her chatter was going seriously downhill.

Sinead walked past and Ann asked her if Walter could eat anything yet.

'Not yet, but we can get sips of water in, which is a start.'

'Do you hear that, Walter? I'm going to have to eat your sandwich again, and I don't even like egg and onion. I hope the smell of it doesn't drive you mad. Maybe that would be a good thing 'cause you'll wake up.'

She thought she felt a wee squeeze from his fingers and she looked up at his face. He looked like an angel, his gaunt pretty face surrounded by blond curls. She squeezed his hand hard and he made an almost inaudible moaning sound. His eyelids fluttered and his eyes opened.

'Sinead, Sinead! He's awake!'

Sinead hurried over and looked closely at Walter. 'He's been doing this more often and longer every time. It's a good sign.'

'Walter! It's Ann.' She kissed his cheek. She saw a flicker of a smile, or did she? She wiped the dribble off his chin with her hanky. 'Wake up. Nobody has any bread in Omagh 'cause you're lying here instead of whizzing round in your wee van firing baps at everyone. The people of Omagh need you, Walter. I need you. Come back to us. Please.' Her whispers trailed off.

He gurgled again and she wiped his chin again. He squeezed her hand again. It felt like the squeeze you would get from a newborn baby, but she felt it.

‘Tap my hand if you can hear me,’ she said and she felt a tiny twitch of his fingers.

Her heart leapt. ‘You’re some operator, Walter Green. Lying here, being attended to hand and foot by the nurses. I hope you don’t fancy any of them. Do they wash you and all? I bet you enjoy that.’ She imagined the wee smile again.

She had a cup of tea, ate the sandwich and then just sat holding his hand, feeling every tiny movement, real or imagined, until the lines seemed increasingly blurred. Then it was time to catch the train home.

It was snowing, but she didn’t care. It was beautiful. Everything was going to be all right.

After mince and onions, Ma looked at her closely. ‘You didn’t eat much.’

‘I’m fine, Ma. Just wrecked, that’s all. Walter’s getting better slowly. There’s slow and there’s Walter slow, but we can’t make him go any faster. All you get is wait and see. Wait and see.’

‘As long as you’re not overdoing things.’

‘I’m okay, honestly. I’m fine.’

‘Church tomorrow?’

‘Of course. Walter needs all the help he can get.’

Everybody at church knew about Walter by that time and even though he wasn’t a Presbyterian, they all kindly asked how he was. Ann couldn’t wait to get away.

CHAPTER 34

It was a strange week. The town was alive with Christmas lights, and carols drifted out from some of the bigger shops. She'd dreamt of going to the New Year's Eve dance in the courthouse ever since she'd been old enough to sneak into the Starr. Last year that dream came true, but not this year. She couldn't imagine going with somebody else. She'd got tickets, but she would pass them on to one of the girls at work. She thought maybe only wee Doris didn't have any, so she would give them to her.

She felt different as she walked around the town, soaking up the festive atmosphere, watching the children staring excitedly into the shop windows. There was nothing she could put her finger on. Just exhaustion and stress, but she was heartened by Walter's progress. She thought about the night of the party and wished with all her heart that Walter hadn't … it should have been beautiful, but it wasn't. No point crying over spilt milk, as Ma would say. Get on with it and keep 'er lit.

Ann was also worried that Ma must feel quite lonely now, with everyone away and her so preoccupied with Walter. She'd get her something special for Christmas. They'd do something nice. One good thing was that Fred was calling more often. She wondered about Fred sometimes, but he made Ma happy and that's all that mattered.

They got a Christmas card and parcel from Hilda; their snow was up to the roof! Muriel's included a long message about planning to come home, but then Al invited her out to his house again and they were having a big party. It was going to be just the best thing ever. Al had taken her to see *Pygmalion* at the Lyric Theatre. There were no famous actors in it. Someone called Alec Clunes played Henry Higgins.

'All right for some,' Ann muttered to Ma as they put the cards on the mantelpiece, though she was tempted to rip Muriel's to shreds and toss it into the fire. 'Can't even be bothered to come home because she's got something more glamorous and exciting going on. I'm not even a wee bit jealous. I wonder what they have for Christmas dinner. Swan? Maybe this year he'll pop the question.' But more than anything she longed to be able to talk to Muriel.

Ma noticed the slight bitterness in her voice, but merely said in her usual world-weary tone, 'I hope she knows what she's doing and doesn't get carried away, with all that frippery and tinsel.'

There was no word from Joe.

Christmas Eve fell on a Saturday and the weather was dreadful. Heavy, freezing rain, almost snow, but not quite, battered against the windows of the train, which was slow and late. Grosvenor Road was dark and bleak. 'In the bleak midwinter,' Ann hummed as she trudged along, bent into the sleet and wind.

The main corridor in the hospital was festooned with paper decorations along its entire length. The ward had been decorated too.

'Happy Christmas, Sinead!' Ann said. 'You've been busy. It looks great.'

'Happy Christmas to you too. Some of the nurses gathered up a few bits and pieces. We all need a touch of festive cheer. Brightens the place up.'

'It does indeed. How is he today?'

'Just the same, I'm afraid.'

'Are you working tomorrow?'

'Yes. No rest for the wicked, but I'll stop into the chapel before I come in. Light a candle or two. I'll light one for Walter.' She knew Ann wasn't a Catholic. 'I should get away about four and we'll have dinner after that.'

'Thanks for the candle, Sinead. You married?'

'Aye, to Sean. He's a porter here. You've probably seen him about without knowing who he is. Big with red hair. We have two little ones. Patrick is four and Kathleen is five.'

'My ma's called Kathleen. There must be great excitement in your house about Santa coming.'

'We can only afford to get them wee things, but they love all the build-up. They're not hard to please. If this sleet turns into snow, that's all they'll need.'

'That sounds lovely. I hope you, Sean and your weans have a great day and Santa is good to you.' Suddenly Ann felt the urge to confide. 'There are four of us kids. Da died just before the war, so Ma had to do it all on her own. I was seven and a half when he died.'

'I'm sorry to hear that,' Sinead said. 'It must have been very tough for you all, especially your ma.'

'Yes, but we got through it. There's just me left at home now. I have a decent job, so things are easier.' She thought about how life might just be about to get very tough again, but it was Christmas. Time for joy and optimism.

'I must get on. Happy Christmas, Ann.'

'Yes, Happy Christmas, Sinead, and thanks for everything. And here's a wee something for you and the other nurses.' She had brought chocolates.

'There was no need. Sure it's what we do, but thank you.' Sinead smiled and went off to attend to another white face in another white bed.

'Hello, Walter,' Ann said.

He gurgled at her. His eyes were open.

'Happy Christmas. I think we're going to have to miss the New Year's Eve ball this year. I hope you don't mind, but I've given our tickets to a wee girl at work. Doris. She's never been and she has a boyfriend, so I think they'll love it, just like we did. We got Christmas cards from Hilda and Muriel. Hilda killed a polar bear with her bare handbag and Muriel is living in a fairy tale in a castle with a psychiatric aristocrat. She's had dinner in the Savoy, you know. How fancy is that? She's too posh to come home and celebrate Christmas with the peasants anymore. Anyway, I haven't bought you anything. You never made a list, but I've got the best present ever. Right here.' She patted her belly.

Walter's eyes moved and his eyelids fluttered.

She continued in a low, bitter tone. 'That quack Dr Bowles was wrong, and his dopey son Soup was wrong, and you were wrong in so, so many ways. But you were right about one thing that night. We *are* going to have to get married and soon, or tongues will wag. So stop messing about, wake up, and get out of this bed. I'm sorry I couldn't tell you over a candlelit dinner with a glass of champagne. That would be a bit difficult in here, but maybe not impossible, seeing as how good Sinead and all are. They probably could have sorted it for us. Anyway, looks like I'm stuck with you after all.' She put his hand on her belly and couldn't stop the tears.

'Remember in Portrush we decided not to get serious and sad and old too quickly? Well, things have got serious pretty quickly, thanks to you, but we're not old yet and things will only get sad if we let them. You have to wake up. That would be the best Christmas present ever. Please, Walter.' He gurgled again and she wiped the spittle off his chin. 'I want to dance with you Walter.' She was shaking.

Sinead came over and asked if she was okay.

'It's … it's just being here on Christmas Eve. I don't know how you do it every day. It's not what we planned, but at least he's alive and everything will get back to normal. Won't it?' Her eyes were pleading for reassurance.

'Whatever will be, will be, Ann. If love could fix him, he'd be going home tomorrow.' But Sinead sensed something. She rested a hand on Ann's shoulder and met her eyes. 'If you need to talk … if there's anything … you know where to find me.'

Ann wondered how could a taig be so nice, and then she grimaced at her stupidity. She's a nurse and a good one. She was her friend. But some secrets were too great to share. 'Thanks again, Sinead. I don't know where I'd be without you.'

'You'll be fine. You're young, you're beautiful, you've got your whole life ahead of you.'

Could this be some kind of message? Was Sinead trying to prepare her for an outcome that might not be a happily ever after?

Sinead wandered off, and Ann could hear her singing 'Jingle Bells' to an old man at the end of the ward.

'I feel it, Walter, but I'll know for absolute certain very soon. So what do we do now? I need you to be okay. Our baby is real.' She held his hand against her belly again to try and get a reaction. Had Sinead noticed? 'Come back to me. Please. I need help. I need you. The baby needs you. How do I tell Ma?'

She sat on, ate his sandwich and talked until she ran out of things to say. She sang 'Silent Night' into his ear. That was his favourite. He smiled his best Mona Lisa smile. She ate the mince pie that Ma had made. She thought she was going to be sick. Then with a kiss on his clammy forehead and a Happy Christmas, she left.

The sleet had stopped. There were a lot of drunk, happy people on the train, but she didn't care. She accepted a bottle of beer from a boy who looked about sixteen and tried to think about what the new year and the new decade would bring. She would be twenty in April; pregnant with no husband and a ma and a house to look after. It really would be a new era in more ways than one.

CHAPTER 35

They'd spent every evening for the past week getting ready for Christmas Day. With only two of them now, it was easier. For the first time, Ma told Mr Reed she didn't want a turkey; they had a small chicken instead.

Ann had bought Ma a new case for her glasses and a string to hang them around her neck so she wouldn't lose them so often. She also got her a box of Milk Tray and fifty Senior Service. Ma got Ann a box of Black Magic and somehow managed to buy her a new raincoat.

They began the day with tea and toast. Then they damped down the fire, put the fireguard in front of it and went to church. Afterwards, they walked home arm in arm. It was dry but very cold. They thought it looked like snow.

The house was lovely and warm when they got back, and they had just hung up their coats and put the kettle on when Fred arrived with a bottle of Harvey's Bristol Cream. The kettle came back off again and they had a Christmas drink instead. They felt like naughty youngsters having a drink at such an early hour, and on Christmas Day, *and* on a Sunday.

Ma reckoned they would be struck down before the day was done.

'God'll hardly want to spoil his big day by killing people, Ma,' Ann said.

Once they'd agreed they might be safe, they had another drink. Then the Greens called. They didn't know Fred but they got on like a house on fire.

Mr Green was pessimistic about his son making a full recovery. Mrs Green cried. Ann was the optimist and she described how Walter responded when she spoke to him. She mentioned an upcoming dance competition in Bangor as an incentive for him to hurry up and get better. She'd become an expert at prattling on and feigning light-heartedness over the past couple of months. She knew he wouldn't be ready; anyhow, she'd be showing by then. What the hell was she going to do?

The chatter brought a wan smile to Mrs Green's pinched face – this and the couple of drinks she'd had. The sherry was finished by early afternoon when the Greens left. Fred stayed to listen to the King's speech. They toasted his Majesty with a wee Bush, then Fred went off into the gathering storm with a gentle list to starboard. As usual, he was having dinner with his two brothers who took it in turn every year. They were all tailors and worked together in the family shop on Castle Street. Both his brothers were married and had two children each, plus there was a young granddaughter, so Christmas was big and noisy.

Now Ma and Ann were alone again, Ann puzzled over how and what to say to Ma. She didn't want to spoil the day, so she said nothing.

The two of them talked about how the absent three were spending Christmas Day. Muriel would be at the mansion eating pheasant and drinking champagne with David Niven, Hilda would be out sledging with polar bears in fifty feet of snow, and Joe would be playing football on the top deck somewhere in the Pacific. Ma was convinced something bad must have happened to him because he hadn't sent a card.

No carol singers came round. The weather was probably too bad for them to venture out. Ann and Ma had their dinner, then sat and stared into the fire and listened to the Christmas music on the radio. Fred didn't come back. They knew he wasn't stupid enough to go out in what was now a full-blown blizzard.

'Staying upright might be beyond him by now,' Ann suggested.

'It's Christmas,' Ma said. 'The man's allowed a wee drink.'

Early in the evening, acrid black sooty smoke blew down the chimney. There was no way to let it out, so they just had to wait for it to settle. As they waited, they had a nightcap and made a toast to Fred, the bringer of good whiskey. Then Ann insisted they have another.

'To Walter and the future, whatever it brings.' They clinked their glasses together, savouring their wee snug oasis.

'Happy Christmas, love. Walter will be all right. I know he will.'

'Happy Christmas, Ma. Me and you against the world,' and she hugged her spindly ma as tightly as she thought was safe. 'I'm going to bed. It's been a lovely day.'

'It has love. I'm going too. I'll sort out the fire.'

'Great.' Ann smiled. 'Get it? Grate.'

'Yes, love. Very good.' They were both a bit tipsy. 'Night, night. No work tomorrow, thank God.'

'Yes, Ma. Thank God.'

* * *

Since it was Boxing Day, Ma had a rare Monday off. She had an even rarer lie-in and didn't get up until nearly nine, by which time Ann had brought in the coal, cleaned out the grate, lit the fire, washed the dishes they'd left soaking overnight, dried them and put them away.

She was singing 'O Come, All Ye Faithful' as she put the kettle back on the hob to make tea. Ma came down in her dressing gown, an ancient threadbare candlewick robe that might have been pink once. Her hair wasn't brushed. It was frizzy and sticking out in all directions.

'Looking good this morning, Ma.'

'No need to be so cheeky. It's my day off.'

'If anyone deserves a day off it's you. No need for airs and graces today. Only Fred might call over later, so you'll need to be looking gorgeous for that.'

'Fred doesn't care what I look like.'

'He'd run a mile if he saw you right now.'

'Fred couldn't run the length of himself. He used to be able to run, before the war.'

'The Boer War?'

'Now, now.'

'Tea?'

'Aye, and a bit of that wheaten.'

'Toasted?'

'That would be lovely.'

The morning passed quietly. They had cold chicken for lunch. The snow had turned to rain during the night. Then the rain stopped and the wind eased and Ann suggested they go for a dander. Ma looked at her as if she was mad.

'Just up the town and back. A breath of air will do us the world of good.'

‘The paths will be all slushy,’ Ma protested.

‘We can put our wellies on. Look at everyone else out in their Christmas style.’

To walk just for the sake of walking was an alien concept, but it was Boxing Day and it seemed like the right thing to do.

Ma smiled. ‘You seem a bit more like your old self,’ she said. ‘I knew a quiet day off was all you needed.’

They got wrapped up with scarves and hats and, arms linked, set off up the town. The shops were all shut, except for Devlin’s, but the Christmas lights were gleaming and the tree outside the courthouse was lit up.

‘Nuala Devlin could be in her grave and she’d still open up,’ Ma said, as they walked past the busy little shop. She struggled up the Courthouse Hill and they stopped at one of the new seats that had been installed outside the post office. Ann dried the seat as best she could with her hanky.

The incline was so steep where the bench was perched, that Ann, who sat on the lower end, couldn’t put her feet on the ground.

They got their breath back, then Ann inhaled deeply and began. ‘Ma?’

‘That sounds like an ominous *Ma* if ever I heard one,’ Ma said.

‘I’ve something to tell you. You’re the first to know, apart from Walter, of course. I’ve thought about how to tell you and I’ve decided the best thing to do is just come out with it.’

‘That’s usually the best way. Don’t beat about the bush. What is it?’

‘I told Walter on Christmas Eve that as soon as he’s better, we’re going to get married.’

Ma patted Ann on the leg. 'Oh, Ann, love, that's great news, but should he not be asking you? You just told him?'

'You know what he's like. He'll be Fred's age before he gets round to asking, and even then, he'll dither, so I made the decision for both of us.'

'I suppose he couldn't say no, could he?'

'No, but I think he smiled, which I took as a yes.'

'Sounds like a yes to me,' Ma paused. 'But I wonder if you shouldn't wait awhile. You're both still very young and you're so bright and ambitious.'

Ann turned her face away and swung her legs as Ma talked.

'Have you any idea, how long it might be before he can ask you properly and you can start to make plans?' Ma went on.

'It can't be too long, because I have other news for you.' Ann looked straight at her mother.

Ma's eyes opened wide; her lips became a tight straight line. She gripped Ann's hand tightly. 'Tell me you're not going to say what I think you're going to say? Tell me you're not,' she pleaded. She looked scared.

Ann's worst fears were instantly realised. Ma looked genuinely shocked, like her world had ended. More than shocked, she looked – disappointed – a dagger into Ann's very being. There was no bigger taboo than being pregnant before you were married.

'I don't know for certain, but I'm pretty sure,' Ann said. 'I've been feeling a bit off. You've noticed it yourself.'

'I thought it was everything you've been having to cope with lately. You're a clever girl and I warned ye often enough!'

'It isn't your fault, Ma.'

Ma leaned back against the back of the bench, shaking her head. 'You'll have to get rid of it. You can try again when Walter's better. No one need ever know. We can sort it out. You could go over to Muriel for a bit. How on earth did it happen? When?'

Ann's heart sank into her shoes, which were dangling three inches above the pavement. Could she tell her mother what had really happened?

'Remember the night of the party?'

'You said you had a row.'

'Walter had a wee drink. He wasn't drunk, he was excited about the party. We both were. We'd planned to do it at the party. It would be our first time and it was supposed to be all romantic. I hoped we'd get engaged. I told him to get something from the barber's, but he got all flustered and sort of rushed things.'

'But you didn't go to the party. Where did it happen?'

'We went out for a fag after the dance. He said that eejit Soup had told him that his da had said that you can't get pregnant if you did it standing up.'

'And you believed him?' Ma shook her head in disbelief.

'I told him Dr Bowles didn't know his arse from his elbow, which was a big problem for a doctor, but he wouldn't listen.'

'Did he force himself on you?' Ma was looking intently at her daughter.

'No … maybe … sort of … not really. I told him to stop, but he wouldn't. He couldn't. It hurt a bit – well, more than a bit – but it was over very fast and I got mad at him and slapped him and told him to eff off and that I never wanted to see him again 'cause he'd ruined everything. He'd wrecked our big romantic night. I stormed off and left him and came home. I heard him shouting that he loved me.'

'And Walter staggered off and got hit by a van?'

'He must have been very upset. He wasn't thinking straight.' Ann was crying

'The sooner you do this, the easier it'll be. You say nobody else knows yet. You need to be realistic.'

This was it now, Ann thought. 'I'm not getting rid of our child, Ma,' she said. 'Walter will be better soon. We'll get married and everything will be all right.'

'You're not thinking straight! What if he doesn't get better before you start to show? Or never gets better?' Another sharp dagger to the heart. 'You might never be able to get married. To anyone. No one will believe that it's Walter's, knowing the state he's in. I see no good outcomes here. You just can't keep it, love. It's not possible. It's for the best.'

They'd never had an argument before, certainly nothing significant. There had never been anything serious to disagree about.

'I'm going to have it, Ma. It's not just mine, it's Walter's. It's ours and we're going to get married.'

'By all means get married as soon as poor Walter is able. But only if he *is* able and can support a family.' Ma was exasperated. 'Then you can have as many weans as you like. But if you go through with this, you'll lose your job. My gentlemen will be scandalised, so I'll be out on my ear too. Then what'll we do? Goodman won't even christen it. You could end up in one of those mother-and-baby places. It can't happen. It just can't.' Ma took her glasses off. Shaking her head she rubbed her eyes.

'I'm having it, Ma, and before you say anything, I'm not going to give it away either – not to the church, not to anyone.'

'So what are you going to do? You can't stay here if you have it,' Ma said.

'I have to stay. Who's going to look after you?'

'I can look after myself. I've always looked after myself, ever since that useless ...' Ma snapped her mouth shut before she said any more.

'You were younger then, Ma – younger than I am now. You'd be alone. I want to stay and look after you, just like you always looked after me.'

Ma could see the determination shining in her youngest daughter's beautiful face and in her fierce green eyes. She had long tried to fathom why her other children had wanted to leave. But she came to understand that to keep them, she had to let them go. They were chasing their dreams, but this was different. This was beyond awful. It wasn't just the wrong man, or the wrong job, or gallivanting off to the four corners of the world. This was much worse. This was as bad as things could get.

'We should go home. We can't talk here. Too many people about,' Ma said. Just then they spotted Mrs Chesney lurching up the hill.

'Yes, Ma. There must be a way out of this ... I was going to say mess, and I know you think there couldn't be a worse mess, but it'll have a happy ending, I know it will.' Ann wasn't sure if she believed a word of of what she'd just said.

Ma looked disgusted. 'And you and Walter and baby Walter will live happily ever after? This isn't a fairy tale, Ann. This is a really big problem. You have to realise that.'

'I do, Ma. I know how hard this is for you – for both of us – but it'll all work out. It has to. It just has to.' Had Ma noticed the desperation in her voice? A new grandchild should be a happy thing. Having Ma disappointed in her was the worst thing of all.

They went home, made tea, had a mince pie and hashed out all the 'what ifs,' and 'what nots' and 'maybes'. Then Fred turned up. Fred could tell that he had arrived in the middle of something huge, so he suggested they have a wee dram – to oil the wheels, as it were.

Ann caught Ma's glance and knew she wanted to tell Fred. He was her most trusted friend. Ann nodded her agreement, so they sat by the fire and talked and by the time Fred got up to leave, his wheels a bit less oiled than he had anticipated, they had an outline of a plan. Ann wanted to dance around the room with Fred she was so relieved, but she settled for a big hug instead.

'See you later, Fred. Can't wait to hear what she says.'

Fred called back at half nine and the plan started to take shape.

Ma was dubious and pessimistic, to say the least. Their crazy idea would never work, she said. Ann and Fred were much more positive. Fred proved vital in convincing Ma. They ganged up on her and gradually, reluctantly, she agreed to go along with it. They all had another wee drop of Coleraine and Ann left them to talk, listen to the radio, and hopefully have a wee dance. As she tried to sleep, she wondered why Ma had never married Fred. Her mind was whirling and spinning, just like it had that day at Barry's. She would take her baby to Barry's as soon as he was old enough and that thought eased her mind enough to allow her to drift into a deep, dreamless sleep.

She didn't hear Ma asking Fred if he really thought their ridiculous plan would work, or Fred replying that it had to work or she would lose Ann as well.

CHAPTER 36

The next day, Ann got into the office early. She'd had a good sleep, had washed her hair and put on her best work dress.

'Good morning, Ann. You look very bright and breezy and full of the joys this morning,' Mrs Crammond said. 'Santa must have been good to you.'

'He was indeed, Mrs Crammond.' Ann did a little twirl. 'New raincoat. What do you think? It's Firestone.'

'Lovely colour. You suit green and you'll certainly need it in this weather.'

'Yes, it's another beautiful day in sunny Omagh. Was Santa good to you as well?'

'Santa ran out of good ideas twenty years ago, love. He must have a lifetime supply of cheap perfume and fags, that's all I can say.'

'Oh dear! You'll have to write to him next year. Get him to buck his ideas up.'

'I think they're unbuckable.' Mrs Crammond smiled the smile of a world-weary wife. 'How's Walter getting on?'

'Getting better, but it could take ages. I was wondering … it's why I'm in so early … I was wondering if there was any way I could get a transfer to Belfast. Just till he gets well enough to come home.'

'How long do you think that will be?'

'No idea. Even the doctors don't know, but I'd like to be able to see him every day. The doctors say it helps if I'm there to talk to him as much as possible.'

'Ach, I feel for you, I really do. Such a tragic thing to happen and on the night you got engaged and all. It's so sad. You're a good worker and I'd hate to lose you, but I'll see what I can do. Can't promise anything, mind, but I'll ask. That's all I can do. It might take a while to sort something out, so don't hold your breath.'

'I understand. Thank you! Thank you so much!' Ann skipped to her desk and the day flew in.

'How can I go to Belfast and leave you here on your own?' she asked Ma later.

'I've been on my own all my life, love. It'll be like a holiday, with only myself to worry about.'

'But you've never been alone before.'

'I have Fred and the neighbours. I'll go to church with Dora or Betty. I'll be fine.'

'Fred doesn't go to church, does he?'

'No, he's a Methodist, God love him.'

'I hope you won't get up to anything while I'm away!'

'We're just friends and that's all we've ever been.' Ma sounded a tad wistful. Could Ann detect the faintest hint of disappointment?

'And you're still certain we can't tell Hilda, or Muriel, or anyone?'

'Absolutely not. No. The fewer people who know the

better. Less lies for us to remember, and what they don't know can't harm them. Or us.'

In bed, Ann longed for the old days when her sisters were still at home and life was simple

* * *

Ann went for a walk on her own after dinner. It was New Year's Eve. She had decided not to go to Belfast. She was too tired. The courthouse was all lit up like a wonderland. She was disappointed to be missing that year's ball, remembering the magical night it had been last year. But she had to deal with all the grown-up, serious, sad stuff now, the stuff she and Walter thought they could put off forever. Now, on the cusp of a new decade, on the brink of a new life, she felt grown up. But she wasn't sad, she was just serious about dealing with whatever lay ahead.

Ma was going along with the plan reluctantly. Her life would be over if anyone discovered what had happened. The 'how' would always remain secret. The Greens were suffering enough. The risks were huge; the shame would be total. The thought of Ma being against her was unbearable. The thought of her being alone was just as bad. She hoped it wouldn't come down to choosing between her ma and her baby. She could and she would do this.

She and Ma sat up with Fred to listen to Big Ben ring in the new year on the radio and raised a glass to 1950. They all agreed it couldn't be worse than the forties. The economy would pick up, rationing would end and the new NHS seemed to be a great idea. Ma still couldn't see how it could work, for her anyway. She got paid in cash and made no National Insurance contributions. Would she still get free treatment? She found this incomprehensible but toasted it anyway.

They reminisced about the war. Fred had very flat feet, so hadn't been allowed to join up, but like everyone else, he had lost a lot of friends and relatives in a conflict that was still very fresh in everyone's minds.

Ma refused to be drawn about her husband, except to say that he ended up with the Gloucestershire Regiment before he had to leave the army on health grounds. That was the pneumonia that eventually killed him in 1937.

Ann tried to prise more information out of her but got nowhere. 'Time for bed,' Ma announced and set her glass down.

'It's your lucky night, Fred,' said Ann and immediately regretted it. 'Sorry, Ma. Sorry, Fred. Didn't mean anything. Just a wee bit tipsy.'

'So you should be. Don't listen to her, Fred. She can have a vicious tongue in her head at times.'

Fred just smiled. When the drink's in and all that.

Ann felt like death warmed up the next morning and blamed that last whiskey. Or was it morning sickness? She was glad she didn't have to go to work, but Ma insisted on church. The service was shorter than normal, but Ann thought the sermon would never end. Her head was throbbing. She felt like boking. That would get the congregation and the whole town talking! Ma looked at her without any semblance of sympathy.

Ann fell into bed early.

'Work tomorrow, love.'

'Yes, Ma.'

Mrs Crammond had no news about a transfer to Belfast. 'Nothing happens over Christmas,' she said. 'Patience. Everything comes to those who wait.'

Ann wondered just how long she could wait as she went to her desk.

CHAPTER 37

Joe's Christmas card arrived on the 7th of January.

> *In Hong Kong. Very hot. Captain of the ship's football team. Ate an octopus. Deelish. I'm well and hope you are too. Happy Xmas. Love Joe. XXX*

The Christmas decorations had been put away, but they placed Joe's card on the mantelpiece. It had a picture of a robin on a piece of holly.

Ann went up to Belfast. No change, but Walter did seem to wriggle more at the sound of her voice.

'What was Christmas like in here then?' She put his hand on her belly. Walter gurgled and moved his index finger. She held it like you would a baby's, crooked around her little finger. She kissed his ghostly white cheek.

'You need to start shaving, Walter Green. Don't do it yourself for God's sake. That would make things worse, if they could be worse. Anyway, we have a plan. I can't tell you too much in case you spill the beans to Sinead or Dr Healy, but it's a good plan. Fred and I think so anyway. Ma thinks it's mad, but she's going along with it because she doesn't want me to leave like the rest of them. She trusts Fred, so we're all ready to go. It means I'm not giving up our baby, not for anyone, not even Ma, and it means that when you get better, we can get married. You have to get better fast, Walter, for us, for the baby.'

She tousled his hair, which had got long and even more curly.

Walter gurgled.

'I hope you stop making that bloody noise before the baby starts. Two of you gurgling at the same time will do my head in. Maybe I should learn to gurgle and then we could have a proper conversation.' She imagined the vaguest hint of a smile on Walter's face.

'The plan means I'll be moving up here to Belfast, so I can visit you every day. The nurses say lots of company and chat will help you recover faster. I know you love to listen to me, so that's something for you to look forward to, eh? But not a word to Sinead or anyone! Especially not your parents.' She put her finger on his pale lips.

She left soon afterwards, wishing Sinead and her family a Happy New Year. This was the first day she'd walked along the Grosvenor Road that it wasn't raining. Sod's law – new raincoat, no rain.

She found the right bus stop near the City Hall and got a bus up the Ravenhill Road. She got off at London Road and walked the short distance to the address she had been given. Ann knocked the brass knocker and Mrs Evans opened the door.

'You must be Ann. Come in. Fred told me you'd probably be calling today. It's very sad about your Walter. Is he going to be all right?'

Mrs Evans was a short round ball of a woman with steely grey hair like a pan scrubber that framed a kindly red face. She looked exactly like her brother, but with hair.

'This is very kind of you, Mrs Evans. I didn't even know Fred had a sister until the other night and when he told us what you did, we couldn't believe it.'

'Fred explained all about you and Walter. That you want to have your baby in secret, away from prying eyes. Obviously, my Henry knows and Pamela – that's my daughter – but absolutely no one else will ever know anything. You'll meet them soon enough. Henry will be home soon for his tea. Between you and me, we've done this before. Absolute discretion is vital, so please, trust me. You and the baby will be fine.'

Ann had no option but to trust the chatty Mrs Evans. They had a cup of tea. *Not strong enough and too much milk.* Ann had a million questions and Mrs Evans answered them all. She certainly seemed to know what she was talking about and Ann relaxed just a bit.

Henry arrived home just after five. He was a thin, wiry wee man and smelled of smoke and beer.

'Henry will run you back down the town. Won't you, Henry?'

Henry looked like a man who had given up disagreeing a long time ago.

'No problem, love. You're getting the train?'

'Yes, back to Omagh.'

'We've been to Omagh many's the time, haven't we, Gladys? Down to visit the brothers. Bogan's is a nice wee bar there on the Main Street.'

They chatted about local landmarks for a few minutes, then it was time to go.

Henry had a little black car with green leather seats. It smelled of smoke and beer as well. It shook itself and backfired a few times before getting going, but they made it in good time. Henry didn't say much or ask questions, but he did tell her not to worry.

'Gladys knows what she's doing,' he added, 'You wouldn't believe some of the great and the good who've used her services and recommended her to their posh friends.'

Ann suddenly wondered if she had to pay for all this. Did she need to pay rent? It hadn't crossed her mind before. Fred would know.

Back in Omagh, she walked up to see Mr and Mrs Green and gave them an update on their son's progress. They all agreed that at least he didn't seem to be in any pain or distress.

'We're the ones in distress,' Mr Green said. 'Walter seems happy in Walterland.'

Ann didn't mention anything else.

The days passed in a whirl of work, trains and exhaustion. Mrs Crammond still had no word of a posting to Belfast. If it didn't happen soon, it might be too late. How would she pay Mrs Evans? She began to pick holes in the plan. Did the posting even matter? She would have to leave work soon anyway. Wouldn't people still talk if she returned in a few months' time, married, with Walter and a baby? Suppose Walter never got better? Nothing for it but to carry on and hope for the best.

She was getting to know the conductors on the trains. Billy was on most Saturdays, but if he wasn't there, it was Sammy. Once they knew why she travelled so regularly, they seemed genuinely concerned about Walter and always asked how he was getting on.

'Tell him you can have a free trip to Portrush on us when

he gets out of that bed,' Billy promised her. He told her to keep smiling. She was young and pretty and obviously had brains. Everything passed. Time took care of that.

Ann realised that she would have to be careful what she said to Billy and Sammy as they obviously knew Mr Green. More potential land mines.

Mr Green spoke to the doctors more than she did. They said the same thing every time – vital signs were good; he had a strong heart; they were able to get soft food into him now.

'Goo stew,' Mr Green called it.

Walter put on weight and they stopped the pain relief. The X-rays were clear, so there wasn't much more the hospital could do, except try and stimulate him and get him more active.

'Like giving a child a rattle,' Mr Green reckoned.

Mrs Green cried again.

Mr Green had asked the big hard question, but the doctors were non-committal. 'Too early to say. Let's wait and see. The brain is a wonderful thing and he could snap out of this any time.'

But Mr Green wasn't convinced. Mrs Green said she wanted to believe more than anything in the world.

Meanwhile, Baby Walter was getting bigger and starting to kick. Ann needed to make a decision. She had to leave. She told Mrs Crammond one Thursday morning that she couldn't wait any longer. She had to go and be with Walter. That was the medical advice and every day counted. Familiar voices talking to him was the best therapy of all. She apologised, said she would work that day but she was off to Belfast in the morning.

'So soon! What will you do for money?' Mrs Crammond seemed genuinely concerned.

'I'm going to stay with an auntie, so I won't have to pay rent. I've a few pounds saved. I'll get a job. But I'll miss everyone here. You've been so good to me through all this.'

'Good luck is all I can say. We'll miss you too. You're a fast learner and you've slotted right in with our wee team. This Walter business is so unfortunate. I hope it all works out for you.'

Unfortunate didn't come close. She thanked Mrs Crammond for everything and after work went home to pack. One little cardboard suitcase with rusty clips that had belonged to her da was all she had and all she needed.

Ma looked old and tired. She was snoozing in her chair when Ann came down. There was no dinner ready.

'Sorry, love. I fell asleep. It won't take long to boil a few spuds, and there's eggs.' She went to stand up.

'Don't worry about it. You sit there. I'll sort it out. You have a wee rest.'

She went out to the privy and sat on the cold, cracked, wooden toilet seat. Elbows on her knees, she put her head in her hands.

The simple thing to do would be to get rid of the baby and stay and look after Ma. Didn't she owe Ma more than she owed Walter? More than she owed the baby? Did she love Walter more than she loved Ma? Stupid questions. Nobody should have to answer questions like that.

She went back to the kitchen and stood hypnotised by the rolling, boiling water in the saucepan. 'A watched pot never boils,' Ma always said, and right then she almost hoped it was true. She wished she could just stand there forever watching the water.

Their last dinner together was spuds and a fried egg. The yolks broke and the eggs stuck to the ancient, blackened pan.

The two women didn't talk much. They didn't have to.

Fred called and pressed a ten-pound note into Ann's hand when Ma wasn't looking. He put his finger up to his lips. Another secret.

'Fred gave me a tenner,' she announced as soon as he left and she held it up for Ma to see.

'He must be made of money. You should give it back to him. He's done enough for us. We don't need charity.'

'It's not charity if a friend gives it to you. It's a gift, but I can leave it here if you want and you can give it back to him tomorrow.'

'No, love. You keep it. You'll probably need it. It's a lot of money, so be careful.'

'Yes, Ma. I'll keep it down my knickers. Nobody'll find it there.' They smiled at each other. They put on the radio. The music was soft and slow. They sat up late, not wanting the evening to end. There was no need to talk.

Friday dawned. There was tea and toast, then hugs and tears.

Mr Green was at the station, resplendent in his porter's uniform. He slipped a fiver into Ann's hand. 'Good luck, love. This is a big thing you're doing.'

'There's no need, honestly.'

'You're giving up your job and leaving your Ma so you can spend more time with my boy to try and make him better. There's a need all right. I'm just sorry I couldn't give you more. But if you're ever stuck, please ask. We'll help if we can, and if you don't need it, sure you can always give it back when you bring Walter home.'

'That's a deal, Mr Green,' and she shook his hand. 'Oh, one more thing. Is it possible to call you, here at the station?'

'Aye. That's a good idea. It's Omagh 279. If I'm about, someone will come and get me.' He lifted her case and carried it to the train. 'Mrs Green and I will still go up to see him on Thursdays, so that could be your day off, if you want. No point all of us going at the same time.'

Ann hadn't thought about meeting the Greens in the hospital. The idea filled her with horror!

'Oh, that's very thoughtful, Mr Green. I want to see him every day, but it might be nice to have a break.'

She breathed a huge sigh of relief as she boarded the train. Mr Green put her case up on the rack for her. 'Good luck, love,' he said and he left her alone.

Same seat, same stops, same views. Different world.

* * *

In Belfast, she got the bus up to London Road. Mrs Evans made her a cup of tea after she'd unpacked in her bedroom. It was at the back of the house overlooking a small overgrown garden.

They had a piece of Battenburg cake. She'd never had such a treat before. The yellow and pink chequerboard cake wrapped in marzipan was very fancy.

She went to see Walter. He got very agitated when she appeared. He started wriggling and gurgling. Was he happy to see her, or was it some sort of fit? Nobody knew. He gradually calmed down and renewed his impersonation of a corpse.

She sat up close to him, held his hand and said into his ear, 'I love you Walter Green.' She squeezed his hand and felt him squeeze back. She wasn't imagining it this time. He knew it was her.

'The plan has started,' she said, 'but remember – not a word to anyone.'

They sat mostly in silence until it was time for her to go.

Back in London Road, Ann was helping Mrs Evans lay the table for dinner.

'Pass me them plates, love.' Ann handed her dishes from the small dresser in the dining room. 'It's been a while since I've had to lay the table for three.'

'How long has Pamela been away?'

'A few years now. She was working in a solicitor's office, and the next thing you know, she's marrying one of them. A solicitor, I mean, not a Catholic.'

'My first job was in a solicitor's office,' Ann said and told Mrs Evans the story of how she met Walter.

'And was it love at first sight?'

'Sort of. He was a bit dozy at the start and I loved teasing him, but I knew he fancied me.' Then she told her about their dancing days.

'I used to love a wee dance myself,' Mrs Evans said.

'I've been going to the dances in the Starr since I was fourteen. I love it more than anything. I dreamt about becoming a dancer.' Her heart sank as the words came out. She knew this dream was dead.

'There's still time. You're still young. You'll get your figure back quickly.'

'There are more important things to do now. No time for dreaming. What does the Bible say about putting away childish things?'

'When you're older maybe.'

In bed that night Ann reflected on the day: a house with an inside toilet, hot water at the turn of a tap, a proper bath, electric lights, and a telephone! She felt a big twang of guilt. Was she being selfish? It was all about her, her and Walter, her and the baby, her and Walter and the baby. How much had Ma been through and done and given and she had nothing? Yet Ma always seemed to want nothing and expect nothing. She knew there was a bitterness there about Da, but Ma seemed to be at the bottom of an ocean of melancholic acceptance of everything. That was just the way life was. Nothing more, nothing less. Nobody's fault.

CHAPTER 38

As the days slowly lengthened and when the weather was good, Ann took the short walk over to Ormeau Park. There was nowhere in Omagh like it – a huge expanse of grass, flower beds and trees. It was still winter, so it was empty and it was beautiful.

She told Walter about the park and what they would do when the baby was born. They would go for walks, pushing the pram, and feed the ducks. They would picnic on egg and onion sandwiches, buns and beer. He seemed to like this idea – but he seemed to like every idea. He gave her the same response to everything.

'Do you know what day it is today? It's Thursday, the 2nd of February. Happy birthday, Walter. You're twenty today. I brought you a piece of cake, but I suppose you don't like fruitcake. I'll eat it if you don't want it.'

She began to sing 'Happy Birthday'. The nurses came and joined in. She cried as she ate the cake.

The day finally arrived when she ran out of things to talk about. They just quietly held hands for hours, her mind blank.

Then suddenly she had an idea: she'd ask Mrs Evans if she could phone Muriel and get her to get Dr Al to give her a call. She could ask him what *he* thought of Walter's condition. She'd offer to pay for the phone call, of course, but she hoped Mrs Evans wouldn't hear of it and would tell her to put her money away.

'How was he today, love?' Mrs Evans asked as she always did when she returned to London Road.

Ann removed her coat and hung it on the wooden hatstand in the hall. 'The same. There are times I think he's making progress, and the next minute I think he's not. Something should be happening. It's been three months!'

'These things take time, love.' Mrs Evans sounded as if she knew about these things. 'You have to trust the doctors, but you have to look after yourself as well. You'll be no good to anyone if you make yourself sick with worry, and too much stress isn't good for the little one. Even now it can tell if you're stressed.'

'Really?'

'If you're poorly, the baby will be poorly. It's part of you. It depends on you for everything, so you need to mind yourself.'

'I will. Can I ask you something?'

'You know you can ask me anything.'

She told Mrs Evans about Dr Tolleshunt-Darcy and how he was a top psychiatrist and she would love to have a chat with him, if possible, about Walter.

'Your sister must have made quite an impression on this chap.'

'Yes, she could charm the birds out of the trees. Could I phone her? I'll pay for it, of course.'

'Of course, you can and don't worry about the money. Henry pays the bills. He never looks at them. He just does what he's told, God love him.'

'Would now be all right?'

'You're exhausted. Maybe best to try her in the morning.'

If only Ma had a telephone, Ann thought as she went up to bed that night, but that dream seemed further away than ever. She knew Fred would pay for it, but Ma would hate that. Why did everything have to be so difficult?

The next morning, she rang Muriel.

'Muriel!' the high-pitched cockney voice pierced Ann's eardrum. 'It's your skin and blister again.'

'Ann, what's wrong? Is Ma sick?'

'Hello to you too and how are you keepin'?'

Muriel ignored the pleasantries. 'Is everything okay?'

Ann hadn't thought through how to explain the situation without creating a minefield of lies that would almost certainly blow up in her face. All Muriel knew was that Walter was in hospital. The last time they'd spoken was just after Christmas.

'We're fine. I've moved up to Belfast. I'm staying up here for a while to be closer to Walter, so I can visit every day.'

'Oh, Ann! Is he still no better? Is Ma on her own? Where are you staying? Have you got a job? What are you doing for money?'

'Slow down, Mu. Too many questions. I'm staying with a lovely lady called Mrs Evans. I bet you didn't know Fred has a younger sister.'

'She must be nice if she's Fred's sister. What about work?'

'I asked for a transfer, but there wasn't one available quickly enough, so I just upped and left.'

'Typical. So what are you doing for money?'

'I have a wee bit saved up and …' And so the lies began. 'Mrs Evans isn't charging me any rent until I can afford it. She's so good. Her husband, Henry, is the manager of a pub. They have a lovely house with an inside loo and everything.'

'You must think Walter's going to be in hospital for a long time, by the sound of it.'

'I don't know. Nobody seems to know. All I get is "wait and see" and "you must be patient" and "these things take time".'

'They're probably right. You sound wrecked. You must be worried sick by all this.'

'I'm coping, but it's been a long few months. Walter still isn't speaking or properly conscious. The thing is, I was wondering if you could ask Al to ring me. I'd love to speak to him and see what he thinks about Walter.'

'I'm sure he'd be happy to, but he might not be able to tell you too much about a patient he's never seen.'

'I know, but I'd still like to have a chat with him. He might have a few ideas. How is he by the way?'

'He's in good form. Very busy trying to put all the ideas he got from Uncle Louis into place here.'

'Have you been out to his castle again? What are the Lord and Lady like?'

'It's not a castle. It's a manor house and his ma and da are lovely. Very down to earth.'

Ann quizzed her a bit more about Al, his posh family and all the famous people he might know, and about their relationship.

'But to get back to you,' Muriel interrupted. 'What'll you do if you get a job and then Walter gets better and they send him home?

'I'll go home too. There's plenty of jobs for the fastest shorthand typist in the world.'

'A shilling in your pocket, young lady.'

'Yes, Ma.'

'And if he doesn't recover?'

'One bridge at a time.' Ann sighed. She was bursting to tell her sister everything. 'Anyhow, no sign of a ring yet?'

'Can't say. It's all top secret and confidential.'

'That's a yes then.' Ann was genuinely excited.

'No, it's not a yes. It's just not a no. It's another wait and see.'

'I hope the wedding's in Omagh.'

'Now you're the one crossing bridges!'

'I'd better go. I'm using Mrs Evans's phone. It's Belfast 942. Ask Al to ring me if he gets a chance.'

'I'll speak to him today. Look after yourself and give my love to Walter and Ma. When will you see her next?'

'Not sure. I ring Fred from here now and again and Walter's da. They both call in to see Ma nearly every day, so they let me know how she's keeping. I think she's all right, but you know she'll never say if she isn't.'

'Yeah, I know what she's like. Anyway, got to go. I'll speak to Al. Love to all. Tell Fred I was asking about him. I miss you. Bye.'

'I miss you too,' Ann said, but Muriel was gone.

Al rang the next day at lunchtime. Mrs Evans answered the phone. 'It's for you,' she whispered to Ann. 'It must be your doctor man. He sounds very posh.'

Ann took the handset and sat on the bottom stair out in the hallway.

'Ann? It's Al here. Is it a convenient time for you to talk? Muriel told me about Walter and I can imagine how worried you must be.'

You could pour his voice over a sponge cake, it was so rich and syrupy. After thanking him for ringing her back so quickly, Ann told him what she knew about Walter – his gurgling, his baby grip, his Mona Lisa smile and his very little else. And the X-ray results.

'I've heard of Mr Butcher. He's an expert in his field, so I've no concerns about the surgical side of things. But it's hard for me to comment on the psychiatric aspects of Walter's condition without seeing him. Not being my patient, it would be difficult and irresponsible for me to make any assessments, either about his condition or his treatment, except please try not to worry too much. I know that's easy to say and much harder to do, but please be patient, if you pardon the pun. Sometimes a patient's recovery is very gradual and sometimes it's very quick. You just have to wait and see.'

Ann sighed. It was more of the same.

'You must think of yourself and your immediate plans. If you make yourself ill with worry, you'll be no good to Walter should he recover, and that's when he'll need you most.'

Ann wanted so much to tell him about her *immediate plans.* 'I understand and you're right, but it's hard to think of anything else.'

'You must focus on your future and your career, as well as visiting Walter as often as possible. He almost certainly knows you're there, and hearing your voice is the best stimulus for him at the moment. Muriel told me you've moved to Belfast to be near him. That's good and it's all you can do. I'm sorry I haven't been much help. Would it make a difference if Muriel took some time off and went home for a while?'

Ann panicked. 'No, no need for that. Thank you. No, you've been a great help. It's good to hear another expert confirming things for me. It's just been so long with no end in sight and no guarantees that he'll ever recover. I can't tell you how much I need him to get better. In the meantime, all I can do is keep er lit and hope for the best.'

'Yes, keep 'er lit. Muriel taught me that. Very good.

Anyway, I must dash, Ann. Look after yourself. Best regards to your mum.'

'Thanks, Al. Goodbye.' Ann got up from the stairs and put the handset back on its cradle. She went into the front room, from where she assumed Mrs Evans had been listening.

'Tea?' she asked, her face confirming that she had heard everything.

CHAPTER 39

Spring brought a sea of daffodils to Ormeau Park.

Ann caressed her bump. 'Wait till your Daddy sees these. I've never seen so many in one place. I'll read you a famous poem about daffodils someday when you're a bit older.'

Her walks took more and more out of her, but the fresh air did her good. She was tired all the time. Mrs Evans, Henry and Pamela couldn't do enough for her. Pamela worked part-time in her husband's office. They had no children but Ann gathered from her conversation that they had been trying for a while. She seemed a bit jealous of Ann – of the baby. She was very friendly and called every other day to see how everyone was and to help out.

As a midwife, Mrs Evans was out a lot, delivering babies left, right and centre, and Pamela filled the gaps.

'Your ma and da have a lovely house here. You're very lucky,' Ann said to her one day when they were alone.

'Yes, it's nice, but I don't know about being lucky. You're the lucky one, with a wee one on the way.'

'And Walter lying up there with a broken brain.'

'My Sammy's brain might not be broken, but I think something else is.' Pamela had a naughty laugh. 'I'm nearly thirty. Time's running out.'

'Have you thought about adopting?'

'It's maybe getting to that stage, but we haven't discussed it much. Sammy is always busy. Typical man. He can't talk about this kind of thing very easily.'

'Walter didn't talk much either. He just did it.'

'And did you not want him to?'

'I did and I didn't, but obviously, things haven't worked out like we'd planned.'

'So you've a baby and no husband and I've a husband and no baby. Whatever happened to happily ever after, that's what I'd like to know.'

The thought flashed through Ann's head that just a few months ago winning a dance competition with Walter would have been her idea of happy ever after.

'I know you're determined to have your baby and I'd be the same, but what if Walter stays like that?' Pamela asked. 'What will you do?'

'He *will* recover and we have a plan.' Ann tried to sound convincing.

Pamela picked up on Ann's shaky confidence and her brow furrowed. 'I hope so, I really do, but if … well … if you change your mind, please let me know. Sammy and I can give your baby a good home and we'd love it to bits.'

Ann was shocked. She hadn't seen that coming. 'I'm so sorry if I gave you the wrong impression, Pamela. I know how much you want a baby, but I don't think I'll be changing my mind. I've never even considered giving up this child and never will, no matter what happens.'

'We can pay. More than the going rate. Ma says she's been offered up to fifty pounds for a healthy baby girl.'

'Oh Pamela! Please ... please don't.'

Pamela got all flustered and embarrassed. 'I better go. Please don't tell Ma we had this conversation. She knows I'm getting desperate and I know she'll be able to help if I ask her.'

When Pamela rushed out, Ann sat in disbelief. Mrs Evans got babies for people for money! Did Fred know? Did Ma know? Were they all in this together? Was there another plan that she didn't know about?

Ann had no idea what to do now. Who could she confide in? Maybe this was all in her head, and there was no master plan to take her baby away from her. She had to think, so she went to the park and counted the daffodils.

When she got back, Mrs Evans was home. They had tea in the sitting room bathed in the spring sunshine.

'Can I ask you something?' Ann said.

'Of course, anything. Is it about the baby? The birth?'

'Sort of. I was wondering about people who can't have children. I've heard they sometimes pay to get a baby – you know, one that the mother can't keep? Would you know anything about that, being a midwife? I mean, how much could I get if I decided not to keep it?'

'Have you been talking to Pamela?'

Ann shook her head unconvincingly.

'Let me explain and perhaps I can put your mind at rest. Yes, I sometimes come across young girls who get pregnant and aren't ready, or more importantly, aren't married. Keeping the baby just isn't possible. They have very few options. They can get an abortion, but it would be backstreet – possibly dangerous and certainly expensive. Or they can go to a mother-and-baby unit where they'll find a home for the baby. The Catholic church runs a few of these, but they aren't nice places. Often the mums end up working in laundries run by the nuns. The church expects the new family to pay.'

Mrs Evans finished her tea and set her cup down. 'They try to keep it quiet, but it's big business for them. The third option is for someone like me to find a new home for the baby. I don't deny that I can make money arranging private adoptions. My clients are usually wealthy and happy to pay to get what they want but can't have. But it happens rarely. Mostly I deliver babies at home to normal, happily married women. But when a desperate woman comes to me in fear of losing her job, her family and her home, what am I supposed to do?' She spread her arms wide.

'The mother is in a complete panic. Her life is ruined if she keeps the baby. At least I can reassure the mother that her baby will be safe and it'll have the best life possible. I don't believe that's a bad thing to be doing for people. Both sides are happy – well, as happy as they can be, I suppose. I'd do it anyway, but if people who have the means are willing to pay me for my trouble, I'd be mad not to take it. The mother receives a few quid for herself too and the child's in a better place, which is more than anyone could hope for from the nuns!'

She looked at Ann like a doctor might when he is delivering a diagnosis. 'I know what you're afraid of. You want to keep your baby and I'll do my best to help. You have my word. Fred says you have it all worked out and I trust him. He wouldn't tell me any details, which is fair enough, but he knows I'll always try and do the right thing.'

'Has he been paying you?'

'No, love, he hasn't, but I understand why you had to ask. He explained the situation and asked me to help and I agreed. He's my brother, your ma's best friend, and that's it.'

'Oh, Gladys,' and Ann started to cry with relief. Panic balloons popped, stress dams burst, and the floods were floods of joy.

Mrs Evans gave her a big hug. 'Finish your tea. I'll go and start the dinner.'

CHAPTER 40

Walter remained very much the same, but Ann didn't. She could no longer hide her bump. She had confided in Sinead some time ago, just telling her that her plan would allow her and Walter to have a baby despite his condition. She had asked her not to say anything to Mr and Mrs Green about her being pregnant. Sinead agreed and didn't ask why. The other nurses made no comment. They remained professional, friendly and kinder than ever.

All she had to do was focus on the plan, keep visiting, and endure.

Then one Wednesday towards the end of May, when she'd told Walter everything she could think of and had fallen silent and was nearly in a doze, Sinead entered the ward. She pulled over a chair from the bed opposite Walter's and drew the curtain around.

'Oh dear. You have your serious face on,' Ann said, suddenly alert.

'It's not serious as such, but it's not *not* serious, if that makes sense.'

'Meaning?' Ann smiled.

'The docs think they've done all they can here. Dr Healy will explain everything to Walter's parents when they're up tomorrow, but between you, me and the gatepost, they're going to send him home. Not home home, but to the Tyrone and Fermanagh, where he can get rehab therapy and his family can spend more time with him – take him out in a wheelchair, try and get him up and about.'

Ann's mind melted. She stared up at the ceiling, searching for God. *You must really hate me and Walter. Is it because he's not a Presbyterian? He made a mistake. A big mistake. I've forgiven him, so why can't you? Is it too much to expect you to look after us now when we need you? I'll be up here in Belfast, the size of a house, and Walter will be in Omagh with his broken brain. You can do miracles, so please make him better. Please help us.'*

'Are you okay?' Sinead asked.

'I don't know. I'm not sure what this means.' Her brain was in a spin. 'Do they think they can really get him up and about?'

'I'm not sure, but I do know they can't do any more for him here.'

The dam burst. 'Shit, shit, shit,' Ann hissed through clenched teeth.

'Can't you just go back to Omagh? Won't this help?'

'NO!' When Sinead looked shocked, Ann stammered, 'It's complicated. I can and I will go back to Omagh, but not yet.'

'The baby?'

Ann nodded and looked up at her friend.

Sinead's eyes glanced at Walter questioningly. Ann nodded imperceptibly.

Sinead gave Ann a hug and whispered, 'You're the strongest person I've ever met. You can do it.'

Ann thought she was going to cry again, but she didn't.

* * *

The first week in June, Walter was transferred to the T&F. This made life a great deal easier for the Greens. At the start, Mr Green rang Ann every day after he'd been to see his son. But there was nothing new to report and the phone calls became less and less frequent. She had to tell him she wasn't coming home yet because she had a job in a shop and it was six days a week, so she couldn't even come to visit. But as long as Walter was getting his daily visits, that was the main thing.

The lies were getting very convoluted by that time. Ann considered writing them all down, so she didn't get caught out.

Fred told her that Ma seemed to be managing but was very quiet these days. Uncle Louis was asking questions about when Ann was coming home. They stuck with the story of Ann's job, but everyone knew she could get a better job in Omagh anytime.

It was a hot summer and Ann was housebound, apart from short waddles up and down the street. The days became long, sweaty and boring. *This is torture ... I want to see Walter. I want my ma.*

But Ma could not help her now. Then one sticky night, at three in the morning, Mrs Evans delivered a little girl in the bedroom of their house on London Road. She weighed six pounds four ounces. Small, but perfectly formed. It wasn't a long or difficult labour. Ann was young and strong and couldn't wait to get home to Omagh.

Mrs Evans made her rest in bed for a few days and she lay in heaven with her baby, feeding her every five minutes, it seemed, and sleeping in between.

'Just wait till your da sees you. You're so gorgeous.'

As soon as she was fit enough, Ann got the train to Omagh. It was a beautiful Saturday morning. She left the baby with Pamela, who would be in her own heaven, at least for a day or two.

It was a long walk out the Hospital Road to the T&F. Breathless and flushed, she raced down the corridor to find Walter. He was in a white ward with white sheets pulled up to his white face.

'Hello, Walter. It's me. I'm sorry it's been so long, but it's complicated. Too complicated for you to understand because you're thick, but I'm here now.' She clasped his hand. 'Can you hear me, Walter? Move your finger once if you can hear me.' His forefinger moved decisively and tapped the back of her hand.

She bent forward and whispered into his ear: 'We have a baby girl, Walter. It's a secret for now, so tell nobody. I've called her Daisy. We can change it if you want.'

The noises Walter was making sounded like he wanted to say something and his fingers were tapping like mad.

'Move your finger just once if you like the name Daisy.'

His finger tapped hard just once.

A sudden wave of pity passed over her at all Walter was missing. 'Oh, Walter, we all need you to get better and come home. I can't do this on my own.' Ann felt the urge to kiss his forehead. He was like another baby. She could smell the clean sheets and the soap. 'I want to dance.'

Walter tapped his finger four times.

'You smell like Daisy. She's beautiful, Walter. She looks a bit like you only not as dopey. And she has normal hair.'

Walter tapped hard.

'I'll bring her to see you as soon as I can, but it's complicated. By the way, did you know there are one million, two hundred and seventy-three daffodils in Ormeau Park? I counted them when they were all out a few months ago. You'd love it. Imagine pushing wee Daisy through a million daffodils. There's lots of daisies in the grass too. That's where I got her name from. I couldn't call her daffodil, could I.'

She didn't sit on for as long as she normally would. She wanted to catch Uncle Louis before she went home. He didn't work on Saturdays, so she walked to his house.

'He's making progress, Ann. Slow but noticeable. You look exhausted, by the way. Are you sure you're looking after yourself properly up there in the big smoke?'

Ann told him excitedly about the finger-tapping in response to questions.

'It's a good sign. Every stimulation is helpful. It would be good for him if you could see and speak to him more often.'

'The shop is very busy in the summer. I'm the manager so it's hard to get away. When they find someone to replace me, I should be able to come home.'

'You'll get a job no bother. What does the shop sell?'

'Everything. Summer stuff. We even have ice cream.'

He tapped his pipe out into a glass ashtray. 'Can I run you home?'

'That would be lovely.'

He stopped right outside the house in Sedan Avenue.

'Are you coming in?' she asked him.

'I'll say a quick hello to Kathleen. I haven't seen her for a while, but I can't stop long. Brenda will have the dinner ready.'

Ma had obviously been asleep and woke as Ann opened the door. 'Ann!' she cried and tried to stand up too quickly. Ann rushed over grabbed her hands and got her upright. She tottered a bit, then stabilised. They hugged until they swayed.

'Sorry, Louis, I'm so glad to have this one back.' Ma disentangled herself.

'No need to apologise. How are you? Long time no see.' Louis gave her a peck on the cheek.

'Oh, I'm grand.' Her eyes were alight as she asked after his family. She was smiling past him at Ann. She didn't hear his answers and asked him to repeat them a couple of times. She paid more attention when they discussed Walter's reaction to Ann.

Ma wrapped her arms around her daughter again, 'It's so good to have you home. I've missed you so much.'

'I'll leave you two to catch up!'

'Thanks for the lift, Uncle Louis,' Ann said as she left him to the door.

'I'd better sit down before I fall down,' Ma said, slumping back into her chair. 'Tell me everything!'

'That could take a while. I'll get some spuds on first. Have we anything else?'

'There's a tin of corned beef.'

'Perfect.'

After dinner, Ann told Ma about the past few months and the birth.

'Daisy? Where did that come from?' Ma exclaimed.

Ann described the carpets of daisies in Ormeau Park. 'I can't call her after you or Mrs Green. People will put two and two together and get twenty-two. I don't even know Mrs Green's Christian name. Even Mr Green calls her Mrs Green and you can't call a baby Mrs Green, can you.'

'She's healthy and feeding well? And sleeping?'

'Oh, Ma, she's beautiful. She looks a wee bit like Walter, but I don't think she'll have the same hair.'

Ma looked relieved. 'And Mrs Evans was good?'

'Better than good. She certainly knows what she's doing. The birth was easy and she couldn't have been more helpful. She explained a heap of things that made a lot of sense.'

'Like what?'

'You know, about looking after babies and stuff, for new mums.'

'Good. Fred will be pleased.'

Somehow the topic of Pamela and her longing for a child came up. 'She's a good sort and would keep Daisy, given half a chance.'

Ma looked up at her.

'No. No chance, Ma,' Ann held up her hands, palms out. 'Don't even think about it. We've agreed. Pamela is happy to look after her when I come down here to see you and Walter. Until I can bring her home, that is.'

Ma looked dubious. How long could Ann stay on in Belfast living off the Evans' generosity?

'I'll have to tell people I'm taking days off from the job I haven't got. Me up there and him down here wasn't part of the plan.'

'Plans have a way of going up the left.' Ma smiled wistfully. 'I never thought you were going to be as strong as you are. I'm proud of you.'

They squeezed each other's hands tightly.

Fred called over. He'd spoken to Gladys on the phone and Daisy was well. She was taking the expressed milk from the bottle without any bother. His eyes met Ann's. He knew that

Gladys had told Ann about the less legal side of her job and it was all okay.

She spoke to Mr Green at the station before she boarded the late train on Sunday evening. They agreed that Walter seemed to be making some headway, but Ann thought Mr Green had aged – he seemed more wrinkled and grey. Visiting every day was tiring. She knew how he felt.

'Do you think you could get your old job back and come home?' he asked. 'Walter obviously knows when you're there. It'd be for the best for both of you, wouldn't it?'

'Yes, of course, it would. I will try to speak to Mrs Crammond again soon.'

Ann boarded the train. The plan was working. Wasn't it?

* * *

Mrs Evans brought a pram home. 'Don't ask,' she said. 'In my line of work and all that.'

The days were still long and warm. Ann was able to take Daisy to the park to see the colourful beds full of all sorts of flowers. They were big, bright and beautiful and made her heart sing.

'Aren't they gorgeous, Daisy? Just like you,' she cooed into the pram. Daisy gurgled and wiggled her wee fingers.

'You sound just like your da,' Ann said. 'Except he's twenty. We'll go and see him soon, I promise. He's not very well at the minute. He's in a place called a hospital. Say hos-pit-al. No? Well, he can't say it either so don't worry. When he gets better, we'll get married and we'll all live happily ever after.' She hoped Daisy couldn't sense her doubt.

* * *

Mrs Evans looked up as Pamela came in. 'Ann's away for a walk in the park with Daisy. You'll have to wait a while longer, I'm afraid, love. She seems very determined to go back to Omagh and take wee Daisy with her. How that's going to work with Walter the way he is, is beyond me.'

'Maybe she'll change her mind when she realises how hard it's going to be.'

'I don't think so. She loves the bones of that child. With or without Walter, she'll be raising her. Fred told me they have some sort of plan, though if it goes pear-shaped, that couple I was telling you about have offered me fifty-five pounds! But I turned them down, of course. You'd have first refusal this time.'

'She's a beautiful wee thing. She's perfect,' Pamela said, trying to smile.

'She is indeed, love. Perfect.'

* * *

The final parts of the plan began to move quickly as the autumn evenings shortened. Ann got her figure back and didn't look as if she'd had a baby just a few months previously. She'd had to borrow some clothes from Pamela initially, but now her own fitted her again, and she felt and looked like her old self.

Daisy moved on to formula and then mushed up mush – goo stew like Walter's.

A Friday afternoon in early October brought rare good news. Ann had left Mrs Evan's number with Mrs Crammond and she phoned to say that one of the girls was moving away to marry, so there was a vacancy. She would like someone with experience, if Ann was still interested. It was wee Doris, the girl Ann had given her New Year's Eve dance tickets to a lifetime ago. It was a nice way to return the favour. Things were falling into place.

Ann moved back to Omagh with Daisy at the end of October. That's when the final piece of the plan began. She pushed the pram around from the station and opened the front door.

Ma was in her chair, dozing. Startled, she woke and her face lit up.

'Ma, say hello to Daisy. Daisy, say hello to your nana.'

Ma's heart melted. 'She's gorgeous. Your eyes, but she does look a bit like her da.'

'She'll grow out of it! Take her.'

Ma and Daisy were made for each other. Old arms formed a natural cradle and Daisy fell asleep.

Ann was out shopping when she met Iris in the street. They hadn't seen each other for ages. They had a lot of catching up to do. They arranged to meet for a proper chat. This was the last, most dangerous piece of the plan.

After a long chat in the Cake Shop, Ann went for it. 'You won't believe what's happened. You know Fred? Fred McPartland?'

Iris shook her head.

'He's a good friend of Ma's.'

Iris shook her head again.

'Well, a friend of his niece up in Belfast had a baby a few months ago. But she wasn't well – the niece's friend, I mean, not the baby – and well, it's very sad, but she passed away shortly afterwards. Her husband said there was no way he could look after a wean, what with his job in the police and all. He has no relatives, and he was going to put the child in an orphanage.' Ann took a deep breath and a long drink of her brown lemonade. 'But when Fred told us the story, we decided – well, I decided – on the spur of the moment, that I would see about maybe adopting this wean. Me and Walter both wanted children, but it might never happen now with Walter being ill. So I decided to go ahead and get one without him.'

Iris was nodding, almost crying and grinning at the same time. She seemed to swallow the fairy tale and said she couldn't wait to see wee Daisy. She couldn't believe how brave Ann was. How sad and tragic it was about her and Walter. Like something from a film. What about work? How would work work with a baby? Who would mind it?

'It's really Ma who had to do the adoption and she *volunteered* to look after her. Work won't even know. We can survive on what I get. She'll not want for anything – the baby, I mean – and Ma as well, of course.'

Iris asked what Ann's plans were if Walter never got better.

'He's getting better and Daisy will only help with that process. I don't think I could ever marry anyone else. Daisy might be the nearest thing I get to having a baby of my own.'

They only had to tell this story to a select few. Once Mrs Chesney knew, they knew the whole town would know. Ma told her gentlemen that she was retiring. Her knees and back were gone. She got three clocks and three twenty-pound notes from them. They told the Reverend Goodman and a few people at church, all of whom got misty-eyed at the part about a child helping Walter recover.

Ma told anyone who would listen that she'd got the short end of the stick. Instead of working three days a week, she'd have to work every day. Back to nappies, at her age! What was Ann thinking about, adopting a wean just like that? But she couldn't stop smiling.

Ann started back at the Ministry of Agriculture and went to see Walter every day after work. On the Friday of her first week back, she found Walter sitting in a wheelchair beside his bed. To the disgust of the matron, she ran and hugged him – awkwardly because of the chair.

She put her forehead on his. 'Did you get into this thing all on your own?'

Was that a smile she saw?

The nurse and a doctor came over and explained this was part of the process to get Walter moving. His muscles were weak and they needed to get him up on his feet.

'Can I push him in this thing?'

'Please do. Take him outside. The gardens are still lovely at this time of year.'

The gardens were indeed still lovely, all gold, red and orange. The sun blinked in and out of the broken clouds as she wheeled the chair to a quiet corner.

She tried to help him to stand up, putting her arms around him and hauling without success.

'I want to dance, Walter. Please get up.'

He was tapping furiously.

'I'm going to bring Daisy out to see you tomorrow. What about that? She'll sort you out.'

The next afternoon she wheeled Daisy out to see Walter for the first time.

She was bursting with pride as she held Daisy in front of him. 'This is your daddy. Daddy, this is your little girl.'

Daisy gurgled. Walter gurgled back.

She carefully set her on his lap. 'Our daughter. Isn't she gorgeous?'

Walter was tapping like a man possessed. Ann beamed at her little family, beside herself with joy.

This is the happiest day of my life, she thought, and at least for a moment, the clouds of doubt and fear cleared.

Father and daughter chatted away in their own secret language as she pushed them out into the sunshine.

CHAPTER 41

Ann was staring into the fire. There were still a few flames flickering. She was reflecting on a good week at work. Daisy was asleep. Ma was dozing in her chair. She was nearly happy. Just then, Patty Paige came on the radio singing 'Tennessee Waltz' and Ann began to sort of hum, sort of sing along, which roused Ma.

'I wonder if every state in America has its own waltz?' Ann said.

'What are you talking about, love?'

'Nothing.'

They listened to the end of the song.

'I was just thinking it would be a lovely tune to dance to.' Ann looked like she was miles away.

'You should go back.'

'To Belfast?'

'No, the Starr. Before you forget how to. Dancing would do you the world of good.'

'I couldn't go back without Walter.'

'He would want you to go back.' Even if he didn't, Ma wanted her to. Her daughter was still young, beautiful and technically unattached, thank God.

'Maybe. I don't know.'

'Do it for me then.'

'Yes, Ma. I'll think about it.'

On Saturday morning she was in Kenwell's buying pork pieces for a Sunday stew.

'Oliver! What are you doing here?'

'Hello, stranger!'

'Are you back back, or just back for a visit?'

'I'm back back.'

'What happened? Did it not work out?'

'It did, but it didn't. I never got to New Orleans. Never got further than New York. I played with some brilliant people and made lots of friends, so I could go back anytime. I saw Charlie Parker playing in his club, Birdland. Probably the greatest thing I've ever heard. That's when I realised that these heroes I've always worshipped are in a different league. I'd never be able to play like that, so here I am home. Back with the dead meat.'

The other butcher smiled but didn't look up from the bacon slicer.

'Come on! You're a brilliant player,' Ann said.

'Thanks. Around here maybe. At least I gave it a go. I've no regrets. I've always loved playing in the dancehalls.'

'Where you're appreciated.'

Oliver smiled. 'What can I get you?'

'Two bob's worth of pork pieces please.'

'No problem.'

'So that means you'll be back in the Starr on Saturdays?'

'If the boys'll have me. As soon as I left, they changed the name of the band to the Premier Showband. They've a good young sax player. But I've had a word with them and I'm joining in next Saturday. Will you be there?'

'You probably heard about Walter. I haven't been to a dance since he got hurt.'

'It's a real shame. You and Walter were great together. How is he now? It must be nearly a year.'

Ann winced. Only a year! How much had changed in that time.

'Aye. He's making progress. It's good to have him back in Omagh. They're very good to him up at the T&F.'

'It's been quite a year for you one way or another. Didn't your Ma adopt a relative's baby or something a few months back?'

Ann smiled. The jungle drums were working just fine. 'Yes. Nothing like having an infant around to cheer up the house. It's been a long time since she's had to look after a wean, but I think she's enjoying it, most of the time! Wee Daisy is just the best thing ever.'

'She was always a grafter, your Ma. Can't even put her feet up when she retires!'

'At least she still has plenty of things to worry about, so she's as happy as Larry.'

'Your mum always enjoyed a good worry, right enough. Is that all I can get you?'

Oliver handed over the parcel of off-cuts and trimmings. 'So you'll come on Saturday? Consider it the big comeback for both of us!'

'Maybe. Thanks, Oliver.' Ann did a little hop as she kicked the sawdust off her shoes outside.

In the afternoon she took Daisy to see Walter. By now, most of the trees were bare and the fallen leaves were mushy and rotten. Ann and the nurse had to be careful when they helped him to stand up, avoiding the slippery leaves. 'One more go, Blondie. Come on, you can do it. Tell him, Daisy. Tell him to stand up.'

Ann grunted with the effort, but with a little more hauling, up he stood.

'Bloody hell, that was easy. Have you been training or something?'

Was he smiling too?

Guided by the nurse on one side and Ann on the other, he tottered unsteadily, shifting from foot to foot. He was making very strange noises, like Joe after a feed of liver and onions. Then his strength gave out and he crashed back down into the wheelchair.

'Well done! We'll try again tomorrow. After church. God will help us. Won't you?' Ann looked heavenwards without any confidence.

She picked Daisy up off the bench where she had been propped up on Ann's raincoat chatting to a friendly robin, tidied Walter up and put Daisy on his lap.

'Mind you hold on to her tight! She's a wriggler. She's going to be a dancer.'

As she wheeled them back inside, she said, 'I'm going back to the Starr tonight. Oliver is back from America and he's playing tonight – first time for a year. His last night was ours too. A year! Can you believe it? Do you remember any of it?'

Walter was tapping as if his life depended on it.

'I'm not asking for permission, but I need you to be okay with it. I don't want to dance with anybody else. I love you, but I need to go back. It's all I've ever wanted to do.'

She thought Walter understood what she was saying. He

was nodding his head. He was agitated and making weird noises.

The nurses came over to calm him down.

'Is he often like this now?' Ann asked them. 'Maybe it was the talk about dancing. Or being on his feet?'

'He seems to be increasingly aware of what's going on around him, and that can make him frustrated because he can't do or say what he wants to.'

'I can't imagine what that must be like. It must be horrible.'

'It's a sign of improvement, but he has a hard road ahead of him,' the older nurse said as she wiped Walter's face.

'I don't know how you do this every day.'

'You get used to it. It's worth it when you see people get better.'

Before Ann left, she whispered, 'I'm here, Walter – forever. You just keep getting better.' She kissed him on the lips.

Back at the house, Ann was alive with the news that Walter had stood up, sort of, and the nurse said he was making progress. Fred called and Ann revelled in recounting the day's events to him.

Fred's old eyes twinkled with joy. 'You deserve some good news, Ann. Great to see you like your old self. And it's a credit to you the way you've looked after that boy. I'm delighted for you.'

'Thanks, Fred. But I couldn't have done any of this without you.'

Saturday could not come fast enough. Ma beamed at Fred and silently clapped her hands when Ann skipped off to get her glad rags on. She came back down in no time and they both drew a sharp breath.

'You look beautiful, love.'

Fred said she looked like Hedy Lamarr. She was wearing the blue dress she'd worn to Portrush. The necklace and earrings were cheap but they looked like Cartier on her. They glowed like proper gemstones in the dim light.

'You two behave yourselves now while I'm out,' Ann said as she opened the front door.

'Don't we always,' Ma said and, much to Ann's surprise, she winked.

Ann was positively crackling with excitement and nerves as she crossed the road to the beckoning lights of the Starr. What if she'd forgotten how to dance properly? Who would be there? What would they say?

She looked down the alley where her world had changed forever. She turned, smiled to herself and straightened her dress. She was ready. She took a deep breath and stepped inside.

About the author

Sam Young was born and raised in Omagh. He went to both Protestant and Catholic schools before university. He worked in financial services before retiring in 2021.

He and his wife, Mae, have travelled extensively, but long haul has become shorter haul following Mae's MS diagnosis.

Sam's other loves are gardening, rugby (Ulster and Ireland), football (Leeds United) and the blues. He reckons these last two are made for each other!

Dancehall Days is his first novel. It has been in his head for over twenty years, but he only started writing it when he retired. It's based very loosely on stories his mother told him about growing up in Omagh just after the war.

Printed in Dunstable, United Kingdom

70095531R00201